ANTHONY TROLLOPE, the fourth of six surviving children, was born on 24 April 1815 in London. As he describes in his *Autobiography*, poverty and debt made his childhood acutely unhappy and disrupted his education: his school fees at Harrow and Winchester were frequently unpaid. His family attempted to restore their fortunes by going to America, leaving the young Anthony alone in England, but it was not until his mother, Frances, began to write that there was any improvement in the family's finances. Her success came too late for her husband, who died in exile in Belgium in 1835. Trollope was unable to afford a university education, and in 1834 he became a junior clerk in the Post Office. He achieved little until he was appointed Surveyor's Clerk in Ireland in 1841. There he worked hard, travelled widely, took up hunting and still found time for his literary career. He married Rose Heseltine, the daughter of a bank manager, in 1844; they had two sons, one of whom emigrated to Australia. Trollope frequently went abroad for the Post Office and did not settle in England again until 1859. He is still remembered as the inventor of the letter-box. In 1867 he resigned from the Post Office and became the editor of *St Paul's Magazine* for the next three years. He failed in his attempt to enter Parliament as a Liberal in 1868. Trollope took his place among London literary society and counted William Thackeray, George Eliot and G. H. Lewes among his friends. He died on 6 December 1882 as the result of a stroke.

Anthony Trollope wrote forty-seven novels and five volumes of short stories as well as travel books, biographies and collections of sketches. The Barsetshire series and the six Palliser or 'political' books were the first novel-sequences to be written in English. His works offer an unsurpassed portrait of the professional and landed classes in Victorian England. In his *Autobiography* (published posthumously in 1883) Trollope describes the self-discipline that enabled his prolific output: he would produce a given number of words per hour in the early morning, before work; he always wrote while travelling by rail or sea, and as soon as he finished one novel he began another. His efforts resulted in his becoming one of England's most successful and popular writers.

Tales of All Countries: First Series was published in book form in 1861; it was to be the first of five collections of short stories, some of which had first appeared in America. Most of them were inspired by Trollope's extensive foreign travels on behalf of the Post Office. Of their publication in Britain, Trollope writes in his *Autobiography*; 'There arose at this time a certain literary project which probably had a great effect upon my career ... I had heard of the *Cornhill Magazine* ... under the editorship of Thackeray. I had at this time written from time to time certain short stories, which had been published in different periodicals ... I wrote to Thackeray ... offering to send him for the magazine certain of these stories.' The offer was accepted and Thackeray replied with 'how very glad indeed I shall be to have you as a co-operator in our new Magazine.'

TALES OF ALL COUNTRIES
FIRST SERIES

ANTHONY TROLLOPE

PENGUIN BOOKS

PENGUIN BOOKS

Published by the Penguin Group
Penguin Books Ltd, 27 Wrights Lane, London W8 5TZ, England
Penguin Books USA Inc., 375 Hudson Street, New York, New York 10014, USA
Penguin Books Australia Ltd, Ringwood, Victoria, Australia
Penguin Books Canada Ltd, 10 Alcorn Avenue, Toronto, Ontario, Canada M4V 3B2
Penguin Books (NZ) Ltd, 182–190 Wairau Road, Auckland 10, New Zealand

Penguin Books Ltd, Registered Offices: Harmondsworth, Middlesex, England

First published 1861
Published in Penguin Books 1993
1 3 5 7 9 10 8 6 4 2

Printed in England by Clays Ltd, St Ives plc

Except in the United States of America, this book is sold subject
to the condition that it shall not, by way of trade or otherwise, be lent,
re-sold, hired out, or otherwise circulated without the publisher's
prior consent in any form of binding or cover other than that in
which it is published and without a similar condition including this
condition being imposed on the subsequent purchaser

CONTENTS.

———

LA MÈRE BAUCHE.

THE Pyreneean valley in which the baths of Vernet are situated is not much known to English, or indeed to any travellers. Tourists in search of good hotels and picturesque beauty combined, do not generally extend their journeys to the Eastern Pyrenees. They rarely get beyond Luchon; and in this they are right, as they thus end their peregrinations at the most lovely spot among these mountains; and are as a rule so deceived, imposed on, and bewildered by guides, inn-keepers, and horse-owners at this otherwise delightful place as to become undesirous of further travel. Nor do invalids from distant parts frequent Vernet. People of fashion go to the Eaux Bonnes and to Luchon, and people who are really ill to Baréges and Cauterets. It is at these places that one meets crowds of Parisians, and the daughters and wives of rich merchants from Bordeaux, with an admixture, now by no means inconsiderable, of Englishmen and Englishwomen. But the Eastern Pyrenees are still unfrequented. And probably they will remain so; for though there are among them

B

lovely valleys—and of all such the valley of Vernet
is perhaps the most lovely—they cannot compete with
the mountain scenery of other tourists-loved regions in
Europe.   At the Port de Venasquez and the Brèche
de Roland in the Western Pyrenees, or rather, to speak
more truly, at spots in the close vicinity of these famous
mountain entrances from France into Spain, one can
make comparisons with Switzerland, Northern Italy,
the Tyrol, and Ireland, which will not be injurious to
the scenes then under view.   But among the eastern
mountains this can rarely be done.   The hills do not
stand thickly together so as to group themselves; the
passes from one valley to another, though not wanting
in altitude, are not close pressed together with over-
hanging rocks, and are deficient in grandeur as well as
loveliness.   And then, as a natural consequence of
all this, the hotels——are not quite as good as they
should be.

But there is one mountain among them which can
claim to rank with the Píc du Midi or the Maledetta.
No one can pooh-pooh the stern old Canigou, standing
high and solitary, solemn and grand, between the two
roads which run from Perpignan into Spain, the one
by Prades and the other by Le Boulon.   Under the
Canigou, towards the west, lie the hot baths of Vernet,
in a close secluded valley, which, as I have said before,
is, as far as I know, the sweetest spot in these Eastern
Pyrenees.

The frequenters of these baths were a few years
back gathered almost entirely from towns not very far

distant, from Perpignan, Narbonne, Carcassonne, and
Bézières, and were not therefore famous, expensive, or
luxurious; but those who believed in them believed
with great faith; and it was certainly the fact that
men and women who went thither worn with toil, sick
with excesses, and nervous through over-care, came
back fresh and strong, fit once more to attack the
world with all its woes. Their character in latter
days does not seem to have changed, though their
circle of admirers may perhaps be somewhat extended.

In those days, by far the most noted and illustrious
person in the village of Vernet was La Mère Bauche.
That there had once been a Père Bauche was known
to the world, for there was a Fils Bauche who lived
with his mother; but no one seemed to remember more
of him than that he had once existed. At Vernet he
had never been known. La Mère Bauche was a native
of the village, but her married life had been passed
away from it, and she had returned in her early widow-
hood to become proprietress and manager, or, as one
may say, the heart and soul of the Hôtel Bauche at
Vernet.

This hotel was a large and somewhat rough establishment, intended for the accommodation of invalids who
came to Vernet for their health. It was built immediately over one of the thermal springs, so that the
water flowed from the bowels of the earth directly into
the baths. There was accommodation for seventy
people, and during the summer and autumn months
the place was always full. Not a few also were to be

found there during the winter and spring, for the charges of Madame Bauche were low, and the accommodation reasonably good.

And in this respect, as indeed in all others, Madame Bauche' had the reputation of being an honest woman. She had a certain price, from which no earthly consideration would induce her to depart; and certain returns for this price in the shape of déjeuners and dinners, baths and beds, which she never failed to give in accordance with the dictates of a strict conscience. These were traits in the character of an hotel-keeper which cannot be praised too highly, and which had met their due reward in the custom of the public. But nevertheless there were those who thought that there was occasionally ground for complaint in the conduct even of Madame Bauche.

In the first place she was deficient in that pleasant smiling softness which should belong to any keeper of a house of public entertainment. In her general mode of life she was stern and silent with her guests, autocratic, authoritative, and sometimes contradictory in her house, and altogether irrational and unconciliatory when any change even for a day was proposed to her, or when any shadow of a complaint reached her ears.

Indeed of complaint, as made against the establishment, she was altogether intolerant. To such she had but one answer. He or she who complained might leave the place at a moment's notice if it so pleased them. There were always others ready to take their places. The power of making this answer came to her from the lowness of her prices; and it was a power which was very dear to her.

The baths were taken at different hours according to medical advice, but the usual time was from five to seven in the morning. The déjeuner or early meal was at nine o'clock, the dinner was at four. After that, no eating or drinking was allowed in the Hôtel Bauche. There was a café in the village, at which ladies and gentlemen could get a cup of coffee or a glass of eau sucré; but no such accommodation was to be had in the establishment. Not by any possible bribery or persuasion could any meal be procured at any other than the authorized hours. A visitor who should enter the salle à manger more than ten minutes after the last bell would be looked at very sourly by Madame Bauche, who on all occasions sat at the top of her own table. Should any one appear as much as half an hour late, he would receive only his share of what had not been handed round. But after the last dish had been so handed, it was utterly useless for any one to enter the room at all.

Her appearance at the period of our tale was perhaps not altogether in her favour. She was about sixty years of age and was very stout and short in the neck. She wore her own gray hair, which at dinner was always tidy enough; but during the whole day previous to that hour she might be seen with it escaping from under her cap in extreme disorder. Her eyebrows were large and bushy, but those alone would

not have given to her face that look of indomitable
sternness which it possessed. Her eyebrows were
serious in their effect, but not so serious as the pair of
green spectacles which she always wore under them.
It was thought by those who had analyzed the subject
that the great secret of Madame Bauche's power lay in
her green spectacles.

Her custom was to move about and through the
whole establishment every day from breakfast till the
period came for her to dress for dinner. She would
visit every chamber and every bath, walk once or twice
round the salle à manger, and very repeatedly round
the kitchen; she would go into every hole and corner,
and peer into everything through her green spectacles:
and in these walks it was not always thought pleasant
to meet her. Her custom was to move very slowly,
with her hands generally clasped behind her back: she
rarely spoke to the guests unless she was spoken to,
and on such occasions she would not often diverge into
general conversation. If any one had aught to say
connected with the business of the establishment, she
would listen, and then she would make her answers,—
often not pleasant in the hearing.

And thus she walked her path through the world,
a stern, hard, solemn old woman, not without gusts of
passionate explosion; but honest withal, and not without some inward benevolence and true tenderness of
heart. Children she had had many, some seven or
eight. One or two had died, others had been married;
she had sons settled far away from home, and at the

time of which we are now speaking but one was left in any way subject to parental authority.

Adolphe Bauche was the only one of her children of whom much was remembered by the present denizens and hangers-on of the hotel. He was the youngest of the number, and having been born only very shortly before the return of Madame Bauche to Vernet, had been altogether reared there. It was thought by the world of those parts, and rightly thought, that he was his mother's darling—more so than had been any of his brothers and sisters,—the very apple of her eye, and gem of her life. At this time he was about twenty-five years of age, and for the last two years had been absent from Vernet—for reasons which will shortly be made to appear. He had been sent to Paris to see something of the world, and learn to talk French instead of the patois of his valley; and having left Paris had come down south into Languedoc, and remained there picking up some agricultural lore which it was thought might prove useful in the valley farms of Vernet. He was now expected home again very speedily, much to his mother's delight.

That she was kind and gracious to her favourite child does not perhaps give much proof of her benevolence; but she had also been kind and gracious to the orphan child of a neighbour; nay, to the orphan child of a rival innkeeper. At Vernet there had been more than one water establishment, but the proprietor of the second had died some few years after Madame Bauche had settled herself at the place. His house had not thrived, and his only child, a little girl, was left altogether without provision.

This little girl, Marie Clavert, La Mère Bauche had taken into her own house immediately after the father's death, although she had most cordially hated that father. Marie was then an infant, and Madame Bauche had accepted the charge without much thought, perhaps, as to what might be the child's ultimate destiny. But since then she had thoroughly done the duty of a mother by the little girl, who had become the pet of the whole establishment, the favourite plaything of Adolphe Bauche,—and at last of course his early sweetheart.

And then and therefore there had come troubles at Vernet. Of course all the world of the valley had seen what was taking place and what was likely to take place, long before Madame Bauche knew anything about it. But at last it broke upon her senses that her son, Adolphe Bauche, the heir to all her virtues and all her riches, the first young man in that or any neighbouring valley, was absolutely contemplating the idea of marrying that poor little orphan, Marie Clavert!

That any one should ever fall in love with Marie Clavert had never occurred to Madame Bauche. She had always regarded the child as a child, as the object of her charity, and as a little thing to be looked on as poor Marie by all the world. She, looking through her green spectacles, had never seen that Marie Clavert was a beautiful creature, full of ripening charms, such as young men love to look on. Marie was of infinite

daily use to Madame Bauche in a hundred little things
about the house, and the old lady thoroughly recognized and appreciated her ability. But for this very
reason she had never taught herself to regard Marie
otherwise than as a useful drudge. She was very fond
of her protégée—so much so that she would listen to
her in affairs about the house when she would listen to
no one else;—but Marie's prettiness and grace and
sweetness as a girl had all been thrown away upon
Maman Bauche, as Marie used to call her.

But unluckily it had not been thrown away upon
Adolphe. He had appreciated, as it was natural that
he should do, all that had been so utterly indifferent to
his mother; and consequently had fallen in love. Consequently also he had told his love; and consequently
also, Marie had returned his love. Adolphe had been
hitherto contradicted but in few things, and thought
that all difficulty would be prevented by his informing
his mother that he wished to marry Marie Clavert.
But Marie, with a woman's instinct, had known better.
She had trembled and almost crouched with fear when
she confessed her love; and had absolutely hid herself
from sight when Adolphe went forth, prepared to ask
his mother's consent to his marriage.

The indignation and passionate wrath of Madame
Bauche were past and gone two years before the date
of this story, and I need not therefore much enlarge
upon that subject. She was at first abusive and bitter,
which was bad for Marie; and afterwards bitter and
silent, which was worse. It was of course determined

that poor Marie should be sent away to some asylum
for orphans or penniless paupers—in short anywhere
out of the way. What mattered her outlook into the
world, her happiness, or indeed her very existence?
The outlook and happiness of Adolphe Bauche,—was
not that to be considered as everything at Vernet?

But this terrible sharp aspect of affairs did not last
very long. In the first place La Mère Bauche had
under those green spectacles a heart that in truth was
tender and affectionate, and after the first two days of
anger she admitted that something must be done for
Marie Clavert; and after the fourth day she acknowledged that the world of the hotel, her world, would
not go as well without Marie Clavert as it would with
her. And in the next place Madame Bauche had a
friend whose advice in grave matters she would sometimes take. This friend had told her that it would be
much better to send away Adolphe, since it was so
necessary that there should be a sending away of some
one; that he would be much benefited by passing
some months of his life away from his native valley;
and that an absence of a year or two would teach him
to forget Marie, even if it did not teach Marie to
forget him.

And we must say a word or two about this friend.
At Vernet he was usually called M. le Capitaine,
though in fact he had never reached that rank. He
had been in the army, and having been wounded in
the leg while still a sous-lieutenant, had been pensioned,
and had thus been interdicted from treading any further

the thorny path that leads to glory. For the last fifteen years he had resided under the roof of Madame Bauche, at first as a casual visitor, going and coming, but now for many years as constant there as she was herself.

He was so constantly called Le Capitaine that his real name was seldom heard. It may however as well be known to us that this was Theodore Campan. He was a tall, well-looking man; always dressed in black garments, of a coarse description certainly, but scrupulously clean and well brushed; of perhaps fifty years of age, and conspicuous for the rigid uprightness of his back—and for a black wooden leg.

This wooden leg was perhaps the most remarkable trait in his character. It was always jet black, being painted, or polished, or japanned, as occasion might require, by the hands of the capitaine himself. It was longer than ordinary wooden legs, as indeed the capitaine was longer than ordinary men; but nevertheless it never seemed in any way to impede the rigid punctilious propriety of his movements. It was never in his way as wooden legs usually are in the way of their wearers. And then to render it more illustrious it had round its middle, round the calf of the leg we may so say, a band of bright brass which shone like burnished gold.

It had been the capitaine's custom, now for some years past, to retire every evening at about seven o'clock into the sanctum sanctorum of Madame Bauche's habitation, the dark little private sitting-room in which she made out her bills and calculated her profits, and there regale himself in her presence—and

indeed at her expense,—for the items never appeared
in the bill, with coffee, and cognac.   I have said that
there was neither eating nor drinking at the establishment after the regular dinner-hours ; but in so saying I
spoke of the world at large. Nothing further was allowed
in the way of trade ; but in the way of friendship so
much was now-a-days always allowed to the capitaine.

It was at these moments that Madame Bauche discussed her private affairs, and asked for and received
advice.   For even Madame Bauche was mortal ; nor
could her green spectacles without other aid carry her
through all the troubles of life.   It was now five years
since the world of Vernet discovered that La Mère
Bauche was going to marry the capitaine ; and for eighteen months the world of Vernet had been full of this
matter : but any amount of patience is at last exhausted,
and as no further steps in that direction were ever taken
beyond the daily cup of coffee, that subject died away—
very much unheeded by La Mère Bauche.

But she, though she thought of no matrimony for
herself, thought much of matrimony for other people ;
and over most of those cups of evening coffee and
cognac a matrimonial project was discussed in these
latter days. It has been seen that the capitaine pleaded
in Marie's favour when the fury of Madame Bauche's
indignation broke forth ; and that ultimately Marie was
kept at home, and Adolphe sent away by his advice.

'But Adolphe cannot always stay away,' Madame
Bauche had pleaded in her difficulty.   The truth of this
the capitaine had admitted ; but Marie, he said, might

be married to some one else before two years were
over. And so the matter had commenced.

But to whom should she be married? To this question the capitaine had answered in perfect innocence of
heart, that La Mère Bauche would be much better able
to make such a choice than himself. He did not know
how Marie might stand with regard to money. If
madame would give some little 'dot,' the affair, the
capitaine thought, would be more easily arranged.

All these things took months to say, during which
period Marie went on with her work in melancholy
listlessness. One comfort she had. Adolphe, before
he went, had promised to her, holding in his hand as
he did so a little cross which she had given him, that no
earthly consideration should sever them ;—that sooner
or later he would certainly be her husband. Marie felt
that her limbs could not work nor her tongue speak
were it not for this one drop of water in her cup.

And then, deeply meditating, La Mère Bauche hit
upon a plan, and herself communicated it to the capitaine over a second cup of coffee into which she poured
a full teaspoonful more than the usual allowance of
cognac. Why should not he, the capitaine himself, be
the man to marry Marie Clavert?

It was a very startling proposal, the idea of matrimony for himself never having as yet entered into the
capitaine's head at any period of his life ; but La
Mère Bauche did contrive to make it not altogether
unacceptable. As to that matter of dowry she was
prepared to be more than generous. She did love

Marie well, and could find it in her heart to give her anything—anything except her son, her own Adolphe. What she proposed was this. Adolphe, himself, would never keep the baths. If the capitaine would take Marie for his wife, Marie, Madame Bauche declared, should be the mistress after her death; subject of course to certain settlements as to Adolphe's pecuniary interests.

The plan was discussed a thousand times, and at last so far brought to bear that Marie was made acquainted with it—having been called in to sit in presence with La Mère Bauche and her future proposed husband. The poor girl manifested no disgust to the stiff ungainly lover whom they assigned to her,—who through his whole frame was in appearance almost as wooden as his own leg. On the whole, indeed, Marie liked the capitaine, and felt that he was her friend; and in her country such marriages were not uncommon. The capitaine was perhaps a little beyond the age at which a man might usually be thought justified in demanding the services of a young girl as his nurse and wife, but then Marie of herself had so little to give—except her youth, and beauty, and goodness.

But yet she could not absolutely consent; for was she not absolutely pledged to her own Adolphe? And therefore, when the great pecuniary advantages were, one by one, displayed before her, and when La Mère Bauche, as a last argument, informed her that as wife of the capitaine she would be regarded as a second mistress in the establishment and not as a servant,—

she could only burst out into tears, and say that she did not know.

'I will be very kind to you,' said the capitaine; 'as kind as a man can be.'

Marie took his hard withered hand and kissed it; and then looked up into his face with beseeching eyes which were not without avail upon his heart.

'We will not press her now,' said the capitaine. 'There is time enough.'

But let his heart be touched ever so much, one thing was certain. It could not be permitted that she should marry Adolphe. To that view of the matter he had given in his unrestricted adhesion; nor could he by any means withdraw it without losing altogether his position in the establishment of Madame Bauche. Nor indeed did his conscience tell him that such a marriage should be permitted. That would be too much. If every pretty girl were allowed to marry the first young man that might fall in love with her, what would the world come to?

And it soon appeared that there was not time enough—that the time was growing very scant. In three months Adolphe would be back. And if everything was not arranged by that time, matters might still go astray.

And then Madame Bauche asked her final question: 'You do not think, do you, that you can ever marry Adolphe?' And as she asked it the accustomed terror of her green spectacles magnified itself tenfold. Marie could only answer by another burst of tears.

The affair was at last settled among them. Marie said that she would consent to marry the capitaine when she should hear from Adolphe's own mouth. that he, Adolphe, loved her no longer. She declared with many tears that her vows and pledges prevented her from promising more than this. It was not her fault, at any rate not now, that she loved her lover. It was not her fault,—not now at least—that she was bound by these pledges. When she heard from his own mouth that he had discarded her, then she would marry the capitaine—or indeed sacrifice herself in any other way that La Mère Bauche might desire. What would anything signify then ?

Madame Bauche's spectacles remained unmoved ; but not her heart. Marie, she told the capitaine, should be equal to herself in the establishment, when once she was entitled to be called Madame Campan, and she should be to her quite as a daughter. She should have her cup of coffee every evening, and dine at the big table, and wear a silk gown at church, and the servants should all call her Madame ; a great career should be open to her, if she would only give up her foolish girlish childish love for Adolphe. And all these great promises were repeated to Marie by the capitaine.

But nevertheless there was but one thing in the whole world which in Marie's eyes was of any value ; and that one thing was the heart of Adolphe Bauche. Without that she would be nothing ; with that,—with that assured, she could wait patiently till doomsday.

Letters were written to Adolphe during all these

eventful doings; and a letter came from him saying
that he greatly valued Marie's love, but that as it had
been clearly proved to him that their marriage would
be neither for her advantage, nor for his, he was willing
to give it up. He consented to her marriage with the
capitaine, and expressed his gratitude to his mother for
the immediate pecuniary advantages which she had
held out to him. Oh, Adolphe, Adolphe! But, alas,
alas! is not such the way of most men's hearts—and
of the hearts of some women?

This letter was read to Marie, but it had no more
effect upon her than would have had some dry legal
document. In those days and in those places men and
women did not depend much upon letters; nor when
they were written, was there expressed in them much of
heart or of feeling. Marie would understand, as she
was well aware, the glance of Adolphe's eye and the
tone of Adolphe's voice; she would perceive at once
from them what her lover really meant, what he wished,
what in the innermost corner of his heart he really desired that she should do. But from that stiff constrained
written document she could understand nothing.

It was agreed therefore that Adolphe should return,
and that she would accept her fate from his mouth.
The capitaine, who knew more of human nature than
did poor Marie, felt tolerably sure of his bride.
Adolphe, who had seen something of the world, would not
care very much for the girl of his own valley. Money
and pleasure, and some little position in the world
would soon wean him from his love; and then Marie

C

would accept her destiny—as other girls in the same position had done since the French world began.

And now it was the evening before Adolphe's expected arrival. La Mère Bauche was discussing the matter with the capitaine over the usual cup of coffee. Madame Bauche had of late become rather nervous on the matter, thinking that they had been somewhat rash in acceding so much to Marie. It seemed to her that it was absolutely now left to the two young lovers to say whether or no they would have each other or not. Now nothing on earth could be further from Madame Bauche's intention than this. Her decree and resolve was to heap down blessings on all persons concerned—provided always that she could have her own way; but, provided she did not have her own way, to heap down,—anything but blessings. She had her code of morality in this matter. She would do good if possible to everybody around her. But she would not on any score be induced to consent that Adolphe should marry Marie Clavert. Should that be in the wind she would rid the house of Marie, of the capitaine, and even of Adolphe himself.

She had become therefore somewhat querulous, and self-opinionated in her discussions with her friend.

'I don't know,' she said on the evening in question; 'I don't know. It may be all right; but if Adolphe turns against me, what are we to do then?'

'Mère Bauche,' said the capitaine, sipping his coffee and puffing out the smoke of his cigar, 'Adolphe will not turn against us.' It had been somewhat remarked by many that the capitaine was more at home in the house, and somewhat freer in his manner of talking with Madame Bauche, since this matrimonial alliance had been on the tapis than he had ever been before. La Mère herself observed it, and did not quite like it; but how could she prevent it now? When the capitaine was once married she would make him know his place, in spite of all her promises to Marie.

'But if he says he likes the girl?' continued Madame Bauche.

'My friend, you may be sure that he will say nothing of the kind. He has not been away two years without seeing girls as pretty as Marie. And then you have his letter.'

'That is nothing, capitaine; he would eat his letter as quick as you would eat an omelet aux fines herbes.' Now the capitaine was especially quick over an omelet aux fines herbes.

'And, Mère Bauche, you also have the purse; he will know that he cannot eat that, except with your good will.'

'Ah!' exclaimed Madame Bauche, 'poor lad! He has not a sous in the world unless I give it to him.' But it did not seem that this reflection was in itself displeasing to her.

'Adolphe will now be a man of the world,' continued the capitaine. 'He will know that it does not do to throw away everything for a pair of red lips. That is the folly of a boy, and Adolphe will be no longer a boy. Believe me, Mère Bauche, things will be right enough.'

'And then we shall have Marie sick and ill and half
dying on our hands,' said Madame Bauche.

This was not flattering to the capitaine, and so he
felt it. 'Perhaps so, perhaps not,' he said. 'But
at any rate she will get over it. It is a malady which
rarely kills young women—especially when another
alliance awaits them.'

'Bah!' said Madame Bauche; and in saying that
word she avenged herself for the too great liberty
which the capitaine had lately taken. He shrugged
his shoulders, took a pinch of snuff, and uninvited
helped himself to a teaspoonful of cognac. Then the
conference ended, and on the next morning before
breakfast Adolphe Bauche arrived.

On that morning poor Marie hardly knew how to
bear herself. A month or two back, and even up to
the last day or two, she had felt a sort of confidence
that Adolphe would be true to her; but the nearer
came that fatal day the less strong was the confidence of the poor girl. She knew that those two long-
headed, aged counsellors were plotting against her
happiness, and she felt that she could hardly dare hope
for success with such terrible foes opposed to her. On
the evening before the day Madame Bauche had met
her in the passages, and kissed her as she wished her
good night. Marie knew little about sacrifices, but
she felt that it was a sacrificial kiss.

In those days a sort of diligence with the mails for
Olette passed through Prades early in the morning, and
a conveyance was sent from Vernet to bring Adolphe

to the baths. Never was prince or princess expected with more anxiety. Madame Bauche was up and dressed long before the hour, and was heard to say five several times that she was sure he would not come. The capitaine was out and on the high road, moving about with his wooden leg, as perpendicular as a lamp-post and almost as black. Marie also was up, but nobody had seen her. She was up and had been out about the place before any of them were stirring; but now that the world was on the move she lay hidden like a hare in its form.

And then the old char-à-banc clattered up to the door, and Adolphe jumped out of it into his mother's arms. He was fatter and fairer than she had last seen him, had a larger beard, was more fashionably clothed, and certainly looked more like a man. Marie also saw him out of her little window, and she thought that he looked like a god. Was it probable, she said to herself, that one so godlike would still care for her?

The mother was delighted with her son, who rattled away quite at his ease. He shook hands very cordially with the capitaine—of whose intended alliance with his own sweetheart he had been informed, and then as he entered the house with his hand under his mother's arm, he asked one question about her. 'And where is Marie?' said he. 'Marie! oh upstairs; you shall see her after breakfast,' said La Mère Bauche. And so they entered the house, and went in to breakfast among the guests. Everybody had heard something of the story, and they were all on the alert to see the young man

whose love or want of love was considered to be of so
much importance.

'You will see that it will be all right,' said the capitaine, carrying his head very high.

'I think so, I think so,' said La Mère Bauche, who,
now that the capitaine was right, no longer desired to
contradict him.

'I know that it will be all right,' said the capitaine.
'I told you that Adolphe would return a man ; and he
is a man. Look at him ; he does not care this for Marie
Clavert ;' and the capitaine, with much eloquence in his
motion, pitched over a neighbouring wall a small stone
which he held in his hand.

And then they all went to breakfast with many signs
of outward joy. And not without some inward joy ;
for Madame Bauche thought she saw that her son was
cured of his love. In the mean time Marie sat up
stairs still afraid to show herself.

'He has come,' said a young girl, a servant in the
house, running up to the door of Marie's room.

'Yes,' said Marie ; 'I could see that he has come.'

'And, oh, how beautiful he is !' said the girl, putting
her hands together and looking up to the ceiling.
Marie in her heart of hearts wished that he was not
half so beautiful, as then her chance of having him
might be greater.

'And the company are all talking to him as though
he were the préfet,' said the girl.

'Never mind who is talking to him,' said Marie ; 'go
away, and leave me—you are wanted for your work.'

Why before this was he not talking to her? Why not, if he were really true to her? Alas, it began to fall upon her mind that he would be false! And what then? What should she do then? She sat still gloomily, thinking of that other spouse that had been promised to her.

As speedily after breakfast as was possible Adolphe was invited to a conference in his mother's private room. She had much debated in her own mind whether the capitaine should be invited to this conference or no. For many reasons she would have wished to exclude him. She did not like to teach her son that she was unable to manage her own affairs, and she would have been well pleased to make the capitaine understand that his assistance was not absolutely necessary to her. But then she had an inward fear that her green spectacles would not now be as efficacious on Adolphe, as they had once been, in old days, before he had seen the world and become a man. It might be necessary that her son, being a man, should be opposed by a man. So the capitaine was invited to the conference.

What took place there need not be described at length. The three were closeted for two hours, at the end of which time they came forth together. The countenance of Madame Bauche was serene and comfortable; her hopes of ultimate success ran higher than ever. The face of the capitaine was masked, as are always the faces of great diplomatists; he walked placid and upright, raising his wooden leg with an ease and skill that was absolutely marvellous. But poor

Adolphe's brow was clouded. Yes, poor Adolphe! for
he was poor in spirit. He had pledged himself to give
up Marie, and to accept the liberal allowance which
his mother tendered him; but it remained for him now
to communicate these tidings to Marie herself.

'Could not you tell her?' he had said to his mother,
with very little of that manliness in his face on which
his mother now so prided herself. But La Mère
Bauche explained to him that it was a part of the
general agreement that Marie was to hear his decision
from his own mouth.

'But you need not regard it,' said the capitaine, with
the most indifferent air in the world. 'The girl
expects it. Only she has some childish idea that she
is bound till you yourself release her. I don't think
she will be troublesome.' Adolphe at that moment did
feel that he should have liked to kick the capitaine out
of his mother's house.

And where should the meeting take place? In the
hall of the bath-house, suggested Madame Bauche;
because, as she observed, they could walk round and
round, and nobody ever went there at that time of day.
But to this Adolphe objected; it would be so cold and
dismal and melancholy.

The capitaine thought that Mère Bauche's little
parlour was the place; but La Mère herself did not like
this. They might be overheard, as she well knew; and
she guessed that the meeting would not conclude without some sobs that would certainly be bitter and might
perhaps be loud.

'Send her up to the grotto, and I will follow her,' said Adolphe. On this therefore they agreed. Now the grotto was a natural excavation in a high rock, which stood precipitously upright over the establishment of the baths. A steep zigzag path with almost never-ending steps had been made along the face of the rock from a little flower garden attached to the house which lay immediately under the mountain. Close along the front of the hotel ran a little brawling river, leaving barely room for a road between it and the door; over this there was a wooden bridge leading to the garden, and some two or three hundred yards from the bridge began the steps by which the ascent was made to the grotto.

When the season was full and the weather perfectly warm the place was much frequented. There was a green table in it, and four or five deal chairs; a green garden seat also was there, which however had been removed into the innermost back corner of the excavation, as its hinder legs were somewhat at fault. A wall about two feet high ran along the face of it, guarding its occupants from the precipice. In fact it was no grotto, but a little chasm in the rock, such as we often see up above our heads in rocky valleys, and which by means of these steep steps had been turned into a source of exercise and amusement for the visitors at the hotel.

Standing at the wall one could look down into the garden, and down also upon the shining slate roof of Madame Bauche's house; and to the left might be

seen the sombre silent snow-capped top of stern old
Canigou, king of mountains among those Eastern
Pyrenees.

And so Madame Bauche undertook to send Marie
up to the grotto, and Adolphe undertook to follow her
thither. It was now spring; and though the winds had
fallen and the snow was no longer lying on the lower
peaks, still the air was fresh and cold, and there was
no danger that any of the few guests at the establishment would visit the place.

'Make her put on her cloak, Mère Bauche,' said the
capitaine, who did not wish that his bride should have
a cold in her head on their wedding-day. La Mère
Bauche pished and pshawed, as though she were not
minded to pay any attention to recommendations on
such subjects from the capitaine. But nevertheless
when Marie was seen slowly to creep across the little
bridge about fifteen minutes after this time, she had a
handkerchief on her head, and was closely wrapped in
a dark brown cloak.

Poor Marie herself little heeded the cold fresh air,
but she was glad to avail herself of any means by
which she might hide her face. When Madame
Bauche sought her out in her own little room, and
with a smiling face and kind kiss bade her go to the
grotto, she knew, or fancied that she knew that it was
all over.

'He will tell you all the truth,—how it all is,' said
La Mère. 'We will do all we can, you know, to
make you happy, Marie. But you must remember

what Monsieur le Curé told us the other day. In this vale of tears we cannot have everything; as we shall have some day, when our poor wicked souls have been purged of all their wickedness. Now go, dear, and take your cloak.'

' Yes, maman.'

' And Adolphe will come to you. And try and behave well, like a sensible girl.'

' Yes, maman,'—and so she went, bearing on her brow another sacrificial kiss—and bearing in her heart such an unutterable load of woe!

Adolphe had gone out of the house before her; but standing in the stable yard, well within the gate so that she should not see him, he watched her slowly crossing the bridge and mounting the first flight of the steps. He had often seen her tripping up those stairs, and had, almost as often, followed her with his quicker feet. And she, when she would hear him, would run; and then he would catch her breathless at the top, and steal kisses from her when all power of refusing them had been robbed from her by her efforts at escape. There was no such running now, no such following, no thought of such kisses.

As for him, he would fain have skulked off and shirked the interview had he dared. But he did not dare; so he waited there, out of heart, for some ten minutes, speaking a word now and then to the bath-man, who was standing by, just to show that he was at his ease. But the bath-man knew that he was not at his ease. Such would-be lies as those rarely achieve

deception;—are rarely believed. And then, at the
end of the ten minutes, with steps as slow as Marie's
had been, he also ascended to the grotto.

Marie had watched him from the top, but so that
she herself should not be seen. He however had not
once lifted up his head to look for her; but, with eyes
turned to the ground had plodded his way up to the
cave. When he entered she was standing in the
middle, with her eyes downcast, and her hands clasped
before her. She had retired some way from the wall,
so that no eyes might possibly see her but those of her
false lover. There she stood when he entered, striving
to stand motionless, but trembling like a leaf in every
limb.

It was only when he reached the top step that he
made up his mind how he would behave. Perhaps
after all, the capitaine was right; perhaps she would
not mind it.

'Marie,' said he, with a voice that attempted to be
cheerful; 'this is an odd place to meet in after such a
long absence,' and he held out his hand to her. But
only his hand! He offered her no salute. He did
not even kiss her cheek as a brother would have done!
Of the rules of the outside world it must be remembered that poor Marie knew but little. He had been
a brother to her, before he had become her lover.

But Marie took his hand saying, 'Yes, it has been
very long.'

'And now that I have come back,' he went on to
say, 'it seems that we are all in a confusion together.

I never knew such a piece of work. However, it is all
for the best, I suppose.'

'Perhaps so,' said Marie still trembling violently,
and still looking down upon the ground. And then
there was silence between them for a minute or so.

'I tell you what it is, Marie,' said Adolphe at last,
dropping her hand and making a great effort to get
through the work before him. 'I am afraid we two have
been very foolish. Don't you think we have now?
It seems quite clear that we can never get ourselves
married. Don't you see it in that light?'

Marie's head turned round and round with her, but
she was not of the fainting order. She took three
steps backwards and leant against the wall of the cave.
She also was trying to think how she might best fight
her battle. Was there no chance for her? Could no
eloquence, no love prevail? On her own beauty she
counted but little; but might not prayers do something, and a reference to those old vows which had
been so frequent, so eager, so solemnly pledged between
them?

'Never get ourselves married!' she said, repeating
his words. 'Never, Adolphe? Can we never be
married?'

'Upon my word, my dear girl, I fear not. You see
my mother is so dead against it.'

'But we could wait; could we not?'

'Ah, but that's just it, Marie. We cannot wait.
We must decide now,—to-day. You see I can do
nothing without money from her—and as for you, you

see she won't even let you stay in the house unless you
marry old Campan at once. He's a very good sort of
fellow though, old as he is. And if you do marry him,
why you see you'll stay here, and have it all your own
way in everything. As for me, I shall come and see
you all from time to time, and shall be able to push
my way as I ought to do.'

'Then, Adolphe, you wish me to marry the capitaine?'

'Upon my honour I think it is the best thing you
can do; I do indeed.'

'Oh, Adolphe!'

'What can I do for you, you know? Suppose I was
to go down to my mother and tell her that I had
decided to keep you myself, what would come of it?
Look at it in that light, Marie.'

'She could not turn you out—you her own son!'

'But she would turn you out; and deuced quick,
too, I can assure you of that; I can, upon my
honour.'

'I should not care that,' and she made a motion
with her hand to show how indifferent she would be to
such treatment as regarded herself. 'Not that—; if
I still had the promise of your love.'

'But what would you do?'

'I would work. There are other houses besides
that one,' and she pointed to the slate roof of the
Bauche establishment.

'And for me—I should not have a penny in the
world,' said the young man.

She came up to him and took his right hand between both of hers and pressed it warmly, oh, so warmly. 'You would have my love,' said she; 'my deepest, warmest, best heart's love. I should want nothing more, nothing on earth, if I could still have yours.' And she leaned against his shoulder and looked with all her eyes into his face.

'But, Marie; that's nonsense, you know.'

'No, Adolphe; it is not nonsense. Do not let them teach you so. What does love mean, if it does not mean that? Oh, Adolphe, you do love me, you do love me; you do love me?'

'Yes;—I love you,' he said slowly;—as though he would not have said it, if he could have helped it. And then his arm crept slowly round her waist, as though in that also he could not help himself.

'And do not I love you?' said the passionate girl. 'Oh I do, so dearly; with all my heart, with all my soul. Adolphe, I so love you, that I cannot give you up. Have I not sworn to be yours; sworn, sworn a thousand times? How can I marry that man! Oh Adolphe, how can you wish that I should marry him?' And she clung to him, and looked at him, and besought him with her eyes.

'I shouldn't wish it;—only—' and then he paused. It was hard to tell her that he was willing to sacrifice her to the old man because he wanted money from his mother.

'Only what! But, Adolphe, do not wish it at all! Have you not sworn that I should be your wife? Look

here, look at this;' and she brought out from her bosom
a little charm that he had given her in return for that
cross. 'Did you not kiss that when you swore before
the figure of the virgin that I should be your wife?
And do you not remember that I feared to swear too,
because your mother was so angry; and then you
made me? After that, Adolphe! Oh, Adolphe!
Tell me that I may have some hope. I will wait; oh,
I will wait so patiently.'

He turned himself away from her and walked backwards and forwards uneasily through the grotto. He did
love her;—love her as such men do love sweet, pretty
girls. The warmth of her hand, the affection of her
touch, the pure bright passion of her tear-laden eye
had reawakened what power of love there was within
him. But what was he to do? Even if he were
willing to give up the immediate golden hopes which
his mother held out to him, how was he to begin, and
then how carry out this work of self-devotion? Marie
would be turned away, and he would be left a victim
in the hands of his mother, and of that stiff, wooden-
legged militaire;—a penniless victim, left to mope
about the place without a grain of influence or a morsel
of pleasure.

'But what can we do?' he exclaimed again, as he
once more met Marie's searching eye.

'We can be true and honest, and we can wait,' she
said, coming close up to him and taking hold of his
arm. 'I do not fear it; and she is not my mother,
Adolphe. You need not fear your own mother.'

'Fear; no, of course I don't fear. But I don't see how the very devil we can manage it.'

'Will you let me tell her that I will not marry the capitaine; that I will not give up your promises; and then I am ready to leave the house?'

'It would do no good.'

'It would do every good, Adolphe, if I had your promised word once more; if I could hear from your own voice one more tone of love. Do you not remember this place? It was here that you forced me to say that I loved you. It is here also that you will tell me that I have been deceived.'

'It is not I that would deceive you,' he said. 'I wonder that you should be so hard upon me. God knows that I have trouble enough.'

'Well; if I am a trouble to you, be it so. Be it as you wish,' and she leaned back against the wall of the rock, and crossing her arms upon her breast looked away from him and fixed her eyes upon the sharp granite peaks of Canigou.

He again betook himself to walk backwards and forwards through the cave. He had quite enough of love for her to make him wish to marry her; quite enough, now, at this moment, to make the idea of her marriage with the capitaine very distasteful to him; enough probably to make him become a decently good husband to her, should fate enable him to marry her; but not enough to enable him to support all the punishment which would be the sure effects of his mother's displeasure. Besides, he had promised his

D

mother that he would give up Marie ;—had entirely
given in his adhesion to that plan of the marriage with
the capitaine.   He had owned that the path of life as
marked out for him by his mother was the one which
it behoved him, as a man, to follow.   It was this view
of his duties as a man which had been specially urged
on him with all the capitaine's eloquence.   And old
Campan had entirely succeeded.   It is so easy to get
the assent of such young men, so weak in mind and
so weak in pocket, when the arguments are backed by
a promise of two thousand francs a year.

'I'll tell you what I'll do,' at last he said.   'I'll
get my mother by herself, and will ask her to let the
matter remain as it is for the present.'

'Not if it be a trouble, M. Adolphe ;' and the proud
girl still held her hands upon her bosom, and still
looked towards the mountain.

'You know what I mean, Marie.   You can understand how she and the capitaine are worrying me.'

'But tell me, Adolphe, do you love me ?'

'You know I love you, only—'

'And you will not give me up ?'

'I will ask my mother.   I will try and make her
yield.'

Marie could not feel that she received much confidence from her lover's promise ; but still, even that,
weak and unsteady as it was, even that was better than
absolute fixed rejection.   So she thanked him, promised
him with tears in her eyes that she would always,
always be faithful to him, and then bade him go down

to the house. She would follow, she said, as soon as
his passing had ceased to be observed.

Then she looked at him as though she expected some
sign of renewed love. But no such sign was vouchsafed to her. Now that she thirsted for the touch of
his lip upon her cheek, it was denied to her. He did
as she bade him; he went down, slowly loitering, by
himself; and in about half an hour she followed him
and unobserved crept to her chamber.

Again we will pass over what took place between the
mother and the son; but late in that evening, after the
guests had gone to bed, Marie received a message,
desiring her to wait on Madame Bauche in a small
salon which looked out from one end of the house. It
was intended as a private sitting-room should any
special stranger arrive who required such accommodation, and therefore was but seldom used. Here she
found La Mère Bauche sitting in an arm-chair behind
a small table on which stood two candles; and on a
sofa against the wall sat Adolphe. The capitaine was
not in the room.

'Shut the door, Marie, and come in and sit down,' said
Madame Bauche. It was easy to understand from the
tone of her voice that she was angry and stern, in an
unbending mood, and resolved to carry out to the very
letter all the threats conveyed by those terrible spectacles.

Marie did as she was bid. She closed the door
and sat down on the chair that was nearest to her.

'Marie,' said La Mère Bauche—and the voice

sounded fierce in the poor girl's ears, and an angry
fire glimmered through the green glasses—' what
is all this about that I hear ?   Do you dare to say that
you hold my son bound to marry you ?'   And then the
august mother paused for an answer.

But Marie had no answer to give.   She looked sup-
pliantly towards her lover, as though beseeching him to
carry on the fight for her.   But if she could not do battle
for herself, certainly he could not do it for her.   What
little amount of fighting he had had in him, had been
thoroughly vanquished before her arrival.

'I will have an answer, and that immediately,' said
Madame Bauche.   'I am not going to be betrayed
into ignominy and disgrace by the object of my own
charity.   Who picked you out of the gutter, miss, and
brought you up and fed you, when you would otherwise
have gone to the foundling?   And is this your gratitude for it all?   You are not satisfied with being fed
and clothed and cherished by me, but you must rob
me of my son!   Know this then, Adolphe shall never
marry a child of charity such as you are.'

Marie sat still, stunned by the harshness of these
words.   La Mère Bauche had often scolded her;
indeed, she was given to much scolding; but she had
scolded her as a mother may scold a child.   And when
this story of Marie's love first reached her ears, she had
been very angry; but her anger had never brought
her to such a pass as this.   Indeed, Marie had not
hitherto been taught to look at the matter in this light.
No one had heretofore twitted her with eating the

bread of charity. It had not occurred to her that on this acco nt she was unfit to be Adolphe's wife. There, in that valley, they were all so nearly equal, that no idea of her own inferiority had ever pressed itself upon her mind. But now—!

When the voice ceased she again looked at him; but it was no longer with a beseeching look. Did he also altogether scorn her? That was now the inquiry which her eyes were called upon to make. No; she could not say that he did. It seemed to her that his energies were chiefly occupied in pulling to pieces the tassel or the sofa cushion.

'And now, miss, let me know at once whether this nonsense is to be over or not,' continued La Mère Bauche; 'and I will tell you at once, I am not going to maintain you here, in my house, to plot against our welfare and happiness. As Marie Clavert you shall not stay here. Capitaine Campan is willing to marry you; and as his wife I will keep my word to you, though you little deserve it. If you refuse to marry him, you must go. As to my son, he is there; and he will tell you now, in my presence, that he altogether declines the honour you propose for him.'

And then she ceased, waiting for an answer, drumming the table with a wafer stamp which happened to be ready to her hand; but Marie said nothing. Adolphe had been appealed to; but Adolphe had not yet spoken.

'Well, miss?' said La Mère Bauche.

Then Marie rose from her seat, and walking round

she touched Adolphe lightly on the shoulder. 'Adolphe,' she said, 'it is for you to speak now. I will do as you bid me.'

He gave a long sigh, looked first at Marie and then at his mother, shook himself slightly, and then spoke : 'Upon my word, Marie, I think mother is right. It would never do for us to marry ; it would not indeed.'

'Then it is decided,' said Marie, returning to her chair.

'And you will marry the capitaine?' said La Mère Bauche.

Marie merely bowed her head in token of acquiescence.

'Then we are friends again. Come here, Marie, and kiss me. You must know that it is my duty to take care of my own son. But I don't want to be angry with you if I can help it ; I don't indeed. When once you are Madame Campan, you shall be my own child ; and you shall have any room in the house you like to choose—there !' And she once more imprinted a kiss on Marie's cold forehead.

How they all got out of the room, and off to their own chambers, I can hardly tell. But in five minutes from the time of this last kiss they were divided. La Mère Bauche had patted Marie, and smiled on her, and called her her dear good little Madame Campan, her young little mistress of the Hôtel Bauche ; and had then got herself into her own room, satisfied with her own victory.

Nor must my readers be too severe on Madame

Bauche. She had already done much for Marie Clavert; and when she found herself once more by her own bedside, she prayed to be forgiven for the cruelty which she felt that she had shown to the orphan. But in making this prayer, with her favourite crucifix in her hand and the little image of the Virgin before her, she pleaded her duty to her son. Was it not right, she asked the Virgin, that she should save her son from a bad marriage? And then she promised ever so much of recompense, both to the Virgin and to Marie; a new trousseau for each, with candles to the Virgin, with a gold watch and chain for Marie, as soon as she should be Marie Campan. She had been cruel; she acknowledged it. But at such a crisis was it not defensible? And then the recompense should be so full!

But there was one other meeting that night, very short indeed, but not the less significant. Not long after they had all separated, just so long as to allow of the house being quiet, Adolphe, still sitting in his room, meditating on what the day had done for him, heard a low tap at his door. 'Come in,' he said, as men always do say; and Marie opening the door, stood just within the verge of his chamber. She had on her countenance neither the soft look of entreating love which she had worn up there in the grotto, nor did she appear crushed and subdued as she had done before his mother. She carried her head somewhat more erect than usual, and looked boldly out at him from under her soft eyelashes. There might still be love there but it was love proudly resolving to quell itself.

Adolphe as he looked at her, felt that he was afraid of her.

'It is all over then between us, M. Adolphe?' she said.

'Well, yes. Don't you think it had better be so, eh, Marie?'

'And this is the meaning of oaths and vows, sworn to each other so sacredly?'

'But, Marie, you heard what my mother said.'

'Oh, sir! I have not come to ask you again to love me. Oh, no! I am not thinking of that. But this, this would be a lie if I kept it now; it would choke me if I wore it as that man's wife. Take it back;' and she tendered to him the little charm which she had always worn round her neck since he had given it to her. He took it abstractedly, without thinking what he did, and placed it on his dressing-table.

'And you,' she continued, 'can you still keep that cross? Oh, no! you must give me back that. It would remind you too often of vows that were untrue.'

'Marie,' he said, 'do not be so harsh to me.'

'Harsh!' said she, 'no; there has been enough of harshness. I would not be harsh to you, Adolphe. But give me the cross; it would prove a curse to you if you kept it.'

He then opened a little box which stood upon the table, and taking out the cross gave it to her.

'And now good-bye,' she said. 'We shall have but little more to say to each other. I know this now, that I was wrong ever to have loved you. I should

have been to you as one of the other poor girls in the
house. But, oh! how was I to help it?' To this he
made no answer, and she, closing the door softly, went
back to her chamber. And thus ended the first day of
Adolphe Bauche's return to his own house.

On the next morning the capitaine and Marie were
formally betrothed. This was done with some little
ceremony, in the presence of all the guests who were
staying at the establishment, and with all manner of
gracious acknowledgments of Marie's virtues. It
seemed as though La Mère Bauche could not be courteous enough to her. There was no more talk of her
being a child of charity; no more allusion now to the
gutter. La Mère Bauche with her own hand brought
her cake with a glass of wine after her betrothal was
over, and patted her on the cheek, and called her her
dear little Marie Campan. And then the capitaine
was made up of infinite politeness, and the guests all
wished her joy, and the servants of the house began to
perceive that she was a person entitled to respect.
How different was all this from that harsh attack that
was made on her the preceding evening! Only
Adolphe,—he alone kept aloof. Though he was present
there he said nothing. He, and he only, offered no
congratulations.

In the midst of all these gala doings Marie herself
said little or nothing. La Mère Bauche perceived this,
but she forgave it. Angrily as she had expressed
herself at the idea of Marie's daring to love her son, she
had still acknowledged within her own heart that such

love had been natural. She could feel no pity for
Marie as long as Adolphe was in danger; but now she
knew how to pity her. So Marie was still petted and
still encouraged, though she went through the day's
work sullenly and in silence.

As to the capitaine it was all one to him. He was
a man of the world. He did not expect that he should
really be preferred, con amore, to a young fellow like
Adolphe. But he did expect that Marie, like other
girls, would do as she was bid; and that in a few days
she would regain her temper and be reconciled to her
life.

And then the marriage was fixed for a very early day;
for as La Mère said, ' What was the use of waiting?
All their minds were made up now, and therefore the
sooner the two were married the better. Did not the
capitaine think so?'

The capitaine said that he did think so.

And then Marie was asked. It was all one to her,
she said. Whatever Maman Bauche liked, that she
would do; only she would not name a day herself.
Indeed she would neither do nor say anything herself which tended in any way to a furtherance of
these matrimonials. But then she acquiesced, quietly
enough if not readily, in what other people did and
said; and so the marriage was fixed for the day week
after Adolphe's return.

The whole of that week passed much in the same
way. The servants about the place spoke among
themselves of Marie's perverseness, obstinacy, and in-

gratitude, because she would not look pleased, or
answer Madame Bauche's courtesies with gratitude;
but La Mère herself showed no signs of anger. Marie
had yielded to her, and she required no more. And
she remembered also the harsh words she had used to
gain her purpose; and she reflected on all that Marie
had lost. On these accounts she was forbearing and
exacted nothing—nothing but that one sacrifice which
was to be made in accordance to her wishes.

And it was made. They were married in the great
salon, the dining-room, immediately after breakfast.
Madame Bauche was dressed in a new puce silk dress
and looked very magnificent on the occasion. She
simpered and smiled, and looked gay even in spite of
her spectacles; and as the ceremony was being performed, she held fast clutched in her hand the gold
watch and chain which were intended for Marie as soon
as ever the marriage should be completed.

The capitaine was dressed exactly as usual, only that
all his clothes were new. Madame Bauche had endeavoured to persuade him to wear a blue coat; but he
answered that such a change would not, he was sure,
be to Marie's taste. To tell the truth, Marie would
hardly have known the difference had he presented
himself in scarlet vestments.

Adolphe, however, was dressed very finely, but he
did not make himself prominent on the occasion. Marie
watched him closely, though none saw that she did so;
and of his garments she could have given an account
with much accuracy—of his garments, ay! and of

every look. 'Is he a man,' she said at last to herself,
'that he can stand by and see all this?'

She too was dressed in silk. They had put on her
what they pleased, and she bore the burden of her
wedding finery without complaint and without pride.
There was no blush on her face as she walked up to
the table at which the priest stood, nor hesitation in
her low voice as she made the necessary answers. She
put her hand into that of the capitaine when required
to do so; and when the ring was put on her finger she
shuddered, but ever so slightly. No one observed it
but La Mère Bauche. 'In one week she will be used
to it, and then we shall all be happy,' said La Mère
to herself. 'And I,—I will be so kind to her!'

And so the marriage was completed, and the watch
was at once given to Marie. 'Thank you, maman,'
said she, as the trinket was fastened to her girdle.
Had it been a pincushion that had cost three sous, it
would have affected her as much.

And then there was cake, and wine, and sweetmeats;
and after a few minutes Marie disappeared. For an
hour or so the capitaine was taken up with the congratulations of his friends, and with the efforts necessary
to the wearing of his new honours with an air of ease;
but after that time he began to be uneasy because his
wife did not come to him. At two or three in the
afternoon he went to La Mère Bauche to complain.
'This lackadaisical nonsense is no good,' he said. 'At
any rate it is too late now. Marie had better come down
among us and show herself satisfied with her husband.'

But Madame Bauche took Marie's part. 'You must
not be too hard on Marie,' she said. 'She has gone
through a good deal this week past, and is very young;
whereas, capitaine, you are not very young.'

The capitaine merely shrugged his shoulders. In
the mean time Mère Bauche went up to visit her protégée in her own room, and came down with a report
that she was suffering from a headache. She could not
appear at dinner, Madame Bauche said; but would
make one at the little party which was to be given in
the evening. With this the capitaine was forced to be
content.

The dinner therefore went on quietly without her,
much as it did on other ordinary days. And then
there was a little time of vacancy, during which the
gentlemen drank their coffee and smoked their cigars at
the café, talking over the event that had taken place
that morning, and the ladies brushed their hair and
added some ribbon or some brooch to their usual
apparel. Twice during this time did Madame Bauche
go up to Marie's room with offers to assist her. 'Not
yet, maman; not quite yet,' said Marie piteously
through her tears, and then twice did the green spectacles leave the room, covering eyes which also were
not dry. Ah! what had she done? What had she
dared to take upon herself to do? She could not
undo it now.

And then it became quite dark in the passages and
out of doors, and the guests assembled in the salon.
La Mère came in and out three or four times, uneasy

in her gait and unpleasant in her aspect, and everybody began to see that things were wrong. 'She is ill,
I am afraid,' said one. 'The excitement has been too
much,' said a second; 'and he is so old,' whispered a
third. And the capitaine stalked about erect on his
wooden leg, taking snuff, and striving to look indifferent;
but he also was uneasy in his mind.

Presently La Mère came in again, with a quicker
step than before, and whispered something, first to
Adolphe and then to the capitaine, whereupon they both
followed her out of the room.

'Not in her chamber?' said Adolphe.

'Then she must be in yours,' said the capitaine.

'She is in neither,' said La Mère Bauche, with her
sternest voice; 'nor is she in the house.'

And now there was no longer an affectation of
indifference on the part of any of them. They were
anything but indifferent. The capitaine was eager in
his demands that the matter should still be kept secret
from the guests. She had always been romantic, he
said, and had now gone out to walk by the river-side.
They three and the old bath-man would go out and
look for her.

'But it is pitch dark,' said La Mère Bauche.

'We will take lanterns,' said the capitaine. And so
they sallied forth with creeping steps over the gravel,
so that they might not be heard by those within, and
proceeded to search for the young wife.

'Marie! Marie!' said La Mère Bauche, in piteous
accents; 'do come to me; pray do!'

'Hush!' said the capitaine. 'They'll hear you if you call.' He could not endure that the world should learn that a marriage with him had been so distasteful to Marie Clavert.

'Marie, dear Marie!' called Madame Bauche, louder than before, quite regardless of the capitaine's feelings; but no Marie answered. In her innermost heart now did La Mère Bauche wish that this cruel marriage had been left undone.

Adolphe was foremost with his lamp, but he hardly dared to look in the spot where he felt that it was most likely that she should have taken refuge. How could he meet her again, alone, in that grotto? Yet he alone of the four was young. It was clearly for him to ascend. 'Marie!' he shouted, 'are you there?' as he slowly began the long ascent of the steps.

But he had hardly begun to mount when a whirring sound struck his ear, and he felt that the air near him was moved; and then there was a crash upon the lower platform of rock, and a moan, repeated twice but so faintly, and a rustle of silk, and a slight struggle somewhere as he knew within twenty paces of him; and then all was again quiet and still in the night air.

'What was that?' asked the capitaine in a harsh voice. He made his way half across the little garden, and he also was within forty or fifty yards of the flat rock. But Adolphe was unable to answer him. He had fainted and the lamp had fallen from his hands, and rolled to the bottom of the steps.

But the capitaine, though even his heart was all but

quenched within him, had still strength enough to make his way up to the rock ; and there, holding the lantern above his eyes, he saw all that was left for him to see of his bride.

As for La Mère Bauche, she never again sat at the head of that table—never again dictated to guests— never again laid down laws for the management of any one. A poor bedridden old woman, she lay there in her house at Vernet for some seven tedious years, and then was gathered to her fathers.

As for the capitaine—but what matters? He was made of sterner stuff. What matters either the fate of such a one as Adolphe Bauche?

THE O'CONORS OF CASTLE CONOR,
COUNTY MAYO.

I SHALL never forget my first introduction to country life in Ireland, my first day's hunting there, or the manner in which I passed the evening afterwards. Nor shall I ever cease to be grateful for the hospitality which I received from the O'Conors of Castle Conor. My acquaintance with the family was first made in the following manner. But before I begin my story, let me inform my reader, that my name is Archibald Green.

I had been for a fortnight in Dublin, and was about to proceed into county Mayo on business which would occupy me there for some weeks. My head-quarters would, I found, be at the town of Ballyglass; and I soon learned that Ballyglass was not a place in which I should find hotel accommodation of a luxurious kind, or much congenial society indigenous to the place itself.

'But you are a hunting man, you say,' said old Sir P—— C——; 'and in that case you will soon know Tom O'Conor. Tom won't let you be dull. I'd write

E

you a letter to Tom, only he'll certainly make you out
without my taking the trouble.'

I did think at the time that the old baronet might
have written the letter for me, as he had been a
friend of my father's in former days; but he did not,
and I started for Ballyglass with no other introduction
to any one in the county than that contained in Sir
P——'s promise that I should soon know Mr. Thomas
O'Conor.

I had already provided myself with a horse, groom,
saddle and bridle, and these I sent down, en avant, that
the Ballyglassians might know that I was somebody.
Perhaps, before I arrived, Tom O'Conor might learn
that a hunting man was coming into the neighbourhood,
and I might find at the inn a polite note intimating
that a bed was at my service at Castle Conor. I had
heard so much of the free hospitality of the Irish
gentry as to imagine that such a thing might be
possible.

But I found nothing of the kind. Hunting gentlemen in those days were very common in county Mayo,
and one horse was no great evidence of a man's standing in the world. Men there, as I learnt afterwards,
are sought for themselves quite as much as they are
elsewhere; and though my groom's top-boots were
neat, and my horse a very tidy animal, my entry into
Ballyglass created no sensation whatever.

In about four days after my arrival, when I was
already infinitely disgusted with the little pot-house in
which I was forced to stay, and had made up my mind

that the people in county Mayo were a churlish set, I
sent my horse on to a meet of the fox-hounds, and
followed after myself on an open car.

No one but an erratic fox-hunter such as I am—a
fox-hunter, I mean, whose lot it has been to wander
about from one pack of hounds to another—can
understand the melancholy feeling which a man has
when he first intrudes himself, unknown by any one,
among an entirely new set of sportsmen. When a
stranger falls thus, as it were out of the moon into a
hunt, it is impossible that men should not stare at him
and ask who he is. And it is so disagreeable to be
stared at, and to have such questions asked! This
feeling does not come upon a man in Leicestershire or
Gloucestershire, where the numbers are large, and a
stranger or two will always be overlooked, but in
small hunting fields it is so painful that a man has to
pluck up much courage before he encounters it.

We met on the morning in question at Bingham's
Grove. There were not above twelve or fifteen men
out, all of whom, or nearly all, were cousins to each
other. They seemed to be all Toms, and Pats, and
Larrys, and Micks. I was done up very knowingly in
pink, and thought that I looked quite the thing; but
for two or three hours nobody noticed me.

I had my eyes about me, however, and soon found
out which of them was Tom O'Conor. He was a fine-
looking fellow, thin and tall, but not largely made,
with a piercing gray eye, and a beautiful voice for
speaking to a hound. He had two sons there also,

short, slight fellows, but exquisite horsemen. I already felt that I had a kind of acquaintance with the father, but I hardly knew on what ground to put in my claim.

We had no sport early in the morning. It was a cold bleak February day, with occasional storms of sleet. We rode from cover to cover, but all in vain. 'I am sorry, sir, that we are to have such a bad day, as you are a stranger here,' said one gentleman to me. This was Jack O'Conor, Tom's eldest son, my bosom friend for many a year after. Poor Jack! I fear that the Encumbered Estates Court sent him altogether adrift upon the world.

'We may still have a run from Poulnaroe, if the gentleman chooses to come on,' said a voice coming from behind with a sharp trot. It was Tom O'Conor.

'Wherever the hounds go, I'll follow,' said I.

'Then come on to Poulnaroe,' said Mr. O'Conor. I trotted on quickly by his side, and before we reached the cover, had managed to slip in something about Sir P. C.

'What the deuce!' said he. 'What! a friend of Sir P——'s? Why the deuce didn't you tell me so? What are you doing down here? Where are you staying,' &c., &c., &c.

At Poulnaroe we found a fox, but before we did so Mr. O'Conor had asked me over to Castle Conor. And this he did in such a way that there was no possibility of refusing him—or, I should rather say, of

disobeying him. For his invitation came quite in the
tone of a command.

' You'll come to us of course when the day is over—
and let me see; we're near Ballyglass now, but the
run will be right away in our direction. Just send
word for them to send your things to Castle Conor.'

' But they're all about, and unpacked,' said I.

'Never mind. Write a note and say what you
want now, and go and get the rest to-morrow yourself.
Here, Patsey!—Patsey! run into Ballyglass for this
gentleman at once. Now don't be long, for the
chances are we shall find here.' And then, after
giving some further hurried instructions he left me to
write a line in pencil to the innkeeper's wife on the
bank of a ditch.

This I accordingly did. 'Send my small portmanteau,' I said, 'and all my black dress clothes, and
shirts, and socks, and all that, and above all my
dressing things which are on the little table, and the
satin neck-handkerchief, and whatever you do, mind
you send my *pumps;*' and I underscored the latter
word; for Jack O'Conor, when his father left me, went
on pressing the invitation. 'My sisters are going to get
up a dance,' said he; 'and if you are fond of that
kind of things perhaps we can amuse you.' Now in
those days I was very fond of dancing—and very fond
of young ladies too, and therefore glad enough to learn
that Tom O'Conor had daughters as well as sons. On
this account I was very particular in underscoring the
word pumps.

'And hurry, you young divil,' he said to Patsey.

'I have told him to take the portmanteau over on a car,' said I.

'All right; then you'll find it there on our arrival.'

We had an excellent run in which I may make bold to say that I did not acquit myself badly. I stuck very close to the hounds, as did the whole of the O'Conor brood; and when the fellow contrived to earth himself, as he did, I received those compliments on my horse, which is the most approved praise which one fox-hunter ever gives to another.

We'll buy that fellow of you before we let you go,' said Peter, the youngest son.

'I advise you to look sharp after your money if you sell him to my brother,' said Jack.

And then we trotted slowly off to Castle Conor, which, however, was by no means near to us. 'We have ten miles to go;—good Irish miles,' said the father. 'I don't know that I ever remember a fox from Poulnaroe taking that line before.'

'He wasn't a Poulnaroe fox,' said Peter.

'I don't know that,' said Jack; and then they debated that question hotly.

Our horses were very tired, and it was late before we reached Mr. O'Conor's house. That getting home from hunting with a thoroughly weary animal, who has no longer sympathy or example to carry him on, is very tedious work. In the present instance I had company with me; but when a man is alone, when his horse toes at every ten steps, when the night is dark and the rain pouring, and there are yet eight miles of road to be conquered,—at such times a man is almost apt to swear that he will give up hunting.

At last we were in the Castle Conor stable yard;—for we had approached the house by some back way; and as we entered the house by a door leading through a wilderness of back passages, Mr. O'Conor said out loud, 'Now, boys, remember I sit down to dinner in twenty minutes.' And then turning expressly to me, he laid his hand kindly upon my shoulder and said, 'I hope you will make yourself quite at home at Castle Conor,—and whatever you do, don't keep us waiting for dinner. You can dress in twenty minutes, I suppose?'

'In ten!' said I, glibly.

'That's well. Jack and Peter will show you your room,' and so he turned away and left us.

My two young friends made their way into the great hall, and thence into the drawing-room, and I followed them. We were all dressed in pink, and had waded deep through bog and mud. I did not exactly know whither I was being led in this guise, but I soon found myself in the presence of two young ladies, and of a girl about thirteen years of age.

'My sisters,' said Jack, introducing me very laconically; 'Miss O'Conor, Miss Kate O'Conor, Miss Tizzy O'Conor.'

'My name is not Tizzy, said the younger; 'it's Eliza. How do you do, sir? I hope you had a fine hunt! Was papa well up, Jack?'

Jack did not condescend to answer this question, but asked one of the elder girls whether anything had come, and whether a room had been made ready for me.

'Oh yes!' said Miss O'Conor; 'they came, I know, for I saw them brought into the house; and I hope Mr. Green will find everything comfortable.' As she said this I thought I saw a slight smile steal across her remarkably pretty mouth.

They were both exceedingly pretty girls. Fanny the elder wore long glossy curls,—for I write, oh reader, of bygone days, as long ago as that, when ladies wore curls if it pleased them so to do, and gentlemen danced in pumps, with black handkerchiefs round their necks —yes, long black, or nearly black silken curls; and then she had such eyes;—I never knew whether they were most wicked or most bright; and her face was all dimples, and each dimple was laden with laughter and laden with love. Kate was probably the prettier girl of the two, but on the whole not so attractive. She was fairer than her sister, and wore her hair in braids; and was also somewhat more demure in her manner.

In spite of the special injunctions of Mr. O'Conor senior, it was impossible not to loiter for five minutes over the drawing-room fire talking to these houris— more especially as I seemed to know them intimately by intuition before half of the five minutes was over. They were so easy, so pretty, so graceful, so kind, they seemed to take it so much as a matter of course that I should stand there talking in my red coat and muddy boots.

'Well; do go and dress yourselves,' at last said Fanny, pretending to speak to her brothers but looking more especially at me. 'You know how mad papa will be. And remember, Mr. Green, we expect great things from your dancing to-night. Your coming just at this time is such a Godsend.' And again that soupçon of a smile passed over her face.

I hurried up to my room. Peter and Jack coming with me to the door. 'Is everything right?' said Peter, looking among the towels and water-jugs. 'They've given you a decent fire for a wonder,' said Jack stirring up the red hot turf which blazed in the grate. 'All right as a trivet,' said I. 'And look alive like a good fellow,' said Jack. We had scowled at each other in the morning as very young men do when they are strangers; and now, after a few hours, we were intimate friends.

I immediately turned to my work, and was gratified to find that all my things were laid out ready for dressing; my portmanteau had of course come open, as my keys were in my pocket, and therefore some of the excellent servants of the house had been able to save me all the trouble of unpacking. There was my shirt hanging before the fire; my black clothes were spread upon the bed, my socks and collar and handkerchief beside them; my brushes were on the toilet table, and everything prepared exactly as though my own man had been there. How nice

I immediately went to work at getting off my spurs
and boots, and then proceeded to loosen the buttons at
my knees. In doing this I sat down in the arm-chair
which had been drawn up for me, opposite the fire.
But what was the object on which my eyes then fell ;—
the objects I should rather say !

Immediately in front of my chair was placed, just
ready for my feet, an enormous pair of shooting-boots
—half-boots, made to lace up round the ankles, with
thick double leather soles, and each bearing half a
stone of iron in the shape of nails and heel-pieces. I
had superintended the making of these shoes in Burlington Arcade with the greatest diligence. I was
never a good shot ; and, like some other sportsmen,
intended to make up for my deficiency in performance
by the excellence of my shooting apparel. 'Those
nails are not large enough,' I had said ; 'nor nearly
large enough.' But when the boots came home they
struck even me as being too heavy, too metalsome.
'He, he, he,' laughed the boot boy as he turned them
up for me to look at. It may therefore be imagined of
what nature were the articles which were thus set out
for the evening's dancing.

And then the way in which they were placed !
When I saw this the conviction flew across my mind
like a flash of lightning that the preparation had been
made under other eyes than those of the servant. The
heavy big boots were placed so prettily before the
chair, and the strings of each were made to dangle
down at the sides, as though just ready for tying ! They

seemed to say, the boots did, 'Now, make haste.
We at any rate are ready—you cannot say that you
were kept waiting for us.' No mere servant's hand
had ever enabled a pair of boots to laugh at one so
completely.

But what was I to do? I rushed at the small
portmanteau, thinking that my pumps also might be
there. The woman surely could not have been such a
fool as to send me those tons of iron for my evening
wear! But alas, alas! no pumps were there. There
was nothing else in the way of covering for my feet;
not even a pair of slippers.

And now what was I to do? The absolute magni-
tude of my misfortune only loomed upon me by degrees. The twenty minutes allowed by that stern old
paterfamilias were already gone and I had done nothing
towards dressing. And indeed it was impossible that
I should do anything that would be of avail. I could
not go down to dinner in my stocking feet, nor could I
put on my black dress trousers over a pair of mud
painted top-boots. As for those iron-soled horrors— ;
and then I gave one of them a kick with the side of
my bare foot which sent it half way under the bed.

But what was I to do? I began washing myself
and brushing my hair with this horrid weight upon my
mind. My first plan was to go to bed, and send down
word that I had been taken suddenly ill in the
stomach; then to rise early in the morning and get
away unobserved. But by such a course of action I
should lose all chance of any further acquaintance with

those pretty girls! That they were already aware of the extent of my predicament, and were now enjoying it—of that I was quite sure.

What if I boldly put on the shooting-boots, and clattered down to dinner in them? What if I took the bull by the horns, and made myself the most of the joke? This might be very well for the dinner, but it would be a bad joke for me when the hour for dancing came. And, alas! I felt that I lacked the courage. It is not every man that can walk down to dinner, in a strange house full of ladies, wearing such boots as those I have described.

Should I not attempt to borrow a pair? This, all the world will say, should have been my first idea. But I have not yet mentioned that I am myself a large-boned man, and that my feet are especially well developed. I had never for a moment entertained a hope that I should find any one in that house whose boot I could wear. But at last I rang the bell. I would send for Jack, and if everything failed, I would communicate my grief to him.

I had to ring twice before anybody came. The servants, I well knew, were putting the dinner on the table. At last a man entered the room, dressed in rather shabby black, whom I afterwards learned to be the butler.

'What is your name, my friend,' said I, determined to make an ally of the man.

'My name? Why Larry sure, yer honor. And the masther is out of his sinses in a hurry, becase yer honer don't come down.'

'Is he though? Well, now Larry; tell me this; which of all the gentlemen in the house has got the largest foot?'

'Is it the largest foot, yer honer?' said Larry, altogether surprised by my question.

Yes; the largest foot,' and then I proceeded to explain to him my misfortune. He took up first my top-boot, and then the shooting-boot—in looking at which he gazed with wonder at the nails;—and then he glanced at my feet, measuring them with his eye; and after this he pronounced his opinion.

'Yer honer couldn't wear a morsel of leather belonging to ere a one of 'em, young or ould. There niver was a foot like that yet among the O'Conors.'

'But are there no strangers staying here?'

'There's three or four on 'em come in to dinner; but they'll be wanting their own boots I'm thinking. And there's young Misther Dillon; he's come to stay. But Lord love you—' and he again looked at the enormous extent which lay between the heel and the toe of the shooting apparatus which he still held in his hand. 'I niver see such a foot as that in the whole barony,' he said, 'barring my own.'

Now Larry was a large man, much larger altogether than myself, and as he said this I looked down involuntarily at his feet; or rather at his foot, for as he stood I could only see one. And then a sudden hope filled my heart. On that foot there glittered a shoe—not indeed such as were my own which were now resting ingloriously at Ballyglass while they were so

sorely needed at Castle Conor; but one which I could
wear before ladies, without shame—and in my present
frame of mind with infinite contentment.

'Let me look at that one of your own,' said I to the
man, as though it were merely a subject for experimental
inquiry. Larry, accustomed to obedience, took off the
shoe and handed it to me. My own foot was immediately in it, and I found that it fitted me like a
glove.

'And now the other,' said I—not smiling, for a
smile would have put him on his guard; but somewhat
sternly, so that that habit of obedience should not
desert him at this perilous moment. And then I
stretched out my hand.

'But yer honer can't keep 'em, you know,' said he.
'I haven't the ghost of another shoe to my feet.' But
I only looked more sternly than before, and still held
out my hand. Custom prevailed. Larry stooped
down slowly, looking at me the while, and pulling off
the other slipper handed it to me with much hesitation.
Alas! as I put it to my foot I found that it was old,
and worn, and irredeemably down at heel;—that it was
in fact no counterpart at all to that other one which
was to do duty as its fellow. But nevertheless I put
my foot into it, and felt that a descent to the drawing-
room was now possible.

'But yer honer will give 'em back to a poor man?'
said Larry almost crying. 'The masther's mad this
minute becase the dinner's not up. Glory to God, only
listhen to that.' And as he spoke a tremendous peal

rang out from some bell down stairs that had evidently been shaken by an angry hand.

'Larry,' said I—and I endeavoured to assume a look of very grave importance as I spoke—'I look to you to assist me in this matter.'

'Och—wirra sthrue then, and will you let me go? just listhen to that,' and another angry peal rang out, loud and repeated.

'If you do as I ask you,' I continued, 'you shall be well rewarded. Look here; look at these boots,' and I held up the shooting-shoes new from Burlington Arcade. 'They cost thirty shillings—thirty shillings! and I will give them to you for the loan of this pair of slippers.'

'They'd be no use at all to me, yer honer; not the laist use in life.'

'You could do with them very well for to-night, and then you could sell them. And here are ten shillings besides,' and I held out half a sovereign which the poor fellow took into his hand.

I waited no further parley but immediately walked out of the room. With one foot I was sufficiently pleased. As regarded that I felt that I had overcome my difficulty. But the other was not so satisfactory. Whenever I attempted to lift it from the ground the horrid slipper would fall off, or only just hang by the toe. As for dancing, that would be out of the question.

'Och, murther, murther,' sang out Larry, as he heard me going down stairs. 'What will I do at all?

'Tare and 'ounds; there, he's at it agin, as mad as blazes.' This last exclamation had reference to another peal which was evidently the work of the master's hand.

I confess I was not quite comfortable as I walked down stairs. In the first place I was nearly half an hour late, and I knew from the vigour of the peals that had sounded that my slowness had already been made the subject of strong remarks. And then my left shoe went flop, flop on every alternate step of the stairs; by no exertion of my foot in the drawing up of my toe could I induce it to remain permanently fixed upon my foot. But over and above and worse than all this was the conviction strong upon my mind that I should become a subject of merriment to the girls as soon as I entered the room. They would understand the cause of my distress, and probably at this moment were expecting to hear me clatter through the stone hall with those odious metal boots.

Hovever, I hurried down and entered the drawing-room, determined to keep my position near the door, so that I might have as little as possible to do on entering and as little as possible in going out. But I had other difficulties in store for me. I had not as yet been introduced to Mrs. O'Conor; nor to Miss O'Conor, the squire's unmarried sister.

'Upon my word I thought you were never coming,' said Mr. O'Conor as soon as he saw me. 'It is just one hour since we entered the house. Jack, I wish you would find out what has come to that fellow Larry,' and again he rang the bell. He was too

angry, or it might be too impatient to go through the
ceremony of introducing me to anybody.

I saw that the two girls looked at me very sharply,
but I stood at the back of an arm-chair so that no one
could see my feet.   But that little imp Tizzy walked
round deliberately, looked at my heels, and then walked
back again.   It was clear that she was in the secret.

There were eight or ten people in the room, but I
was too much fluttered to notice well who they were.

'Mamma,' said Miss O'Conor, 'let me introduce Mr.
Green to you.'

It luckily happened that Mrs. O'Conor was on the
same side of the fire as myself, and I was able to take
the hand which she offered me without coming round
into the middle of the circle.   Mrs. O'Conor was a
little woman, apparently not of much importance in
the world, but, if one might judge from first appearance,
very good-natured.

'And my aunt Die, Mr. Green,' said Kate, pointing
to a very straight-backed, grim-looking lady, who occupied a corner of a sofa, on the opposite side of the
hearth.   I knew that politeness required that I should
walk across the room and make acquaintance with her.
But under the existing circumstances how was I to
obey the dictates of politeness?   I was determined
therefore to stand my ground, and merely bowed across
the room at Miss O'Conor.   In so doing I made an
enemy who never deserted me during the whole of my
intercourse with the family.   But for her, who knows who
might have been sitting opposite to me as I now write?

'Upon my word, Mr. Green, the ladies will expect much from an Adonis who takes so long over his toilet,' said Tom O'Conor in that cruel tone of banter which he knew so well how to use.

'You forget, father, that men in London can't jump in and out of their clothes as quick as we wild Irishmen,' said Jack.

'Mr. Green knows that we expect a great deal from him this evening. I hope you polk well, Mr. Green,' said Kate.

I muttered something about never dancing, but I knew that that which I said was inaudible.

'I don't think Mr. Green will dance,' said Tizzy; 'at least not much.' The impudence of that child was, I think, unparalleled by any that I have ever witnessed.

'But in the name of all that's holy, why don't we have dinner?' And Mr. O'Conor thundered at the door. 'Larry, Larry, Larry!' he screamed.

'Yes, yer honer, it'll be all right in two seconds,' answered Larry, from some bottomless abyss. 'Tare an' ages; what'll I do at all,' I heard him continuing, as he made his way into the hall. Oh what a clatter he made upon the pavement,—for it was all stone! And how the drops of perspiration stood upon my brow as I listened to him!

And then there was a pause, for the man had gone into the dining-room. I could see now that Mr. O'Conor was becoming very angry, and Jack the eldest son—oh, how often he and I have laughed over all

this since—left the drawing-room for the second time.
Immediately afterwards, Larry's footsteps were again
heard, hurrying across the hall, and then there was a
great slither, and an exclamation, and the noise of a
fall—and I could plainly hear poor Larry's head strike
against the stone floor.

'Ochone, ochone !' he cried at the top of his voice—
' I'm murthered with 'em now intirely ; and d—— 'em
for boots—St. Peter be good to me.'

There was a general rush into the hall, and I was
carried with the stream. The poor fellow who had
broken his head would be sure to tell how I had
robbed him of his shoes. The coachman was already
helping him up, and Peter good-naturedly lent a hand.

'What on earth is the matter ?' said Mr. O'Conor.

'He must be tipsy,' whispered Miss O'Conor, the
maiden sister.

' I aint tipsy at all thin,' said Larry, getting up and
rubbing the back of his head, and sundry other parts
of his body. ' Tipsy indeed !' And then he added when
he was quite upright, ' The dinner is sarved—at last.'

And he bore it all without telling. ' I'll give that
fellow a guinea to-morrow morning,' said I to myself—
' if it's the last that I have in the world.'

I shall never forget the countenance of the Miss
O'Conors as Larry scrambled up cursing the unfortu-
nate boots—' What on earth has he got on,' said Mr.
O'Conor.

' Sorrow take 'em for shoes,' ejaculated Larry. But
his spirit was good and he said not a word to betray me.

We all then went in to dinner how we best could. It was useless for us to go back into the drawing-room, that each might seek his own partner. Mr. O'Conor 'the masther,' not caring much for the girls who were around him, and being already half beside himself with the confusion and delay, led the way by himself. I as a stranger should have given my arm to Mrs. O'Conor; but as it was I took her eldest daughter instead, and contrived to shuffle along into the dining-room without exciting much attention, and when there I found myself happily placed between Kate and Fanny.

'I never knew anything so awkward,' said Fanny; 'I declare I can't conceive what has come to our old servant Larry. He's generally the most precise person in the world, and now he is nearly an hour late—and then he tumbles down in the hall.'

'I am afraid I am responsible for the delay,' said I.

'But not for the tumble I suppose,' said Kate from the other side. I felt that I blushed up to the eyes, but I did not dare to enter into explanations.

'Tom,' said Tizzy, addressing her father across the table, 'I hope you had a good run to-day.' It did seem odd to me that a young lady should call her father Tom, but such was the fact.

'Well; pretty well,' said Mr. O'Conor.

'And I hope you were up with the hounds.'

'You may ask Mr. Green that. He at any rate was with them, and therefore he can tell you.'

'Oh, he wasn't before you, I know. No Englishman could get before you—I am quite sure of that.'

'Don't you be impertinent, miss,' said Kate. 'You can easily see, Mr. Green, that papa spoils my sister Eliza.'

'Do you hunt in top-boots, Mr. Green?' said Tizzy.

To this I made no answer. She would have drawn me into a conversation about my feet in half a minute, and the slightest allusion to the subject threw me into a fit of perspiration.

'Are you fond of hunting, Miss O'Conor? asked I, blindly hurrying into any other subject of conversation.

Miss O'Conor owned that she was fond of hunting— just a little; only papa would not allow it. When the hounds met anywhere within reach of Castle Conor, she and Kate would ride out to look at them; and if papa was not there that day—an omission of rare occurrence—they would ride a few fields with the hounds.

'But he lets Tizzy keep with them the whole day,' said she, whispering.

'And has Tizzy a pony of her own?'

'Oh yes, Tizzy has everything. She's papa's pet, you know.'

'And whose pet are you?' I asked.

'Oh—I am nobody's pet, unless sometimes Jack makes a pet of me when he's in a good humour. Do you make pets of your sisters, Mr. Green?'

'I have none. But if I had I should not make pets of them.'

'Not of your own sisters?'

'No. As for myself I'd sooner make a pet of my friend's sister; a great deal.'

'How very unnatural,' said Miss O'Conor with the prettiest look of surprise imaginable.

'Not at all unnatural I think,' said I, looking tenderly and lovingly into her face. Where does one find girls so pretty, so easy, so sweet, so talkative as the Irish girls? And then with all their talking and all their ease, who ever hears of their misbehaving? They certainly love flirting as they also love dancing. But they flirt without mischief and without malice.

I had now quite forgotten my misfortune, and was beginning to think how well I should like to have Fanny O'Conor for my wife. In this frame of mind I was bending over towards her as a servant took away a plate from the other side, when a sepulchral note sounded in my ear. It was like the memento mori of the old Roman;—as though some one pointed in the midst of my bliss to the sword hung over my head by a thread. It was the voice of Larry, whispering in his agony just above my head—

'They's disthroying my poor feet intirely, intirely; so they is! I can't bear it much longer, yer honer.' I had committed murder like Macbeth; and now my Banquo had come to disturb me at my feast.

'What is it he says to you?' asked Fanny.

'Oh nothing,' I answered, once more in my misery.

'There seems to be some point of confidence between you and our Larry,' she remarked.

'Oh no,' said I, quite confused; 'not at all.'

'You need not be ashamed of it. Half the gentlemen in the county have their confidences with Larry;

—and some of the ladies too, I can tell you. He was
born in this house, and never lived anywhere else ; and
I am sure he has a larger circle of acquaintance than
any one else in it.'

I could not recover my self-possession for the next
ten minutes. Whenever Larry was on our side of the
table I was afraid he was coming to me with another
agonized whisper. When he was opposite I could not
but watch him as he hobbled in his misery. It was
evident that the boots were too tight for him, and had
they been made throughout of iron they could not have
been less capable of yielding to the feet. I pitied him
from the bottom of my heart. And I pitied myself
also, wishing that I was well in bed upstairs with some
feigned malady, so that Larry might have had his own
again.

And then for a moment I missed him from the room.
He had doubtless gone to relieve his tortured feet in
the servants-hall, and as he did so was cursing my
cruelty. But what mattered it ? Let him curse. If
he would only stay away and do that I would appease
his wrath when we were alone together with pecuniary
satisfaction.

But there was no such rest in store for me. 'Larry,
Larry,' shouted Mr. O'Conor, 'where on earth has the
fellow gone to ?' They were all cousins at the table
except myself, and Mr. O'Conor was not therefore re-
strained by any feeling of ceremony. 'There is something wrong with that fellow to-day ; what is it, Jack ?'

'Upon my word, sir, I don't know,' said Jack.

'I think he must be tipsy,' whispered Miss O'Conor, the maiden sister, who always sat at her brother's left hand. But a whisper though it was, it was audible all down the table.

'No, ma'am; it aint dhrink at all,' said the coachman. 'It is his feet as does it.'

'His feet!' shouted Tom O'Conor.

'Yes; I know it's his feet,' said that horrid Tizzy. 'He's got on great thick nailed shoes. It was that that made him tumble down in the hall.'

I glanced at each side of me, and could see that there was a certain consciousness expressed in the face of each of my two neighbours;—on Kate's mouth there was decidedly a smile, or rather perhaps the slightest possible inclination that way; whereas on Fanny's part I thought I saw something like a rising sorrow at my distress. So at least I flattered myself.

'Send him back into the room immediately,' said Tom, who looked at me as though he had some consciousness that I had introduced all this confusion into his household. What should I do? Would it not be best for me to make a clean breast of it before them all? But alas! I lacked the courage.

The coachman went out, and we were left for five minutes without any servant, and Mr. O'Conor the while became more and more savage. I attempted to say a word to Fanny, but failed—Vox faucibus hæsit.

'I don't think he has got any others,' said Tizzy— 'at least none others left.'

On the whole I am glad I did not marry into the

family, as I could not have endured that girl to stay in
my house as a sister-in-law.

'Where the d—— has that other fellow gone to?'
said Tom. 'Jack, do go out and see what is the
matter. If anybody is drunk send for me.'

'Oh, there is nobody drunk,' said Tizzy.

Jack went out, and the coachman returned; but
what was done and said I hardly remember. The
whole room seemed to swim round and round, and as
far as I can recollect the company sat mute, neither
eating nor drinking. Presently Jack returned.

'It's all right,' said he. I always liked Jack. At
the present moment he just looked towards me and
laughed slightly.

'All right?' said Tom. 'But is the fellow coming?'

'We can do with Richard, I suppose,' said Jack.

'No—I can't do with Richard,' said the father.
'And I will know what it all means. Where is that
fellow Larry?'

Larry had been standing just outside the door, and
now he entered gently as a mouse. No sound came
from his footfall, nor was there in his face that look of
pain which it had worn for the last fifteen minutes. But
he was not the less abashed, frightened, and unhappy.

'What is all this about, Larry?' said his master,
turning to him. 'I insist upon knowing.'

'Och thin, Mr. Green, yer honer, I wouldn't be
afther telling agin yer honer; indeed I wouldn't
thin, av' the masther would only let me hould my

tongue.' And he looked across at me, deprecating my anger.

'Mr. Green! said Mr. O'Conor.

'Yes, yer honer. It's all along of his honer's thick shoes,' and Larry stepping backwards towards the door, lifted them up from some corner, and coming well forward, exposed them with the soles uppermost to the whole table.

'And that's not all, yer honer; but they've squoze the very toes of me into a jelly.'

There was now a loud laugh, in which Jack and Peter and Fanny and Kate and Tizzy all joined; as too did Mr. O'Conor—and I also myself after a while.

'Whose boots are they?' demanded Miss O'Conor senior, with her severest tone and grimmest accent.

''Deed then and the divil may have them for me, Miss,' answered Larry. 'They war Mr. Green's, but the likes of him won't wear them agin afther the likes of me—barring he wanted them very particular,' added he, remembering his own pumps.

I began muttering something, feeling that the time had come when I must tell the tale. But Jack with great good nature, took up the story and told it so well, that I hardly suffered in the telling.

'And that's it,' said Tom O'Conor, laughing till I thought he would have fallen from his chair. 'So you've got Larry's shoes on—'

'And very well he fills them,' said Jack.

'And it's his honer that's welcome to 'em,' said

Larry, grinning from ear to ear now that he saw that 'the masther' was once more in a good humour.

'I hope they'll be nice shoes for dancing,' said Kate.

'Only there's one down at the heel I know,' said Tizzy.

'The servant's shoes!' This was an exclamation made by the maiden lady, and intended apparently only for her brother's ear. But it was clearly audible by all the party.

'Better that than no dinner,' said Peter.

'But what are you to do about the dancing?' said Fanny, with an air of dismay on her face which flattered me with an idea that she did care whether I danced or no.

In the mean time Larry, now as happy as an emperor, was tripping round the room without any shoes to encumber him as he withdrew the plates from the table.

'And it's his honer that's welcome to 'em,' said he again, as he pulled off the table-cloth with a flourish. 'And why wouldn't he, and he able to folly the hounds betther nor any Englishman that iver war in these parts before,—anyways so Mick says!'

Now Mick was the huntsman, and this little tale of eulogy from Larry went far towards easing my grief. I had ridden well to the hounds that day, and I knew it.

There was nothing more said about the shoes, and I was soon again at my ease, although Miss O'Conor did say something about the impropriety of Larry walking

about in his stocking feet. The ladies however soon
withdrew,—to my sorrow, for I was getting on swim-
mingly with Fanny; and then we gentlemen gathered
round the fire and filled our glasses.

In about ten minutes a very light tap was heard,
the door was opened to the extent of three inches,
and a female voice which I readily recognized called
to Jack.

Jack went out, and in a second or two put his head
back into the room and called to me—'Green,' he
said, 'just step here a moment, there's a good fellow.'
I went out, and there I found Fanny standing with her
brother.

'Here are the girls at their wits' ends,' said he,
'about your dancing. So Fanny has put a boy upon one
of the horses, and proposes that you should send another
line to Mrs. Meehan at Ballyglass. It's only ten miles,
and he'll be back in two hours.'

I need hardly say that I acted in conformity with
this advice. I went into Mr. O'Conor's book room,
with Jack and his sister, and there scribbled a note.
It was delightful to feel how intimate I was with them,
and how anxious they were to make me happy.

'And we won't begin till they come,' said Fanny.

'Oh, Miss O'Conor, pray don't wait,' said I.

'Oh, but we will,' she answered. 'You have your
wine to drink, and then there's the tea; and then we'll
have a song or two. I'll spin it out; see if I don't.'
And so we went to the front door where the boy was
already on his horse—her own nag as I afterwards found.

'And Patsey,' said she, 'ride for your life now; and Patsey, whatever you do, don't come back without Mr. Green's pumps—his dancing-shoes you know.'

And in about two hours the pumps did arrive; and I don't think I ever spent a pleasanter evening or got more satisfaction out of a pair of shoes. They had not been two minutes on my feet before Larry was carrying a tray of negus across the room in those which I had worn at dinner.

'The Dillon girls are going to stay here,' said Fanny as I wished her good night at two o'clock. 'And we'll have dancing every evening as long as you remain.'

'But I shall leave to-morrow,' said I.

'Indeed you won't. Papa will take care of that.'

And so he did. 'You had better go over to Ballyglass yourself to-morrow,' said he, 'and collect your own things. There's no knowing else what you may have to borrow of Larry.'

I stayed there three weeks, and in the middle of the third I thought that everything would be arranged between me and Fanny. But the aunt interfered; and in about a twelvemonth after my adventures she consented to make a more fortunate man happy for his life.

JOHN BULL ON THE GUADALQUIVIR.

I AM an Englishman living, as all Englishmen should
do, in England, and my wife would not, I think, be
well pleased were any one to insinuate that she were
other than an Englishwoman, but in the circumstances
of my marriage I became connected with the south of
Spain, and the narrative which I am to tell requires
that I should refer to some of those details.

The Pomfrets and Daguilars have long been in
trade together in this country, and one of the partners
has usually resided at Seville for the sake of the works
which the firm there possesses. My father, James
Pomfret, lived there for ten years before his marriage;
and since that, and up to the present period, old
Mr. Daguilar has been always on the spot. He was,
I believe, born in Spain, but he came very early to
England; he married an English wife, and his sons
have been educated exclusively in England. His only
daughter, Maria Daguilar, did not pass so large a
proportion of her early life in this country, but she
came to us for a visit at the age of seventeen, and

when she returned I made up my mind that I most
assuredly would go after her. So I did, and she is
now sitting on the other side of the fireplace with a
legion of small linen habiliments in a huge basket by
her side.

I felt, at the first, that there was something lacking to
make my cup of love perfectly delightful. It was very
sweet, but there was wanting that flower of romance
which is generally added to the heavenly draught
by a slight admixture of opposition. I feared that
the path of my true love would run too smooth.
When Maria came to our house my mother and elder
sister seemed to be quite willing that I should be con-
tinually alone with her; and she had not been there
ten days before my father, by chance, remarked that
there was nothing old Mr. Daguilar valued so highly
as a thorough feeling of intimate alliance between the
two families which had been so long connected in
trade. I was never told that Maria was to be my
wife, but I felt that the same thing was done without
words; and when, after six weeks of somewhat elaborate attendance upon her, I asked her to be Mrs. John
Pomfret, I had no more fear of a refusal, or even of
hesitation on her part, than I now have when I suggest
to my partner some commercial transaction of un-
doubted advantage.

But Maria, even at that age, had about her a quiet
sustained decision of character quite unlike anything I
had seen in English girls. I used to hear, and do still
hear, how much more flippant is the education of girls

in France and Spain than in England; and I know
that this is shown to be the result of many causes—
the Roman Catholic religion being, perhaps, the chief
offender; but, nevertheless, I rarely see in one of our
own young women the same power of a self-sustained
demeanour as I meet on the Continent. It goes no
deeper than the demeanour, people say. I can only
answer that I have not found that shallowness in my
own wife.

Miss Daguilar replied to me that she was not prepared with an answer; she had only known me six
weeks, and wanted more time to think about it;
besides, there was one in her own country with whom
she would wish to consult. I knew she had no
mother; and as for consulting old Mr. Daguilar on
such a subject, that idea, I knew, could not have
troubled her. Besides, as I afterwards learned, Mr.
Daguilar had already proposed the marriage to his
partner exactly as he would have proposed a division
of assets. My mother declared that Maria was a
foolish chit—in which, by-the-by, she showed her
entire ignorance of Miss Daguilar's character; my
eldest sister begged that no constraint might be put on
the young lady's inclinations—which provoked me to
assert that the young lady's inclinations were by no
means opposed to my own; and my father, in the
coolest manner, suggested that the matter might stand
over for twelve months, and that I might then go to
Seville, and see about it! Stand over for twelve
months! Would not Maria, long before that time,

G

have been snapped up and carried off by one of those inordinately rich Spanish grandees who are still to be met with occasionally in Andalucia?

My father's dictum, however, had gone forth; and Maria, in the calmest voice, protested that she thought it very wise. I should be less of a boy by that time, she said, smiling on me, but driving wedges between every fibre of my body as she spoke. 'Be it so,' I said, proudly. 'At any rate, I am not so much of a boy that I shall forget you.' 'And, John, you still have the trade to learn,' she added, with her deliciously foreign intonation—speaking very slowly, but with perfect pronunciation. The trade to learn! However, I said not a word, but stalked out of the room. meaning to see her no more before she went. But I could not resist attending on her in the hall as she started; and, when she took leave of us, she put her face up to be kissed by me, as she did by my father, and seemed to receive as much emotion from one embrace as from the other. 'He'll go out by the packet of the 1st April,' said my father, speaking of me as though I were a bale of goods. 'Ah! that will be so nice,' said Maria, settling her dress in the carriage; 'the oranges will be ripe for him then!'

On the 17th April I did sail, and felt still very like a bale of goods. I had received one letter from her, in which she merely stated that her papa would have a room ready for me on my arrival; and, in answer to that, I had sent an epistle somewhat longer, and, as I then thought, a little more to the purpose. Her turn of mind was more practical than mine, and I must confess my belief that she did not appreciate my poetry.

I landed at Cadiz and was there joined by an old family friend, one of the very best fellows that ever lived. He was to accompany me up as far as Seville ; and, as he had lived for a year or two at Xeres, was supposed to be more Spanish almost than a Spaniard. His name was Johnson, and he was in the wine trade ; and whether for travelling or whether for staying at home—whether for paying you a visit in your own house, or whether for entertaining you in his—there never was (and I am prepared to maintain there never will be) a stancher friend, a choicer companion, or a safer guide than Thomas Johnson. Words cannot produce a eulogium sufficient for his merits. But, as I have since learned, he was not quite so Spanish as I had imagined. Three years among the *bodegas* of Xeres had taught him, no doubt, to appreciate the exact twang of a good, dry sherry ; but not, as I now conceive, the exactest flavour of the true Spanish character. I was very lucky, however, in meeting such a friend, and now reckon him as one of the stanchest allies of the house of Pomfret, Daguilar, and Pomfret.

He met me at Cadiz, took me about the town which appeared to me to be of no very great interest ;—though the young ladies were all very well. But, in this respect, I was then a Stoic, till such time as I might be able to throw myself at the feet of her whom I was ready to

proclaim the most lovely of all the Dulcineas of Andalucia. He carried me up by boat and railway to Xeres;
gave me a most terrific headache, by dragging me out
into the glare of the sun, after I had tasted some half
a dozen different wines, and went through all the
ordinary hospitalities. On the next day we returned
to Puerto, and from thence getting across to St. Lucar
and Bonanza, found ourselves on the banks of the
Guadalquivir, and took our places in the boat for
Seville. I need say but little to my readers respecting
that far-famed river. Thirty years ago we in England
generally believed that on its banks was to be found a
pure elysium of pastoral beauty; that picturesque
shepherds and lovely maidens here fed their flocks in
fields of asphodel; that the limpid stream ran cool and
crystal over bright stones and beneath perennial shade;
and that everything on the Guadalquivir was as lovely
and as poetical as its name. Now, it is pretty widely
known that no uglier river oozes down to its bourn in
the sea through unwholesome banks of low mud. It
is brown and dirty; ungifted by any scenic advantage;
margined for miles upon miles by huge, flat, expansive
fields, in which cattle are reared—the bulls wanted for
the bull-fights among other—and birds of prey sit constant on the shore, watching for the carcasses of such
as die. Such are the charms of the golden Guadalquivir.

At first we were very dull on board that steamer.
I never found myself in a position in which there was
less to do. There was a nasty smell about the little

boat which made me almost ill; every turn in the river
was so exactly like the last, that we might have been
standing still; there was no amusement except eating,
and that, when once done, was not of a kind to make
an early repetition desirable.. Even Johnson was becoming dull, and I began to doubt whether I was so
desirous as I once had been to travel the length and
breadth of all Spain.   But about noon a little incident
occurred which did for a time remove some of our
tedium.   The boat had stopped to take in passengers
on the river; and, among others, a man had come on
board dressed in a fashion that, to my eyes, was equally
strange and picturesque.   Indeed, his appearance was
so singular, that I could not but regard him with care,
though I felt at first averse to stare at a fellow-pas-
senger on account of his clothes.   He was a man of
about fifty, but as active apparently as though not
more than twenty-five; he was of low stature, but of
admirable make; his hair was just becoming grizzled,
but was short and crisp and well cared for; his face
was prepossessing, having a look of good humour
added to courtesy, and there was a pleasant, soft smile
round his mouth which ingratiated one at the first sight.
But it was his dress rather than his person which
attracted attention.   He wore the ordinary Andalucian
cap—of which such hideous parodies are now making
themselves common in England—but was not contented
with the usual ornament of the double tuft.   The cap
was small, and jaunty; trimmed with silk velvet—as is
common here with men careful to adorn their persons;

but this man's cap was finished off with a jewelled
button and golden filigree work. He was dressed in a
short jacket with a stand-up collar; and that also was
covered with golden buttons and with golden button-
holes. It was all gilt down the front, and all lace
down the back. The rows of buttons were double; and
those of the more backward row hung down in heavy
pendules. His waistcoat was of coloured silk—very
pretty to look at; and ornamented with a small sash,
through which gold threads were worked. All the
buttons of his breeches also were of gold; and there
were gold tags to all the button-holes. His stockings
were of the finest silk, and clocked with gold from the
knee to the ankle.

Dress any Englishman in such a garb and he will
at once give you the idea of a hog in armour. In
the first place he will lack the proper spirit to carry
it off, and in the next place the motion of his limbs
will disgrace the ornaments they bear. 'And so
best,' most Englishmen will say. Very likely; and,
therefore, let no Englishman try it. But my Spaniard
did not look at all like a hog in armour. He walked
slowly down the plank into the boat, whistling lowly
but very clearly, a few bars from an opera tune.
It was plain to see that he was master of himself,
of his ornaments, and of his limbs. He had no appearance of thinking that men were looking at him,
or of feeling that he was beauteous in his attire;—
nothing could be more natural than his foot-fall, or
the quiet glance of his cheery gray eye. He walked

up to the captain, who held the helm, and lightly
raised his hand to his cap. The captain, taking one
hand from the wheel, did the same, and then the
stranger, turning his back to the stern of the vessel,
and fronting down the river with his face, continued
to whistle slowly, clearly, and in excellent time.
Grand as were his clothes they were no burthen on
his mind.

'What is he?' said I, going up to my friend Johnson,
with a whisper.

'Well, I've been looking at him,' said Johnson—
which was true enough; 'he's a——an uncommonly
good-looking fellow, isn't he?'

'Particularly so,' said I; 'and got up quite irre-
spective of expense. Is he a—a—a gentleman, now,
do you think?'

'Well, those things are so different in Spain, that
it's almost impossible to make an Englishman understand them. One learns to know all this sort of
people by being with them in the country, but one
can't explain.'

'No; exactly. Are they real gold?'

'Yes, yes; I dare say they are. They sometimes
have them silver gilt.'

'It is quite a common thing, then, isn't it?' asked I.

'Well, not exactly; that—— Ah! yes; I see! of
course. He is a torero.'

'A what?'

'A mayo. I will explain it all to you. You will
see them about in all places, and will get used to them.'

'But I haven't seen one other as yet.'

'No, and they are not all so gay as this, nor so new in their finery, you know.'

'And what is a torero?'

'Well, a torero is a man engaged in bull-fighting.'

'Oh! he is a matador, is he?' said I, looking at him with more than all my eyes.

'No, not exactly that;—not of necessity. He is probably a mayo. A fellow that dresses himself smart for fairs, and will be seen hanging about with the bull-fighters. What would be a sporting fellow in England—only he won't drink and curse like a low man on the turf there. Come, shall we go and speak to him?'

'I can't talk to him,' said I, diffident of my Spanish. I had received lessons in England from Maria Daguilar; but six weeks is little enough for making love, let alone the learning of a foreign language.

'Oh! I'll do the talking. You'll find the language easy enough before long. It soon becomes the same as English to you, when you live among them.' And then Johnson, walking up to the stranger, accosted him with that good-natured familiarity with which a thoroughly nice fellow always opens a conversation with his inferior. Of course I could not understand the words which were exchanged; but it was clear enough that the 'mayo' took the address in good part, and was inclined to be communicative and social.

'They are all of pure gold,' said Johnson, turning
to me after a minute, making as he spoke a motion
with his head to show the importance of the information.

'Are they indeed?' said I. 'Where on earth did
a fellow like that get them?' Whereupon Johnson
again returned to his conversation with the man.
After another minute he raised his hand, and began
to finger the button on the shoulder; and to aid him
in doing so, the man of the bull-ring turned a little on
one side.

'They are wonderfully well made,' said Johnson,
talking to me, and still fingering the button. 'They
are manufactured, he says, at Osuna, and he tells
me that they make them better there than anywhere
else.'

'I wonder what the whole set would cost?' said I.
'An enormous deal of money for a fellow like him, I
should think!'

'Over twelve ounces,' said Johnson, having asked
the question; 'and that will be more than forty
pounds.'

'What an uncommon ass he must be!' said I.

As Johnson by this time was very closely scrutinizing
the whole set of ornaments I thought I might do so
also, and going up close to our friend, I too began
to handle the buttons and tags on the other side.
Nothing could have been more good-humoured than
he was—so much so that I was emboldened to hold up
his arm that I might see the cut of his coat, to take

off his cap and examine the make, to stuff my finger in beneath his sash, and at last to kneel down while I persuaded him to hold up his legs that I might look to the clocking. The fellow was thoroughly good-natured, and why should I not indulge my curiosity?

'You'll upset him if you don't take care,' said Johnson; for I had got fast hold of him by one ankle, and was determined to finish the survey completely.

'Oh, no, I sha'n't,' said I; 'a bull-fighting chap can surely stand on one leg. But what I wonder at is, how on earth he can afford it!' Whereupon Johnson again began to interrogate him in Spanish.

'He says he has got no children,' said Johnson, having received a reply, 'and that as he has nobody but himself to look after, he is able to allow himself such little luxuries.'

'Tell him that I say he would be better with a wife and couple of babies,' said I—and Johnson interpreted.

'He says that he'll think of it some of these days, when he finds that the supply of fools in the world is becoming short,' said Johnson.

We had nearly done with him now; but after regaining my feet, I addressed myself once more to the heavy pendules, which hung down almost under his arm. I lifted one of these, meaning to feel its weight between my fingers; but unfortunately I gave a lurch, probably through the motion of the boat, and still holding by the button, tore it almost off from our friend's coat.

'Oh, I am so sorry!' I said, in broad English.

'It do not matter at all,' he said, bowing, and speaking with equal plainness.   And then, taking a knife from his pocket, he cut the pendule off, leaving a bit of torn cloth on the side of his jacket.

'Upon my word, I am quite unhappy,' said I ; 'but I always am so awkward.'   Whereupon he bowed low.

'Couldn't I make it right!' said I, bringing out my purse.

He lifted his hand, and I saw that it was small and white; he lifted it, and gently put it upon my purse, smiling sweetly as he did so.   'Thank you, no, señor ; thank you, no.'   And then, bowing to us both, he walked away down into the cabin.

'Upon my word, he is a deuced well-mannered fellow,' said I.

'You shouldn't have offered him money,' said Johnson ; 'a Spaniard does not like it.'

'Why, I thought you could do nothing without money in this country.   Doesn't every one take bribes?'

'Ah! yes; that is a different thing; but not the price of a button.   By Jove! he understood English, too.   Did you see that?'

'Yes; and I called him an ass!   I hope he doesn't mind it.'

'Oh! no; he won't think anything about it,' said Johnson.   'That sort of fellows don't.   I dare say we shall see him in the bull-ring next Sunday, and then we'll make all right with a glass of lemonade.'

And so our adventure ended with the man of the gold ornaments. I was sorry that I had spoken English before him so heedlessly, and resolved that I would never be guilty of such *gaucherie* again. But, then, who would think that a Spanish bull-fighter would talk a foreign language? I was sorry, also, that I had torn his coat;—it had looked so awkward; and sorry again that I had offered the man money. Altogether I was a little ashamed of myself; but I had too much to look forward to at Seville to allow any heaviness to remain long at my heart; and before I had arrived at the marvellous city I had forgotten both him and his buttons.

Nothing could be nicer than the way in which I was welcomed at Mr. Daguilar's house, or more kind—I may almost say affectionate—than Maria's manner to me. But it was too affectionate; and I am not sure that I should not have liked my reception better had she been more diffident in her tone, and less inclined to greet me with open warmth. As it was, she again gave me her cheek to kiss, in her father's presence, and called me dear John, and asked me specially after some rabbits which I had kept at home merely for a younger sister; and then it seemed as though she were in no way embarrassed by the peculiar circumstances of our position. Twelve months since I had asked her to be my wife, and now she was to give me an answer; and yet she was as assured in her gait, and as serenely

joyous in her tone, as though I were a brother just
returned from college. It could not be that she meant
to refuse me, or she would not smile on me and be so
loving; but I could almost have found it in my heart
to wish that she would. 'It is quite possible,' said I
to myself, 'that I may not be found so ready for this
family bargain. A love that is to be had like a bale of
goods is not exactly the love to suit my taste.' But
then, when I met her again in the morning, I could
no more have quarrelled with her than I could have
flown.

I was inexpressibly charmed with the whole city, and
especially with the house in which Mr. Daguilar lived.
It opened from the corner of a narrow, unfrequented
street—a corner like an elbow—and, as seen from the
exterior, there was nothing prepossessing to recommend
it; but the outer door led by a short hall or passage to
an inner door or *grille*, made of open ornamental iron-
work, and through that we entered a court, or patio,
as they called it. Nothing could be more lovely or
deliciously cool than was this small court. The building on each side was covered by trellis-work; and beautiful creepers, vines, and parasite flowers, now in the full
magnificence of the early summer, grew up and clustered round the window. Every inch of wall was
covered, so that none of the glaring whitewash wounded
the eye. In the four corners of the patio were four
large orange-trees, covered with fruit. I would not say
a word in special praise of these, remembering that
childish promise she had made on my behalf. In the

middle of the court there was a fountain, and round
about on the marble floor there were chairs, and here
and there a small table, as though the space were really
a portion of the house. It was here that we used to
take our cup of coffee and smoke our cigarettes, I and
old Mr. Daguilar, while Maria sat by, not only approv-
ing, but occasionally rolling for me the thin paper round
the fragrant weed with her taper fingers. Beyond the
patio was an open passage or gallery, filled also with
flowers in pots; and then, beyond this, one entered the
drawing-room of the house. It was by no means a
princely palace or mansion, fit for the owner of untold
wealth. The rooms were not over large nor very numerous; but the most had been made of a small space,
and everything had been done to relieve the heat of an
almost tropical sun.

'It is pretty, is it not?' she said, as she took me
through it.

'Very pretty,' I said. 'I wish we could live in
such houses.'

'Oh, they would not do at all for dear old fat,
cold, cozy England. You are quite different, you
know, in everything from us in the south; more phleg-
matic, but then so much steadier. The men and the
houses are all the same.'

I can hardly tell why, but even this wounded me.
It seemed to me as though she were inclined to put
into one and the same category things English, dull,
useful, and solid; and that she was disposed to show
a sufficient appreciation for such necessaries of life,

though she herself had another and inner sense—a sense
keenly alive to the poetry of her own southern clime ; and
that I, as being English, was to have no participation in
this latter charm.   An English husband might do very
well, the interests of the firm might make such an
arrangement desirable, such a *mariage de convenance*—
so I argued to myself—might be quite compatible
with—with heaven only knows what delights of super-
terrestrial romance, from which I, as being an English
thick-headed lump of useful coarse mortality, was to
be altogether debarred.   She had spoken to me of
oranges, and having finished the survey of the house,
she offered me some sweet little cakes.   It could not
be that of such things were the thoughts which lay
undivulged beneath the clear waters of those deep
black eyes—undivulged to me, though no one else
could have so good a right to read those thoughts !
It could not be that that noble brow gave index of a
mind intent on the trade of which she spoke so often !
Words of other sort than any that had been vouchsafed
to me must fall at times from the rich curves of that
perfect mouth.

So felt I then, pining for something to make me
unhappy.   Ah. me !   I know all about it now, and am
content.   But I wish that some learned pundit would
give us a good definition of romance, would describe
in words that feeling with which our hearts are so
pestered when we are young, which makes us sigh
for we know not what, and forbids us to be contented with what God sends us.   We invest female

beauty with impossible attributes, and are angry because our women have not the spiritualized souls of angels, anxious as we are that they should also be human in the flesh. A man looks at her he would love as at a distant landscape in a mountainous land. The peaks are glorious with more than the beauty of earth and rock and vegetation. He dreams of some mysterious grandeur of design which tempts him on under the hot sun, and over the sharp rock, till he has reached the mountain goal which he had set before him. But when there, he finds that the beauty is well-nigh gone, and as for that delicious mystery on which his soul had fed, it has vanished for ever.

I know all about it now, and am, as I said, content. Beneath those deep black eyes there lay a well of love, good, honest, homely love, love of father and husband and children that were to come—of that love which loves to see the loved ones prospering in honesty. That noble brow—for it is noble; I am unchanged in that opinion, and will go unchanged to my grave— covers thoughts as to the welfare of many, and an intellect fitted to the management of a household, of servants, namely, and children and perchance a husband. That mouth can speak words of wisdom, of very useful wisdom—though of poetry it has latterly uttered little that was original. Poetry and romance! They are splendid mountain views seen in the distance. So let men be content to see them, and not attempt to tread upon the fallacious heather of the mystic hills.

In the first week of my sojourn in Seville I spoke
no word of overt love to Maria, thinking, as I confess, to induce her thereby to alter her mode of conduct to myself. 'She knows that I have come here
to make love to her—to repeat my offer; and she
will at any rate be chagrined if I am slow to do so.'
But it had no effect. At home my mother was rather
particular about her table, and Maria's greatest efforts
seemed to be used in giving me as nice dinners as
we gave her. In those days I did not care a straw
about my dinner, and so I took an opportunity of
telling her. 'Dear me,' said she, looking at me
almost with grief, 'do you not? What a pity! And
do you not like music either?' 'Oh, yes, I adore
it,' I replied. I felt sure at the time that had I
been born in her own sunny clime, she would never
have talked to me about eating. But that was my
mistake.

I used to walk out with her about the city, seeing
all that is there of beauty and magnificence. And in
what city is there more that is worth the seeing? At
first this was very delightful to me, for I felt that I was
blessed with a privilege that would not be granted to
any other man. But its value soon fell in my eyes, for
others would accost her, and walk on the other side,
talking to her in Spanish, as though I hardly existed,
or were a servant there for her protection. And I was
not allowed to take her arm, and thus to appropriate
her, as I should have done in England. 'No, John,'
she said, with the sweetest, prettiest smile, 'we don't

H

do that here; only when people are married.' And she made this allusion to married life out, openly, with no slightest tremor on her tongue.

'Oh, I beg pardon,' said I, drawing back my hand, and feeling angry with myself for not being fully acquainted with all the customs of a foreign country.

'You need not beg pardon,' said she, 'when we were in England we always walked so. It is just a custom, you know.' And then I saw her drop her large dark eyes to the ground, and bow gracefully in answer to some salute.

I looked round, and saw that we had been joined by a young cavalier,—a Spanish nobleman, as I saw at once; a man with jet black hair, and a straight nose, and a black moustache, and patent leather boots, very slim and very tall, and—though I would not confess it then—uncommonly handsome. I myself am inclined to be stout, my hair is light, my nose broad, I have no hair on my upper lip, and my whiskers are rough and uneven. 'I could punch your head though, my fine fellow,' said I to myself, when I saw that he placed himself at Maria's side, 'and think very little of the achievement.'

The wretch went on with us round the plaza for some quarter of an hour, talking Spanish with the greatest fluency, and she was every whit as fluent. Of course, I could not understand a word that they said. Of all positions that a man can occupy, I think that that is about the most uncomfortable; and I cannot

say that, even up to this day, I have quite forgiven her
for that quarter of an hour.

'I shall go in,' said I, unable to bear my feelings,
and preparing to leave her. 'The heat is unendurable.'

'Oh dear, John, why did you not speak before?' she
answered. 'You cannot leave me here, you know, as
I am in your charge; but I will go with you almost
directly.' And then she finished her conversation with
the Spaniard, speaking with an animation she had
never displayed in her conversations with me.

It had been agreed between us for two or three days
before this, that we were to rise early on the following
morning for the sake of ascending the tower of the
cathedral, and visiting the Giralda, as the iron figure
is called, which turns upon a pivot on the extreme
summit. We had often wandered together up and
down the long dark gloomy aisle of the stupendous
building, and had, together, seen its treasury of art;
but as yet we had not performed the task which has to
be achieved by all visitors to Seville; and in order that
we might have a clear view over the surrounding country, and not be tormented by the heat of an advanced
sun, we had settled that we would ascend the Giralda
before breakfast.

And now, as I walked away from the plaza towards
Mr. Daguilar's house, with Maria by my side, I made
up my mind that I would settle my business during
this visit to the cathedral. Yes, and I would so
manage the settlement that there should be no doubt
left as to my intentions and my own ideas. I would not

be guilty of shilly-shally conduct; I would tell her
frankly what I felt and what I thought, and would
make her understand that I did not desire her hand if
I could not have her heart. I did not value the kindness of her manner, seeing that that kindness sprung
from indifference rather than passion; and so I would
declare to her. And I would ask her, also, who was
this young man with whom she was intimate—for whom
all her volubility and energy of tone seemed to be
employed? She had told me once that it behoved her
to consult a friend in Seville as to the expediency of
her marriage with me. Was this the friend whom she
had wished to consult? If so, she need not trouble
herself. Under such circumstances I should decline
the connection! And I resolved that I would find out
how this might be. A man who proposes to take a
woman to his bosom as his wife, has a right to ask for
information—ay, and to receive it too. It flashed upon
my mind at this moment that Donna Maria was well
enough inclined to come to me as my wife, but——. I
could hardly define the 'buts' to myself, for there
were three or four of them. Why did she always speak
to me in a tone of childish affection, as though I were
a schoolboy home for the holidays? I would have all
this out with her on the tower on the following morning, standing under the Giralda.

On that morning we met together in the patio, soon
after five o'clock, and started for the cathedral. She
looked beautiful, with her black mantilla over her head,
and with black gloves on, and her black morning silk

dress—beautiful, composed, and at her ease, as though she were well satisfied to undertake this early morning walk from feelings of good nature—sustained, probably, by some under-current of a deeper sentiment.   Well; I would know all about it before I returned to her father's house.

There hardly stands, as I think, on the earth a building more remarkable than the cathedral of Seville, and hardly one more grand.   Its enormous size ; its gloom and darkness ; the richness of ornamentation in the details, contrasted with the severe simplicity of the larger outlines ; the variety of its architecture ; the glory of its paintings ; and the wondrous splendour of its metallic decoration, its altar-friezes, screens, rails, gates, and the like, render it, to my mind, the first in interest among churches.   It has not the coloured glass of Chartres, or the marble glory of Milan, or such a forest of aisles as Antwerp, or so perfect a hue in stone as Westminster, nor in mixed beauty of form and colour does it possess anything equal to the choir of Cologne ; but, for combined magnificence and awe-compelling grandeur, I regard it as superior to all other ecclesiastical edifices.

It is its deep gloom with which the stranger is so greatly struck on his first entrance.   In a region so hot as the south of Spain, a cool interior is a main object with the architect, and this it has been necessary to effect by the exclusion of light ; consequently the church is dark, mysterious, and almost cold.   On the morning in question, as we entered, it seemed to be filled with

gloom, and the distant sound of a slow footstep here
and there beyond the transept inspired one almost with
awe. Maria, when she first met me, had begun to
talk with her usual smile, offering me coffee and a
biscuit before I started. 'I never eat biscuit,' I said,
with almost a severe tone, as I turned from her. That
dark, horrid man of the plaza—would she have offered
him a cake had she been going to walk with him in the
gloom of the morning? After that little had been
spoken between us. She walked by my side with her
accustomed smile; but she had, as I flattered myself,
begun to learn that I was not to be won by a meaning-
less good nature. 'We are lucky in our morning for
the view;' that was all she said, speaking with that
peculiarly clear, but slow, pronunciation which she
had assumed in learning our language.

We entered the cathedral, and, walking the whole
length of the aisle, left it again at the porter's porch at
the further end. Here we passed through a low door
on to the stone flight of steps, and at once began to
ascend. 'There are a party of your countrymen up
before us,' said Maria; 'the porter says that they went
through the lodge half an hour since.' 'I hope they
will return before we are on the top,' said I, bethinking
myself of the task that was before me. And indeed
my heart was hardly at ease within me, for that which
I had to say would require all the spirit of which I was
master.

The ascent to the Giralda is very long and very
fatiguing; and we had to pause on the various landings

and in the singular belfry in order that Miss Daguilar
might recruit her strength and breath. As we rested
on one of these occasions, in a gallery which runs round
the tower below the belfry, we heard a great noise
of shouting, and a clattering of sticks among the balls.
'It is the party of your countrymen who went up before
us,' said she. 'What a pity that Englishmen should
always make so much noise!' And then she spoke in
Spanish to the custodian of the bells, who is usually to
be found in a little cabin up there within the tower.
'He says that they went up shouting like demons,'
continued Maria; and it seemed to me that she looked
as though I ought to be ashamed of the name of an
Englishman. 'They may not be so solemn in their
demeanour as Spaniards,' I answered; 'but, for all that,
there may be quite as much in them.'

We then again began to mount, and before we had
ascended much further we passed my three countrymen.
They were young men, with gray coats and gray
trousers, with slouched hats, and without gloves. They
had fair faces and fair hair, and swung big sticks in
their hands, with crooked handles. They laughed and
talked loud, and when we met them, seemed to be
racing with each other; but nevertheless they were
gentlemen. No one who knows by sight what an
English gentleman is, could have doubted that; but I
did acknowledge to myself that they should have remembered that the edifice they were treading was a
church, and that the silence they were invading was
the cherished property of a courteous people.

'They are all just the same as big boys,' said Maria. The colour instantly flew into my face, and I felt that it was my duty to speak up for my own countrymen. The word 'boys' especially wounded my ears. It was as a boy that she treated me; but, on looking at that befringed young Spanish Don—who was not, apparently, my elder in age—she had recognized a man. However, I said nothing further till I reached the summit. One cannot speak with manly dignity while one is out of breath on a staircase.

'There, John,' she said, stretching her hands away over the fair plain of the Guadalquivir, as soon as we stood against the parapet; 'is not that lovely?'

I would not deign to notice this. 'Maria,' I said, 'I think that you are too hard upon my countrymen!'

'Too hard! No; for I love them. They are so good and industrious; and they come home to their wives, and take care of their children. But why do they make themselves so—so—what the French call *gauche?*'

'Good and industrious, and come home to their wives!' thought I. 'I believe you hardly understand us as yet,' I answered. 'Our domestic virtues are not always so very prominent; but, I believe, we know how to conduct ourselves as gentlemen: at any rate, as well as Spaniards.' I was very angry—not at the faults, but at the good qualities imputed to us.

'In affairs of business, yes,' said Maria, with a look of firm confidence in her own opinion—that look of confidence she has never lost, and I pray that she may

never lose it while I remain with her—' but in the little
intercourses of the world, no! A Spaniard never
forgets what is personally due either to himself or his
neighbours. If he is eating an onion, he eats it as an
onion should be eaten.'

'In such matters as that he is very grand, no doubt,'
said I, angrily.

'And why should you not eat an onion properly,
John? Now, I heard a story yesterday from Don
—— about two Englishmen, which annoyed me very
much.' I did not exactly catch the name of the Don
in question, but I felt through every nerve in my
body that it was the man who had been talking to her
on the plaza.

'And what have they done?' said I. 'But it is
the same everywhere. We are always abused; but,
nevertheless, no people are so welcome. At any rate,
we pay for the mischief we do.' I was angry with
myself the moment the words were out of my mouth,
for, after all, there is no feeling more mean than that
pocket-confidence with which an Englishman sometimes
swaggers.

'There was no mischief done in this case,' she
answered. 'It was simply that two men have made
themselves ridiculous for ever. The story is all about
Seville, and, of course, it annoys me that they should
be Englishmen.'

'And what did they do?'

'The Marquis D'Almavivas was coming up to
Seville in the boat, and they behaved to him in the

most outrageous manner. He is here now, and is
going to give a series of *fêtes*. Of course he will not
ask a single Englishman.'

'We shall manage to live, even though the Marquis
D'Almavivas may frown upon us,' said I, proudly.

'He is the richest, and also the best of our noblemen,' continued Maria; 'and I never heard of anything so absurd as what they did to him. It made me
blush when Don —— told me.' Don Tomàs, I thought
she said.

'If he be the best of your noblemen, how comes it
that he is angry because he has met two vulgar men?
It is not to be supposed that every Englishman is a
gentleman.'

'Angry! Oh, no! he was not angry; he enjoyed
the joke too much for that. He got completely the
best of them, though they did not know it; poor fools!
How would your Lord John Russell behave if two
Spaniards in an English railway carriage were to pull
him about and tear his clothes?'

'He would give them in charge to a policeman, of
course,' said I, speaking of such a matter with the
contempt it deserved.

'If that were done here your ambassador would be
demanding national explanations. But Almavivas did
much better;—he laughed at them without letting them
know it.'

'But do you mean that they took hold of him
violently, without any provocation? They must have
been drunk.'

'Oh, no, they were sober enough. I did not see it, so I do not quite know exactly how it was, but I understand that they committed themselves most absurdly, absolutely took hold of his coat and tore it, and—; but they did such ridiculous things that I cannot tell you.' And yet Don Tomàs, if that was the man's name, had been able to tell her, and she had been able to listen to him.

'What made them take hold of the marquis?' said I.

'Curiosity, I suppose,' she answered. 'He dresses somewhat fancifully, and they could not understand that any one should wear garments different from their own.' But even then the blow did not strike home upon me.

'Is it not pretty to look down upon the quiet town?' she said, coming close up to me, so that the skirt of her dress pressed me, and her elbow touched my arm. Now was the moment I should have asked her how her heart stood towards me; but I was sore and uncomfortable, and my destiny was before me. She was willing enough to let these English faults pass by without further notice, but I would not allow the subject to drop.

'I will find out who these men were,' said I, 'and learn the truth of it. When did it occur?'

'Last Thursday, I think he said.'

'Why, that was the day we came up in the boat, Johnson and myself. There was no marquis there then, and we were the only Englishmen on board.'

'It was on Thursday, certainly, because it was well known in Seville that he arrived on that day. You must have remarked him because he talks English perfectly—though, by-the-by, these men would go on chattering before him about himself as though it were impossible that a Spaniard should know their language. They are ignorant of Spanish, and they cannot bring themselves to believe that any one should be better educated than themselves.'

Now the blow had fallen, and I straightway appreciated the necessity of returning immediately to Clapham, where my family resided, and giving up for ever all idea of Spanish connections. I had resolved to assert the full strength of my manhood on that tower, and now words had been spoken which left me weak as a child. I felt that I was shivering, and did not dare to pronounce the truth which must be made known. As to speaking of love, and signifying my pleasure that Don Tomàs should for the future be kept at a distance, any such effort was quite beyond me. Had Don Tomàs been there, he might have walked off with her from before my face without a struggle on my part. 'Now I remember about it,' she continued, 'I think he must have been in the boat on Thursday.'

'And now that I remember,' I replied, turning away to hide my embarrassment, 'he was there. Your friend down below in the plaza seems to have made out a grand story. No doubt he is not fond of the English. There was such a man there, and I did take hold——'

'O, John, was it you?'

'Yes, Donna Maria, it was I; and if Lord John Russell were to dress himself in the same way——' But I had no time to complete my description of what might occur under so extravagantly impossible a combination of circumstances, for as I was yet speaking, the little door leading out on to the leads of the tower was opened, and my friend, the mayo of the boat, still bearing all his gewgaws on his back, stepped up on to the platform. My eye instantly perceived that the one pendule was still missing from his jacket. He did not come alone, but three other gentlemen followed him, who, however, had no peculiarities in their dress. He saw me at once, and bowed and smiled; and then observing Donna Maria, he lifted his cap from his head, and addressing himself to her in Spanish, began to converse with her as though she were an old friend.

'Señor,' said Maria, after the first words of greeting had been spoken between them; 'you must permit me to present to you my father's most particular friend, and my own,—Mr. Pomfret; John, this is the Marquis D'Almavivas.'

I cannot now describe the grace with which this introduction was effected, or the beauty of her face as she uttered the word. There was a boldness about her as though she had said, 'I know it all—the whole story. But, in spite of that, you must take him on my representation, and be gracious to him in spite of what he has done. You must be content to do that; or in quarrelling with him you must quarrel with me also.' And it

was done at the spur of the moment—without delay.
She, who not five minutes since had been loudly con-
demning the unknown Englishman for his rudeness, had
already pardoned him, now that he was known to be
her friend; and had determined that he should be
pardoned by others also or that she would share his
disgrace. I recognized the nobleness of this at the
moment; but, nevertheless, I was so sore that I would
almost have preferred that she should have disowned
me.

The marquis immediately lifted his cap with his left
hand while he gave me his right. 'I have already had
the pleasure of meeting this gentleman,' he said; 'we
had some conversation in the boat together.'

'Yes,' said I, pointing to his rent, 'and you still bear
the marks of our encounter.'

'Was it not delightful, Donna Maria,' he continued,
turning to her; 'your friend's friend took me for a
torero?'

'And it served you properly, señor,' said Donna
Maria, laughing; 'you have no right to go about with
all those rich ornaments upon you.'

'Oh! quite properly; indeed, I make no complaint;
and I must beg your friend to understand, and his
friend also, how grateful I am for their solicitude as to
my pecuniary welfare. They were inclined to be severe
on me for being so extravagant in such trifles. I was
obliged to explain that I had no wife at home kept
without her proper allowance of dresses, in order that
I might be gay.'

'They are foreigners, and you should forgive their error,' said she.

'And in token that I do so,' said the marquis, 'I shall beg your friend to accept the little ornament which attracted his attention.' And so saying, he pulled the identical button out of his pocket, and gracefully proffered it to me.

'I shall carry it about with me always,' said I, accepting it, 'as a memento of humiliation. When I look at it, I shall ever remember the folly of an Englishman and the courtesy of a Spaniard;' and as I made the speech I could not but reflect whether it might, under any circumstances, be possible that Lord John Russell should be induced to give a button off his coat to a Spaniard.

There were other civil speeches made, and before we left the tower the marquis had asked me to his parties, and exacted from me an unwilling promise that I would attend them. 'The señora,' he said, bowing again to Maria, 'would, he was sure, grace them. She had done so on the previous year; and as I had accepted his little present I was bound to acknowledge him as my friend.' All this was very pretty, and of course I said that I would go, but I had not at that time the slightest intention of doing so. Maria had behaved admirably; she had covered my confusion, and shown herself not ashamed to own me, delinquent as I was; but, not the less, had she expressed her opinion, in language terribly strong, of the awkwardness of which I had been guilty, and had shown almost an aversion to my English character. I should leave Seville as quickly as I could, and should certainly not again put myself in the way of the Marquis D'Almavivas. Indeed, I dreaded the moment that I should be first alone with her, and should find myself forced to say something indicative of my feelings—to hear something also indicative of her feelings. I had come out this morning resolved to demand my rights and to exercise them—and now my only wish was to run away. I hated the marquis, and longed to be alone that I might cast his button from me. To think that a man should be so ruined by such a trifle!

We descended that prodigious flight without a word upon the subject, and almost without a word at all. She had carried herself well in the presence of Almavivas, and had been too proud to seem ashamed of her companion; but now, as I could well see, her feelings of disgust and contempt had returned. When I begged her not to hurry herself, she would hardly answer me; and when she did speak, her voice was constrained and unlike herself. And yet how beautiful she was! Well, my dream of Spanish love must be over. But I was sure of this: that having known her, and given her my heart, I could never afterwards share it with another.

We came out at last on the dark, gloomy aisle of the cathedral, and walked together without a word up along the side of the choir, till we came to the transept. There was not a soul near us, and not a sound was to be heard but the distant, low pattering of a mass, then in course of celebration at some far-off chapel in the cathedral. When we got to the transept Maria turned a little, as though she was going to the transept door, and then stopped herself. She stood still; and when I stood also, she made two steps towards me, and put her hand on my arm. 'Oh, John!' she said.

'Well,' said I; 'after all it does not signify. You can make a joke of it when my back is turned.'

'Dearest John!'—she had never spoken to me in that way before—'you must not be angry with me. It is better that we should explain to each other, is it not?'

'Oh, much better. I am very glad you heard of it at once. I do not look at it quite in the same light that you do; but nevertheless——'

'What do you mean? But I know you are angry with me. And yet you cannot think that I intended those words for you. Of course I know now that there was nothing rude in what passed.'

'Oh, but there was.

'No, I am sure there was not. You could not be rude though you are so free hearted. I see it all now, and so does the marquis. You will like him so much when you come to know him. Tell me that you won't be cross with me for what I have said. Sometimes I think that I have displeased you, and yet my whole wish has been to welcome you to Seville, and to make you comfortable as an old friend. Promise me that you will not be cross with me.'

Cross with her! I certainly had no intention of being

cross, but I had begun to think that she would not care what my humour might be. 'Maria,' I said, taking hold of her hand.

'No, John, do not do that. It is in the church, you know.'

'Maria, will you answer me a question?'

'Yes,' she said, very slowly, looking down upon the stone slabs beneath our feet.

'Do you love me?'

'Love you!'

'Yes, do you love me? You were to give me an answer here, in Seville, and now I ask for it. I have almost taught myself to think that it is needless to ask; and now this horrid mischance——'

'What do you mean?' said she, speaking very quickly.

'Why this miserable blunder about the marquis's button! After that I suppose——'

'The marquis! Oh, John, is that to make a difference between you and me?—a little joke like that?'

'But does it not?'

'Make a change between us!—such a thing as that! Oh, John!'

'But tell me, Maria, what am I to hope? If you will say that you can love me, I shall care nothing for the marquis. In that case I can bear to be laughed at.'

'Who will dare to laugh at you? Not the marquis, whom I am sure you will like.'

'Your friend in the plaza, who told you of all this.'

'What, poor Tomàs!'

'I do not know about his being poor. I mean the gentleman who was with you last night.'

'Yes, Tomàs. You do not know who he is?'

'Not in the least.'

'How droll! He is your own clerk—partly your own, now that you are one of the firm. And, John, I mean to make you do something for him; he is such a good fellow; and last year he married a young girl whom I love—oh, almost like a sister.'

Do something for him! Of course I would. I promised, then and there, that I would raise his salary to any conceivable amount that a Spanish clerk could desire; which promise I have since kept, if not absolutely to the letter, at any rate, to an extent which has been considered satisfactory by the gentleman's wife.

'But, Maria—dearest Maria——'

'Remember, John, we are in the church; and poor papa will be waiting breakfast.'

I need hardly continue the story further. It will be known to all that my love-suit throve in spite of my unfortunate raid on the button of the Marquis D'Almavivas, at whose series of *fêtes* through that month I was, I may boast, an honoured guest. I have since that had the pleasure of entertaining him in my own poor house in England, and one of our boys bears his Christian name.

From that day in which I ascended the Giralda to this present day in which I write, I have never once had occasion to complain of a deficiency of romance either in Maria Daguilar or in Maria Pomfret.

MISS SARAH JACK, OF SPANISH TOWN,
JAMAICA.

THERE is nothing so melancholy as a country in its decadence, unless it be a people in their decadence. I am not aware that the latter misfortune can be attributed to the Anglo-Saxon race in any part of the world; but there is reason to fear that it has fallen on an English colony in the island of Jamaica.

Jamaica was one of those spots on which fortune shone with the full warmth of all her noonday splendour. That sun has set;—whether for ever or no none but a prophet can tell; but, as far as a plain man may see, there are at present but few signs of a coming morrow, or of another summer.

It is not just or proper that one should grieve over the misfortunes of Jamaica with a stronger grief because her savannahs are so lovely, her forests so rich, her mountains so green, and her rivers so rapid; but it is so. It is piteous that a land so beautiful should be one which fate has marked for misfortune. Had Guiana, with its flat level unlovely soil, become poverty-stricken, one would hardly sorrow over it as one does sorrow for Jamaica.

As regards scenery she is the gem of the western tropics. It is impossible to conceive spots on the earth's surface more gracious to the eye than those steep green valleys which stretch down to the south-west from the Blue Mountain peak towards the sea ; and but little behind these in beauty are the rich wooded hills which in the western part of the island divide the counties of Hanover and Westmoreland. The hero of the tale which I am going to tell was a sugar-grower in the latter district, and the heroine was a girl who lived under that Blue Mountain peak.

The very name of a sugar-grower as connected with Jamaica savours of fruitless struggle, failure, and desolation. And from his earliest growth fruitless struggle, failure, and desolation had been the lot of Maurice Cumming. At eighteen years of age he had been left by his father sole possessor of the Mount Pleasant estate, than which in her palmy days Jamaica had little to boast of that was more pleasant or more palmy. But those days had passed by before Roger Cumming, the father of our friend, had died.

These misfortunes coming on the head of one another, at intervals of a few years, had first stunned and then killed him. His slaves rose against him, as they did against other proprietors around him, and burned down his house and mills, his homestead and offices. Those who know the amount of capital which a sugar-grower must invest in such buildings will understand the extent of this misfortune. Then the slaves were emancipated. It is not perhaps possible that we, now-a-days, should regard this as a calamity; but it was quite impossible that a Jamaica proprietor of those days should not have done so. Men will do much for philanthropy, they will work hard, they will give the coat from their back;—nay the very shirt from their body; but few men will endure to look on with satisfaction while their commerce is destroyed.

But even this Mr. Cumming did bear after a while, and kept his shoulder to the wheel. He kept his shoulder to the wheel till that third misfortune came upon him—till the protection duty on Jamaica sugar was abolished. Then he turned his face to the wall and died.

His son at this time was not of age, and the large but lessening property which Mr. Cumming left behind him was for three years in the hands of trustees. But nevertheless Maurice, young as he was, managed the estate. It was he who grew the canes, and made the sugar;—or else failed to make it. He was the 'massa' to whom the free negroes looked as the source from whence their wants should be supplied, notwithstanding that being free, they were ill inclined to work for him let his want of work be ever so sore.

Mount Pleasant had been a very large property. In addition to his sugar-canes Mr. Cumming had grown coffee; for his land ran up into the hills of Trelawney to that altitude which in the tropics seems necessary for the perfect growth of the coffee berry.

But it soon became evident that labour for the double produce could not be had, and the coffee plantation was abandoned. Wild brush and the thick undergrowth of forest reappeared on the hill-sides which had been rich with produce. And the evil re-created and exaggerated itself. Negroes squatted on the abandoned property; and being able to live with abundance from their stolen gardens, were less willing than ever to work in the cane pieces.

And thus things went from bad to worse. In the good old times Mr. Cumming's sugar produce had spread itself annually over some three hundred acres; but by degrees this dwindled down to half that extent of land. And then in those old golden days they had always taken a full hogshead from the acre;—very often more. The estate had sometimes given four hundred hogsheads in the year. But in the days of which we now speak the crop had fallen below fifty.

At this time Maurice Cumming was eight-and-twenty, and it is hardly too much to say that misfortune had nearly crushed him. But nevertheless it had not crushed him. He, and some few like him, had still hoped against hope;—had still persisted in looking forward to a future for the island which once was so generous with its gifts. When his father died he might still have had enough for the wants of life had he sold his property for what it would fetch. There was money in England, and the remains of large wealth. But he would not sacrifice Mount Pleasant or abandon Jamaica; and now after ten years' struggling he still kept Mount Pleasant, and the mill was still going; but all other property had parted from his hands.

By nature Maurice Cumming would have been gay and lively, a man with a happy spirit and easy temper; but struggling had made him silent if not morose, and had saddened if not soured his temper. He had lived alone at Mount Pleasant, or generally alone. Work or want of money, and the constant difficulty of getting labour for his estate, had left him but little time for a young man's ordinary amusements. Of the charms of ladies' society he had known but little. Very many of the estates around him had been absolutely abandoned, as was the case with his own coffee plantation, and from others men had sent away their wives and daughters. Nay, most of the proprietors had gone themselves, leaving an overseer to extract what little might yet be extracted out of the property. It too often happened that that little was not sufficient to meet the demands of the overseer himself.

The house at Mount Pleasant had been an irregular, low-roofed, picturesque residence, built with only one floor, and surrounded on all sides by large verandahs. In the old days it had always been kept in perfect order, but now this was far from being the case. Few young bachelors can keep a house in order, but no bachelor young or old can do so under such a doom as that of Maurice Cumming. Every shilling that Maurice Cumming could collect was spent in bribing negroes to work for him. But bribe as he would the negroes would not work. 'No, massa; me pain here; me no workee to-day,' and Sambo would lay his fat hand on his fat stomach.

I have said that he lived generally alone. Occasionally his house at Mount Pleasant was enlivened by visits of an aunt, a maiden sister of his mother, whose usual residence was at Spanish Town. It is or should be known to all men that Spanish Town was and is the seat of the Jamaica legislature.

But Maurice was not overfond of his relative. In this he was both wrong and foolish, for Miss Sarah Jack—such was her name—was in many respects a good woman, and was certainly a rich woman. It is true that she was not a handsome woman, nor a fashionable woman, nor perhaps altogether an agreeable woman. She was tall, thin, ungainly, and yellow. Her voice, which she used freely, was harsh. She was a politician and a patriot. She regarded England as the greatest of countries, and Jamaica as the greatest of colonies. But much as she loved England she was very loud in denouncing what she called the perfidy of the mother to the brightest of her children. And much as she loved Jamaica she was equally severe in her taunts against those of her brother-islanders who would not believe that the island might yet flourish as it had flourished in her father's days.

'It is because you and men like you will not do your duty by your country,' she had said some score of times to Maurice—not with much justice considering the laboriousness of his life.

But Maurice knew well what she meant. 'What could I do there up at Spanish Town,' he would answer, 'among such a pack as there are there? Here I may do something.'

And then she would reply with the full swing of her eloquence. 'It is because you and such as you think only of yourself and not of Jamaica, that Jamaica has come to such a pass as this. Why is there a pack there as you call them in the honourable House of Assembly? Why are not the best men in the island to be found there, as the best men in England are to be found in the British House of Commons? A pack, indeed! My father was proud of a seat in that house, and I remember the day, Maurice Cumming, when your father also thought it no shame to represent his own parish. If men like you, who have a stake in the country, will not go there, of course the house is filled with men who have no stake. If they are a pack, it is you who send them there;—you, and others like you.'

All this had its effect, though at the moment Maurice would shrug his shoulders and turn away his head from the torrent of the lady's discourse. But Miss Jack, though she was not greatly liked, was greatly respected. Maurice would not own that she convinced him; but at last he did allow his name to be put up as candidate for his own parish, and in due time he became a member of the honourable House of Assembly in Jamaica.

This honour entails on the holder of it the necessity

of living at or within reach of Spanish Town for some
ten weeks towards the close of every year. Now on
the whole face of the uninhabited globe there is perhaps
no spot more dull to look at, more Lethean in its
aspect, more corpse-like or more cadaverous than
Spanish Town. It is the head-quarters of the govern-
ment, the seat of the legislature, the residence of the
governor;—but nevertheless it is, as it were, a city of
the very dead.

Here, as we have said before, lived Miss Jack in a
large forlorn ghost-like house in which her father and
all her family had lived before her. And as a matter
of course Maurice Cumming when he came up to
attend to his duties as a member of the legislature took
up his abode with her.

Now at the time of which we are specially speaking
he had completed the first of these annual visits. He
had already benefited his country by sitting out one
session of the colonial parliament, and had satisfied
himself that he did no other good than that of keeping
away some person more objectionable than himself.
He was however prepared to repeat this self-sacrifice
in a spirit of patriotism for which he received a very
meagre meed of eulogy from Miss Jack, and an
amount of self-applause which was not much more
extensive.

'Down at Mount Pleasant I can do something,' he
would say over and over again, 'but what good can
any man do up here?'

'You can do your duty,' Miss Jack would answer,

' as others did before you when the colony was made to
prosper.'   And then they would run off into a long
discussion about free labour and protective duties.
But at the present moment Maurice Cumming had
another vexation on his mind over and above that
arising from his wasted hours at Spanish Town and
his fruitless labours at Mount Pleasant.   He was in
love, and was not altogether satisfied with the conduct
of his lady love.

Miss Jack had other nephews besides Maurice
Cumming, and nieces also, of whom Marian Leslie was
one.   The family of the Leslies lived up near Newcastle—in the mountains, that is, which stand over
Kingston—at a distance of some eighteen miles from
Kingston, but in a climate as different from that of the
town as the climate of Naples is from that of Berlin.
In Kingston the heat is all but intolerable throughout
the year, by day and by night, in the house and out of
it.   In the mountains round Newcastle, some four
thousand feet above the sea, it is merely warm during
the day, and cool enough at night to make a blanket
desirable.

It is pleasant enough living up among those green
mountains.   There are no roads there for wheeled
carriages, nor are there carriages with or without
wheels.   All journeys are made on horseback.   Every
visit paid from house to house is performed in this
manner.   Ladies old and young live before dinner in
their riding-habits.   The hospitality is free, easy, and
unembarrassed.   The scenery is magnificent.   The

tropical foliage is wild and luxuriant beyond measure. There may be enjoyed all that a southern climate has to offer of enjoyment, without the penalties which such enjoyments usually entail.

Mrs. Leslie was a half-sister of Miss Jack, and Miss Jack had been a half-sister also of Mrs. Cumming; but Mrs. Leslie and Mrs. Cumming had in no way been related. And it had so happened that up to the period of his legislative efforts Maurice Cumming had seen nothing of the Leslies. Soon after his arrival at Spanish Town he had been taken by Miss Jack to Shandy Hall, for so the residence of the Leslies was called, and having remained there for three days, had fallen in love with Marian Leslie. Now in the West Indies all young ladies flirt; it is the first habit of their nature—and few young ladies in the West Indies were more given to flirting, or understood the science better, than Marian Leslie.

Maurice Cumming fell violently in love, and during his first visit at Shandy Hall found that Marian was perfection—for during this first visit her propensities were exerted altogether in his own favour. That little circumstance does make such a difference in a young man's judgment of a girl! He came back full of admiration, not altogether to Miss Jack's dissatisfaction; for Miss Jack was willing enough that both her nephew and her niece should settle down into married life.

But then Maurice met his fair one at a governor's ball—at a ball where red coats abounded, and aides-de-camp dancing in spurs, and narrow-waisted lieutenants with sashes or epaulets! The aides-de-camp and narrow-waisted lieutenants waltzed better than he did; and as one after the other whisked round the ball-room with Marian firmly clasped in his arms, Maurice's feelings were not of the sweetest. Nor was this the worst of it. Had the whisking been divided equally among ten, he might have forgiven it; but there was one specially narrow-waisted lieutenant, who towards the end of the evening kept Marian nearly wholly to himself. Now to a man in love, who has had but little experience of either balls or young ladies, this is intolerable.

He only met her twice after that before his return to Mount Pleasant, and on the first occasion that odious soldier was not there. But a specially devout young clergyman was present, an unmarried evangelical handsome young curate fresh from England; and Marian's piety had been so excited that she had cared for no one else. It appeared moreover that the curate's gifts for conversion were confined, as regarded that opportunity, to Marian's advantage. 'I will have nothing more to say to her,' said Maurice to himself, scowling. But just as he went away Marian had given him her hand, and called him Maurice—for she pretended that they were cousins—and had looked into his eyes and declared that she did hope that the assembly at Spanish Town would soon be sitting again. Hitherto, she said, she had not cared one straw about it. Then poor Maurice pressed the little fingers which

lay within his own, and swore that he would be at
Shandy Hall on the day before his return to Mount
Pleasant. So he was; and there he found the narrow-
waisted lieutenant, not now bedecked with sash and
epaulettes, but lolling at his ease on Mrs. Leslie's sofa
in a white jacket, while Marian sat at his feet telling
his fortune with a book about flowers.

'Oh, a musk rose, Mr. Ewing; you know what a
musk rose means!' Then she got up and shook hands
with Mr. Cumming; but her eyes still went away to
the white jacket and the sofa. Poor Maurice had often
been nearly broken-hearted in his efforts to manage his
free black labourers; but even that was easier than
managing such as Marian Leslie.

Marian Leslie was a Creole—as also were Miss Jack
and Maurice Cumming—a child of the tropics; but by
no means such a child as tropical children are generally
thought to be by us in more northern latitudes. She
was black-haired and black-eyed, but her lips were as
red and her cheeks as rosy as though she had been born
and bred in regions where the snow lies in winter. She
was a small, pretty, beautifully made little creature,
somewhat idle as regards the work of the world, but
active and strong enough when dancing or riding were
required from her. Her father was a banker, and
was fairly prosperous in spite of the poverty of his
country. His house of business was at Kingston, and
he usually slept there twice a week; but he always
resided at Shandy Hall, and Mrs. Leslie and her children
knew but very little of the miseries of Kingston. For

be it known to all men, that of all towns Kingston, Jamaica, is the most miserable.

I fear that I shall have set my readers very much against Marian Leslie;—much more so than I would wish to do. As a rule they will not know how thoroughly flirting is an institution in the West Indies— practised by all young ladies, and laid aside by them when they marry, exactly as their young-lady names and young-lady habits of various kinds are laid aside. All I would say of Marian Leslie is this, that she understood the working of the institution more thoroughly than others did. And I must add also in her favour that she did not keep her flirting for sly corners, nor did her admirers keep their distance till mamma was out of the way. It mattered not to her who was present. Had she been called on to make one at a synod of the clergy of the island, she would have flirted with the bishop before all his priests. And there have been bishops in the colony who would not have gainsayed her!

But Maurice Cumming did not rightly calculate a.. this; nor indeed did Miss Jack do so as thoroughly as she should have done, for Miss Jack knew more about such matters than did poor Maurice. 'If you like Marian, why don't you marry her?' Miss Jack had once said to him; and this coming from Miss Jack, who was made of money, was a great deal.

'She wouldn't have me,' Maurice had answered.

'That's more than you know or I either,' was Miss Jack's reply. 'But if you like to try, I'll help you.'

K

With reference to this, Maurice as he left Miss
Jack's residence on his return to Mount Pleasant, had
declared that Marian Leslie was not worth an honest
man's love.

'Psha!' Miss Jack replied; 'Marian will do like
other girls. When you marry a wife I suppose you
mean to be master?'

'At any rate I sha'n't marry her,' said Maurice.
And so he went his way back to Hanover with a sore
heart. And no wonder, for that was the very day on
which Lieutenant Ewing had asked the question about
the musk rose.

But there was a dogged constancy of feeling about
Maurice which could not allow him to disburden himself of his love. When he was again at Mount Pleasant among his sugar-canes and hogsheads he could
not help thinking about Marian. It is true he always
thought of her as flying round that ball-room in Ewing's
arms, or looking up with rapt admiration into that
young parson's face; and so he got but little pleasure
from his thoughts. But not the less was he in love
with her;—not the less, though he would swear to
himself three times in the day that for no earthly consideration would he marry Marian Leslie.

The early months of the year from January to May
are the busiest with a Jamaica sugar-grower, and in
this year they were very busy months with Maurice
Cumming. It seemed as though there were actually
some truth in Miss Jack's prediction that prosperity
would return to him if he attended to his country; for

the prices of sugar had risen higher than they had ever been since the duty had been withdrawn, and there was more promise of a crop at Mount Pleasant than he had seen since his reign commenced. But then the question of labour? How he slaved in trying to get work from those free negroes; and alas, how often he slaved in vain! But it was not all in vain; for as things went on it became clear to him that in this year he would, for the first time since he commenced, obtain something like a return from his land. What if the turning-point had come, and things were now about to run the other way?

But then the happiness which might have accrued to him from this source was dashed by his thoughts of Marian Leslie. Why had he thrown himself in the way of that syren? Why had he left Mount Pleasant at all? He knew that on his return to Spanish Town his first work would be to visit Shandy Hall; and yet he felt that of all places in the island, Shandy Hall was the last which he ought to visit.

And then about the beginning of May, when he was hard at work turning the last of his canes into sugar and rum, he received his annual visit from Miss Jack And whom should Miss Jack bring with her but Mr. Leslie.

'I'll tell you what it is,' said Miss Jack; 'I have spoken to Mr. Leslie about you and Marian.'

'Then you had no business to do anything of the kind,' said Maurice, blushing up to his ears.

'Nonsense,' replied Miss Jack, 'I understand what I

am about. Of course Mr. Leslie will want to know
something about the estate.'

'Then he may go back as wise as he came, for he'll
learn nothing from me. Not that I have anything to
hide.'

'So I told him. Now there are a large family of
them, you see; and of course he can't give Marian much.'

'I don't care a straw if he doesn't give her a shilling. If she cared for me, or I for her, I shouldn't
look after her for her money.'

'But a little money is not a bad thing, Maurice,'
said Miss Jack, who in her time had had a good deal,
and had managed to take care of it.

'It is all one to me.'

'But what I was going to say is this—hum—ha—.
I don't like to pledge myself for fear I should raise
hopes which mayn't be fulfilled.'

'Don't pledge yourself to anything, aunt, in which
Marian Leslie and I are concerned.'

'But what I was going to say is this; my money,
what little I have, you know, must go some day either
to you or to the Leslies.'

'You may give all to them if you please.'

'Of course I may, and I dare say I shall,' said Miss
Jack, who was beginning to be irritated. 'But at any
rate you might have the civility to listen to me when I
am endeavouring to put you on your legs. I am sure
I think about nothing else, morning, noon, and night,
and yet I never get a decent word from you. Marian
is too good for you; that's the truth.'

But at length Miss Jack was allowed to open her budget, and to make her proposition ; which amounted to this—that she had already told Mr. Leslie that she would settle the bulk of her property conjointly on Maurice and Marian if they would make a match of it. Now as Mr. Leslie had long been casting a hankering eye after Miss Jack's money, with a strong conviction however that Maurice Cumming was her favourite nephew and probable heir, this proposition was not unpalatable. So he agreed to go down to Mount Pleasant and look about him.

' But you may live for the next thirty years, my dear Miss Jack,' Mr. Leslie had said.

' Yes, I may,' Miss Jack replied, looking very dry.

' And I am sure I hope you will,' continued Mr. Leslie. And then the subject was allowed to drop ; for Mr. Leslie knew that it was not always easy to talk to Miss Jack on such matters.

Miss Jack was a person in whom I think we may say that the good predominated over the bad. She was often morose, crabbed, and self-opinionated ; but then she knew her own imperfections, and forgave those she loved for evincing their dislike of them. Maurice Cumming was often inattentive to her, plainly showing that he was worried by her importunities and ill at ease in her company. But she loved her nephew with all her heart ; and though she dearly liked to tyrannize over him, never allowed herself to be really angry with him, though he so frequently refused to bow to her dictation. And she loved Marian Leslie also, though

Marian was so sweet and lovely and she herself so harsh and ill-favoured. She loved Marian, though Marian would often be impertinent. She forgave the flirting, the light-heartedness, the love of amusement. Marian, she said to herself, was young and pretty. She, Miss Jack, had never known Marian's temptation. And so she resolved in her own mind that Marian should be made a good and happy woman ;— but always as the wife of Maurice Cumming.

But Maurice turned a deaf ear to all these good tidings—or rather he turned to them an ear that seemed to be deaf. He dearly, ardently loved that little flirt ; but seeing that she was a flirt, that she had flirted so grossly when he was by, he would not confess his love to a human being. He would not have it known that he was wasting his heart for a worthless little chit, to whom every man was the same—except that those were most eligible whose toes were the lightest and their outside trappings the brightest. That he did love her he could not help, but he would not disgrace himself by acknowledging it.

He was very civil to Mr. Leslie, but he would not speak a word that could be taken as a proposal for Marian. It had been part of Miss Jack's plan that the engagement should absolutely be made down there at Mount Pleasant, without any reference to the young lady ; but Maurice could not be induced to break the ice. So he took Mr. Leslie through his mills and over his cane-pieces, talked to him about the laziness of the ' niggers,' while the ' niggers ' themselves stood by tittering, and rode with him away to the high grounds where the coffee plantation had been in the good old days; but not a word was said between them about Marian. And yet Marian was never out of his heart.

And then came the day on which Mr. Leslie was to go back to Kingston. 'And you won't have her then?' said Miss Jack to her nephew early that morning. 'You won't be said by me?'

'Not in this matter, aunt.'

'Then you will live and die a poor man; you mean that, I suppose?'

'It's likely enough that I shall. There's this comfort, at any rate, I'm used to it.' And then Miss Jack was silent again for a while.

'Very well, sir; that's enough,' she said angrily. And then she began again. 'But, Maurice, you wouldn't have to wait for my death, you know.' And she put out her hand and touched his arm, entreating him as it were to yield to her. 'Oh, Maurice,' she said, 'I do so want to make you comfortable. Let us speak to Mr. Leslie.'

But Maurice would not. He took her hand and thanked her, but said that on this matter he must be his own master. 'Very well, sir,' she exclaimed, 'I have done. In future you may manage for yourself. As for me, I shall go back with Mr. Leslie to Kingston.' And so she did. Mr. Leslie returned that day, taking her with him. When he took his leave, his invitation to Maurice to come to Shandy Hall was not very ressing. 'Mrs. Leslie and the children will always be lad to see you,' said he.

'Remember me very kindly to Mrs. Leslie and the children,' said Maurice. And so they parted.

'You have brought me down here on a regular fool's errand,' said Mr. Leslie, on their journey back to town.

'It will all come right yet,' replied Miss Jack. 'Take my word for it, he loves her.'

'Fudge,' said Mr. Leslie. But he could not afford to quarrel with his rich connection.

In spite of all that he had said and thought to the contrary, Maurice did look forward during the remainder of the summer to his return to Spanish Town with something like impatience. It was very dull work, being there alone at Mount Pleasant; and let him do what he would to prevent it, his very dreams took him to Shandy Hall. But at last the slow time made itself away, and he found himself once more in his aunt's house.

A couple of days passed and no word was said about the Leslies. On the morning of the third day he determined to go to Shandy Hall. Hitherto he had never been there without staying for the night; but on this occasion he made up his mind to return the same day. 'It would not be civil of me not to go there,' he said to his aunt.

'Certainly not,' she replied, forbearing to press the matter further. 'But why make such a terrible hard day's work of it?'

'Oh, I shall go down in the cool, before breakfast;

and then I need not have the bother of taking a bag.'

And in this way he started. Miss Jack said nothing further; but she longed in her heart that she might be at Marian's elbow unseen during the visit.

He found them all at breakfast, and the first to welcome him at the hall door was Marian. 'Oh, Mr. Cumming, we are so glad to see you;' and she looked into his eyes with a way she had, that was enough to make a man's heart wild. But she did not call him Maurice now.

Miss Jack had spoken to her sister Mrs. Leslie, as well as to Mr. Leslie about this marriage scheme. 'Just let them alone,' was Mrs. Leslie's advice. 'You can't alter Marian by lecturing her. If they really love each other they'll come together; and if they don't, why then they'd better not.'

'And you really mean that you're going back to Spanish Town to-day?' said Mrs. Leslie to her visitor.

'I'm afraid I must. Indeed I haven't brought my things with me.' And then he again caught Marian's eye, and began to wish that his resolution had not been so sternly made.

'I suppose you are so fond of that house of assembly,' said Marian, 'that you cannot tear yourself away for more than one day. You'll not be able, I suppose, to find time to come to our picnic next week?'

Maurice said he feared that he should not have time to go to a picnic.

'Oh, nonsense,' said Fanny—one of the younger

girls—'you must come. We can't do without him, can we?'

'Marian has got your name down the first on the list of the gentlemen,' said another.

'Yes; and Captain Ewing's second,' said Bell, the youngest.

'I'm afraid I must induce your sister to alter her list,' said Maurice, in his sternest manner. 'I cannot manage to go, and I'm sure she will not miss me.'

Marian looked at the little girl who had so unfortunately mentioned the warrior's name, and the little girl knew that she had sinned.

'Oh, we cannot possibly do without you; can we Marian?' said Fanny. 'It's to be at Bingley's dell, and we've got a bed for you at Newcastle; quite near, you know.'

'And another for ——,' began Bell, but she stopped herself.

'Go away to your lessons, Bell,' said Marian. 'You know how angry mamma will be at your staying here all the morning;' and poor Bell with a sorrowful look left the room.

'We are all certainly very anxious that you should come; very anxious for a great many reasons,' said Marian, in a voice that was rather solemn, and as though the matter were one of considerable import. 'But if you really cannot, why of course there is no more to be said.'

'There will be plenty without me, I am sure.'

'As regards numbers, I dare say there will; for we

shall have pretty nearly the whole of the two regiments;' and Marian as she alluded to the officers spoke in a tone which might lead one to think that she would much rather be without them; 'but we counted on you as being one of ourselves; and as you had been away so long, we thought—we thought—,' and then she turned away her face, and did not finish her speech. Before he could make up his mind as to his answer she had risen from her chair, and walked out of the room. Maurice almost thought that he saw a tear in her eye as she went.

He did ride back to Spanish Town that afternoon, after an early dinner; but before he went Marian spoke to him alone for one minute.

'I hope you are not offended with me,' she said.

'Offended! oh no; how could I be offended with you?'

'Because you seem so stern. I am sure I would do anything I could to oblige you, if I knew how. It would be so shocking not to be good friends with a cousin like you.'

'But there are so many different sorts of friends,' said Maurice.

'Of course there are There are a great many friends that one does not care a bit for,—people that one meets at balls and places like that—.'

'And at picnics,' said Maurice.

'Well, some of them there too; but we are not like that; are we?'

What could Maurice do but say, 'no,' and declare

that their friendship was of a warmer description? And how could he resist promising to go to the picnic, though as he made the promise he knew that misery would be in store for him? He did promise, and then she gave him her hand and called him Maurice.

'Oh! I am so glad,' she said. 'It seemed so shocking that you should refuse to join us. And mind and be early, Maurice; for I shall want to explain it all. We are to meet, you know, at Clifton Gate at one o'clock, but do you be a little before that, and we shall be there.'

Maurice Cumming resolved within his own breast as he rode back to Spanish Town, that if Marian behaved to him all that day at the picnic as she had done this day at Shandy Hall, he would ask her to be his wife before he left her.

And Miss Jack also was to be at the picnic.

'There is no need of going early,' said she, when her nephew made a fuss about the starting. 'People are never very punctual at such affairs as that; and then they are always quite long enough.' But Maurice explained that he was anxious to be early, and on this occasion he carried his point.

When they reached Clifton Gate the ladies were already there; not in carriages, as people go to picnics in other and tamer countries, but each on her own horse or her own pony. But they were not alone. Beside Miss Leslie was a gentleman, whom Maurice knew as Lieutenant Graham, of the flag ship at Port Royal; and at a little distance which quite enabled him to join in the conversation was Captain Ewing, the lieutenant with the narrow waist of the previous year.

'We shall have a delightful day, Miss Leslie,' said the lieutenant.

'Oh, charming, isn't it?' said Marian.

'But now to choose a place for dinner, Captain Ewing;—what do you say?'

'Will you commission me to select? You know I'm very well up in geometry, and all that.'

'But that won't teach you what sort of a place does for a picnic dinner;—will it, Mr. Cumming?' And then she shook hands with Maurice, but did not take any further special notice of him. 'We'll all go together, if you please. The commission is too important to be left to one.' And then Marian rode off, and the lieutenant and the captain rode with her.

It was open for Maurice to join them if he chose, but he did not choose. He had come there ever so much earlier than he need have done, dragging his aunt with him, because Marian had told him that his services would be specially required by her. And now as soon as she saw him she went away with those two officers!—went away without vouchsafing him a word. He made up his mind, there on the spot, that he would never think of her again—never speak to her otherwise than he might speak to the most indifferent of mortals.

And yet he was a man that could struggle right manfully with the world's troubles; one who had struggled with them from his boyhood, and had never

been overcome. Now he was unable to conceal the
bitterness of his wrath because a little girl had ridden
off to look for a green spot for her tablecloth without
asking his assistance!

Picnics are, I think, in general, rather tedious for
the elderly people who accompany them. When the
joints become a little stiff dinners are eaten most
comfortably with the accompaniment of chairs and
tables, and a roof overhead is an agrément de plus.
But, nevertheless, picnics cannot exist without a
certain allowance of elderly people. The Miss
Marians and Captains Ewing cannot go out to dine on
the grass without some one to look after them. So
the elderly people go to picnics, in a dull tame way,
doing their duty, and wishing the day over. Now on
the morning in question, when Marian rode off with
Captain Ewing and Lieutenant Graham, Maurice
Cumming remained among the elderly people.

A certain Mr. Pomken, a great Jamaica agri-
culturist, one of the Council, a man who had known
the good old times, got him by the button and held
him fast, discoursing wisely of sugar and rum, of
Gadsden pans and recreant negroes, on all of which
subjects Maurice Cumming was known to have an
opinion of his own. But as Mr. Pomken's words
sounded into one ear, into the other fell notes, listened
to from afar,—the shrill laughing voice of Marian
Leslie as she gave her happy order to her satellites
around her, and ever and anon the bass haw-haw of
Captain Ewing, who was made welcome as the chief of

her attendants. That evening in a whisper to a brother
councillor Mr. Pomken communicated his opinion that
after all there was not so much in that young Cumming
as some people said. But Mr. Pomken had no idea
that that young Cumming was in love.

And then the dinner came, spread over half an acre.
Maurice was among the last who seated himself; and
when he did so it was in an awkward comfortless
corner, behind Mr. Pomken's back, and far away from
the laughter and mirth of the day. But yet from his
comfortless corner he could see Marian as she sat in
her pride of power, with her friend Julia Davis near
her, a flirt as bad as herself, and her satellites around
her, obedient to her nod, and happy in her smiles.

'Now I won't allow any more champagne,' said
Marian; 'or who will there be steady enough to help
me over the rocks to the grotto?'

'Oh, you have promised me!' cried the captain.

'Indeed, I have not; have I, Julia?'

'Miss Davis has certainly promised me,' said the
lieutenant.

'I have made no promise, and don't think I shall go
at all,' said Julia, who was sometimes inclined to
imagine that Captain Ewing should be her own property.

All which and much more of the kind Maurice
Cumming could not hear; but he could see—and
imagine, which was worse. How innocent and inane
are, after all, the flirtings of most young ladies, if all
their words and doings in that line could be brought to

paper! I do not know whether there be as a rule more vocal expression of the sentiment of love between a man and woman than there is between two thrushes! They whistle and call to each other, guided by instinct rather than by reason.

'You are going home with the ladies to-night, I believe,' said Maurice to Miss Jack, immediately after dinner. Miss Jack acknowledged that such was her destination for the night.

'Then my going back to Spanish Town at once won't hurt any one—for, to tell the truth, I have had enough of this work.'

'Why, Maurice, you were in such a hurry to come.'

'The more fool I; and so now I am in a hurry to go away. Don't notice it to anybody.'

Miss Jack looked in his face and saw that he was really wretched; and she knew the cause of his wretchedness.

'Don't go yet, Maurice,' she said; and then added, with a tenderness that was quite uncommon with her, 'Go to her, Maurice, and speak to her openly and freely, once for all; you will find that she will listen then. Dear Maurice, do, for my sake.'

He made no answer, but walked away, roaming sadly by himself among the trees. 'Listen!' he exclaimed to himself. 'Yes, she will alter a dozen times in as many hours. Who can care for a creature that can change as she changes?' And yet he could not help caring for her.

As he went on, climbing among rocks, he again came upon the sound of voices, and heard especially that of Captain Ewing. 'Now, Miss Leslie, if you will take my hand you will soon be over all the difficulty.' And then a party of seven or eight, scrambling over some stones, came nearly on the level on which he stood, in full view of him; and leading the others were Captain Ewing and Miss Leslie.

He turned on his heel to go away, when he caught the sound of a step following him, and a voice saying, 'Oh, there is Mr. Cumming, and I want to speak to him;' and in a minute a light hand was on his arm.

'Why are you running away from us?' said Marian.

'Because—oh, I don't know. I am not running away. You have your party made up, and I am not going to intrude on it.'

'What nonsense! Do come now; we are going to this wonderful grotto. I thought it so ill-natured of you, not joining us at dinner. Indeed you know you had promised.'

He did not answer her, but he looked at her—full in the face, with his sad eyes laden with love. She half understood his countenance, but only half understood it.

'What is the matter, Maurice?' she said. 'Are you angry with me? Will you come and join us?'

'No, Marian, I cannot do that. But if you can leave them and come with me for half an hour, I will not keep you longer.'

She stood hesitating a moment, while her companion remained on the spot where she had left him. 'Come

L

Miss Leslie,' called Captain Ewing. 'You will have it dark before we can get down.'

'I will come with you,' whispered she to Maurice, 'but wait a moment.' And she tripped back, and in some five minutes returned after an eager argument with her friends. 'There,' she said, 'I don't care about the grotto, one bit, and I will walk with you now;—only they will think it so odd.' And so they started off together.

Before the tropical darkness had fallen upon them Maurice had told the tale of his love,—and had told it in a manner differing much from that of Marian's usual admirers. He spoke with passion and almost with violence; he declared that his heart was so full of her image that he could not rid himself of it for one minute; 'nor would he wish to do so,' he said, 'if she would be his Marian, his own Marian, his very own. But if not ——' and then he explained to her, with all a lover's warmth, and with almost more than a lover's liberty, what was his idea of her being 'his own, his very own,' and in doing so inveighed against her usual light-heartedness in terms which at any rate were strong enough.

But Marian bore it all well. Perhaps she knew that the lesson was somewhat deserved; and perhaps she appreciated at its value the love of such a man as Maurice Cumming, weighing in her judgment the difference between him and the Ewings and the Grahams.

And then she answered him well and prudently,

with words which startled him by their prudent serious-
ness as coming from her. She begged his pardon
heartily, she said, for any grief which she had caused
him; but yet how was she to be blamed, seeing that she
had known nothing of his feelings? Her father and
mother had said something to her of this proposed
marriage; something, but very little; and she had
answered by saying that she did not think Maurice
had any warmer regard for her than of a cousin. After
this answer neither father nor mother had pressed the
matter further. As to her own feelings she could then
say nothing, for she then knew nothing;—nothing but
this, that she loved no one better than him, or rather
that she loved no one else. She would ask herself if
she could love him; but he must give her some little
time for that. In the mean time—and she smiled
sweetly at him as she made the promise—she would
endeavour to do nothing that would offend him; and
then she added that on that evening she would dance
with him any dances that he liked. Maurice, with a
self-denial that was not very wise, contented himself
with engaging her for the first quadrille.

They were to dance that night in the mess-room of
the officers at Newcastle. This scheme had been added
on as an adjunct to the picnic, and it therefore became
necessary that the ladies should retire to their own
or their friends' houses at Newcastle to adjust their
dresses. Marian Leslie and Julia Davis were there
accommodated with the loan of a small room by the
major's wife, and as they were brushing their hair,

and putting on their dancing-shoes, something was said between them about Maurice Cumming.

'And so you are to be Mrs. C. of Mount Pleasant,' said Julia. 'Well; I didn't think it would come to that at last.'

'But it has not come to that, and if it did why should I not be Mrs. C., as you call it?'

'The knight of the rueful countenance, I call him.'

'I tell you what then, he is an excellent young man, and the fact is you don't know him.'

'I don't like excellent young men with long faces. I suppose you won't be let to dance quick dances at all now.'

'I shall dance whatever dances I like, as I have always done,' said Marian, with some little asperity in her tone.

'Not you; or if you do, you'll lose your promotion. You'll never live to be my Lady Rue. And what will Graham say? You know you've given him half a promise.'

'That's not true, Julia;—I never gave him the tenth part of a promise.'

'Well, he says so;' and then the words between the young ladies became a little more angry. But, nevertheless, in due time they came forth with faces smiling as usual, with their hair properly brushed, and without any signs of warfare.

But Marian had to stand another attack before the business of the evening commenced, and this was from no less doughty an antagonist than her aunt, Miss Jack. Miss Jack soon found that Maurice had not

kept his threat of going home; and though she did not
absolutely learn from him that he had gone so far towards perfecting her dearest hopes as to make a formal
offer to Marian, nevertheless she did gather that things
were fast that way tending.   If only this dancing were
over! she said to herself, dreading the unnumbered
waltzes with Ewing, and the violent polkas with
Graham. So Miss Jack resolved to say one word to
Marian—'A wise word in good season,' said Miss Jack
to herself, ' how sweet a thing it is.'

'Marian,' said she.   ' Step here a moment, I want
to say a word to you.'

'Yes, aunt Sarah,' said Marian, following her aunt
into a corner, not quite in the best humour in the world;
for she had a dread of some further interference.

' Are you going to dance with Maurice to-night?'

' Yes, I believe so,—the first quadrille.'

' Well, what I was going to say is this. I don't want
you to dance many quick dances to-night, for a reason
I have :—that is, not a great many.'

' Why, aunt, what nonsense!'

' Now my dearest, dearest girl, it is all for your
own sake. Well, then, it must out. He does not like
it, you know.'

' What he?'

' Maurice.'

' Well, aunt, I don't know that I'm bound to dance
or not to dance just as Mr. Cumming may like. Papa
does not mind my dancing. The people have come
here to dance, and you can hardly want to make me

ridiculous by sitting still.' And so that wise word did not appear to be very sweet.

And then the amusement of the evening commenced, and Marian stood up for a quadrille with her lover. She however was not in the very best humour. She had, as she thought, said and done enough for one day in Maurice's favour. And she had no idea, as she declared to herself, of being lectured by aunt Sarah.

'Dearest Marian,' he said to her, as the quadrille came to a close, 'it is in your power to make me so happy,—so perfectly happy.'

'But then people have such different ideas of happiness,' she replied. 'They can't all see with the same eyes, you know.' And so they parted.

But during the early part of the evening she was sufficiently discreet; she did waltz with Lieutenant Graham, and polk with Captain Ewing, but she did so in a tamer manner than was usual with her, and she made no emulous attempts to dance down other couples. When she had done she would sit down, and then she consented to stand up for two quadrilles with two very tame gentlemen, to whom no lover could object.

'And so, Marian, your wings are regularly clipped at last,' said Julia Davis coming up to her.

'No more clipped than your own,' said Marian.

'If Sir Rue won't let you waltz now, what will he require of you when you're married to him?'

'I am just as well able to waltz with whom I like as you are, Julia; and if you say so in that way, I shall think it's envy.'

'Ha—ha—ha; I may have envied you some of your beaux before now; I dare say I have. But I certainly do not envy you Sir Rue.' And then she went off to her partner.

All this was too much for Marian's weak strength, and before long she was again whirling round with Captain Ewing. 'Come, Miss Leslie,' said he, 'let us see what we can do. Graham and Julia Davis have been saying that your waltzing days are over, but I think we can put them down.'

Marian as she got up, and raised her arm in order that Ewing might put his round her waist, caught Maurice's eye as he leaned against a wall, and read in it a stern rebuke. 'This is too bad,' she said to herself. 'He shall not make a slave of me, at any rate as yet.' And away she went as madly, more madly than ever, and for the rest of the evening she danced with Captain Ewing and with him alone.

There is an intoxication quite distinct from that which comes from strong drink. When the judgment is altogether overcome by the spirits this species of drunkenness comes on, and in this way Marian Leslie was drunk that night. For two hours she danced with Captain Ewing, and ever and anon she kept saying to herself that she would teach the world to know—and of all the world Mr. Cumming especially—that she might be led but not driven.

Then about four o'clock she went home, and as she attempted to undress herself in her own room she burst into violent tears and opened her heart to her sister—

'Oh, Fanny, I do love him, I do love him so dearly! and now he will never come to me again!'

Maurice stood still with his back against the wall, for the full two hours of Marian's exhibition, and then he said to his aunt before he left—'I hope you have now seen enough ; you will hardly mention her name to me again.' Miss Jack groaned from the bottom of her heart but she said nothing. She said nothing that night to any one ; but she lay awake in her bed, thinking, till it was time to rise and dress herself. 'Ask Miss Marian to come to me,' she said to the black girl who came to assist her. But it was not till she had sent three times, that Miss Marian obeyed the summons.

At three o'clock on the following day Miss Jack arrived at her own hall door in Spanish Town. Long as the distance was she ordinarily rode it all, but on this occasion she had provided a carriage to bring her over as much of the journey as it was practicable for her to perform on wheels. As soon as she reached her own hall door she asked if Mr. Cumming was at home. 'Yes,' the servant said. 'He was in the small book room, at the back of the house, up stairs.' Silently, as if afraid of being heard, she stepped up her own stairs into her own drawing-room ; and very silently she was followed by a pair of feet lighter and smaller than her own.

Miss Jack was usually somewhat of a despot in her own house, but there was nothing despotic about her now as she peered into the book-room. This she did with her bonnet still on, looking round the half-opened

door as though she were afraid to disturb her nephew.
He sat at the window looking out into the verandah
which ran behind the house, so intent on his thoughts
that he did not hear her.

'Maurice,' she said, 'can I come in?'

'Come in? oh yes, of course;' and he turned round
sharply at her. 'I tell you what, aunt; I am not well
here, and I cannot stay out the session. I shall go
back to Mount Pleasant.'

'Maurice,' and she walked close up to him as she
spoke, 'Maurice, I have brought some one with me to
ask your pardon.'

His face became red up to the roots of his hair as he
stood looking at her without answering. 'You would
grant it certainly,' she continued, 'if you knew how
much it would be valued.'

'Whom do you mean? who is it?' he asked at last.

'One who loves you as well as you love her—and
she cannot love you better. Come in, Marian.' The
poor girl crept in at the door, ashamed of what she was
induced to do, but yet looking anxiously into her
lover's face. 'You asked her yesterday to be your
wife,' said Miss Jack, 'and she did not then know her
own mind. Now she has had a lesson. You will ask
her once again; will you not, Maurice?'

What was he to say? How was he to refuse, when
that soft little hand was held out to him; when those
eyes laden with tears just ventured to look into his face?

'I beg your pardon if I angered you last night,'
she said.

In half a minute Miss Jack had left the room, and in the space of another thirty seconds Maurice had forgiven her. 'I am your own now, you know,' she whispered to him in the course of that long evening. 'Yesterday, you know—,' but the sentence was never finished.

It was in vain that Julia Davis was ill natured and sarcastic, in vain that Ewing and Graham made joint attempt upon her constancy. From that night to the morning of her marriage—and the interval was only three months—Marian Leslie was never known to flirt.

THE COURTSHIP OF SUSAN BELL.

JOHN MUNROE BELL had been a lawyer in Albany, State of New York, and as such had thriven well. He had thriven well as long as thrift and thriving on this earth had been allowed to him. But the Almighty had seen fit to shorten his span.

Early in life he had married a timid, anxious, pretty good little wife, whose whole heart and mind had been given up to do his bidding and deserve his love. She had not only deserved it but had possessed it, and as long as John Munroe Bell had lived, Henrietta Bell— Hetta as he called her—had been a woman rich in blessings. After twelve years of such blessings he had left her, and had left with her two daughters, a second Hetta, and the heroine of our little story, Susan Bell.

A lawyer in Albany may thrive passing well for eight or ten years, and yet not leave behind him any very large sum of money if he dies at the end of that time. Some small modicum, some few thousand dollars, John Bell had amassed, so that his widow and daughters were not absolutely driven to look for work or bread.

In those happy days when cash had begun to flow in plenteously to the young father of the family he had taken it into his head to build for himself, or rather for his young female brood, a small neat house in the out-skirts of Saratoga Springs. In doing so he was insti-gated as much by the excellence of the investment for his pocket as by the salubrity of the place for his girls. He furnished the house well, and then during some sum-mer weeks his wife lived there, and sometimes he let it.

How the widow grieved when the lord of her heart and master of her mind was laid in the grave, I need not tell. She had already counted ten years of widow-hood, and her children had grown to be young women beside her at the time of which I am now about to speak. Since that sad day on which they had left Albany they had lived together at the cottage at the Springs. In winter their life had been lonely enough ; but as soon as the hot weather began to drive the fainting citizens out from New York, they had always received two or three boarders—old ladies generally, and occasionally an old gentleman—persons of very steady habits, with whose pockets the widow's moderate demands agreed better than the hotel charges. And so the Bells lived for ten years.

That Saratoga is a gay place in July, August, and September the world knows well enough. To girls who go there with trunks full of muslin and crinoline, for whom a carriage and pair of horses is always wait-ing immediately after dinner, whose fathers' pockets are bursting with dollars, it is a very gay place.

Dancing and flirtations come as a matter of course, and matrimony follows after with only too great rapidity. But the place was not very gay for Hetta or Susan Bell.

In the first place the widow was a timid woman, and among other fears feared greatly that she should be thought guilty of setting traps for husbands. Poor mothers ! how often are they charged with this sin when their honest desires go no further than that their bairns may be 'respectit like the lave.' And then she feared flirtations ; flirtations that should be that and nothing more, flirtations that are so destructive of the heart's sweetest essence. She feared love also, though she longed for that as well as feared it ;—for her girls, I mean ; all such feelings for herself were long laid under ground ;—and then, like a timid creature as she was, she had other indefinite fears, and among them a great fear that those girls of hers would be left husbandless,—a phase of life which after her twelve years of bliss she regarded as anything but desirable. But the upshot was,—the upshot of so many fears and such small means, —that Hetta and Susan Bell had but a dull life of it.

Were it not that I am somewhat closely restricted in the number of my pages, I would describe at full the merits and beauties of Hetta and Susan Bell. As it is I can but say a few words. At our period of their lives Hetta was nearly one-and-twenty, and Susan was just nineteen. Hetta was a short, plump, demure young woman, with the softest smoothed hair, and the brownest brightest eyes. She was very useful in the house, good at corn cakes, and thought much, particu-

larly in these latter months, of her religious duties.
Her sister in the privacy of their own little room would
sometimes twit her with the admiring patience with
which she would listen to the lengthened eloquence of
Mr. Phineas Beckard, the Baptist minister.   Now Mr.
Phineas Beckard was a bachelor.

Susan was not so good a girl in the kitchen or about
the house as was her sister ; but she was bright in the
parlour, and if that motherly heart could have been
made to give out its inmost secret—which, however, it
could not have been made to give out in any way painful to dear Hetta—perhaps it might have been found
that Susan was loved with the closest love.   She
was taller than her sister, and lighter ; her eyes were
blue as were her mother's ; her hair was brighter than
Hetta's, but not always so singularly neat.   She had a
dimple on her chin, whereas Hetta had none ; dimples on
her cheeks too, when she smiled ; and, oh, such a mouth !
There ; my allowance of pages permits no more.

One piercing cold winter's day there came knocking
at the widow's door—a young man.   Winter days, when
the ice of January is refrozen by the wind of February,
are very cold at Saratoga Springs.   In these days there
was not often much to disturb the serenity of Mrs.
Bell's house ; but on the day in question there came
knocking at the door—a young man.

Mrs. Bell kept an old domestic, who had lived with
them in those happy Albany days.   Her name was
Kate O'Brien, but though picturesque in name she was
hardly so in person.   She was a thick-set, noisy, good-

natured old Irishwoman, who had joined her lot to that
of Mrs. Bell when the latter first began housekeeping,
and knowing when she was well off, had remained in
the same place from that day forth. She had known
Hetta as a baby, and, so to say, had seen Susan's birth.

' And what might you be wanting, sir ?' said Kate
O'Brien, apparently not quite pleased as she opened
the door and let in all the cold air.

'I wish to see Mrs. Bell. Is not this Mrs. Bell's
house ?' said the young man, shaking the snow from out
of the breast of his coat.

He did see Mrs. Bell, and we will now tell who he
was, and why he had come, and how it came to pass
that his carpet-bag was brought down to the widow's
house and one of the front bedrooms was prepared for him,
and that he drank tea that night in the widow's parlour.

His name was Aaron Dunn, and by profession he
was an engineer. What peculiar misfortune in those
days of frost and snow had befallen the line of rails
which runs from Schenectady to Lake Champlain, I
never quite understood. Banks and bridges had in
some way come to grief, and on Aaron Dunn's shoulders
was thrown the burden of seeing that they were duly
repaired. Saratoga Springs was the centre of these
mishaps, and therefore at Saratoga Springs it was
necessary that he should take up his temporary abode.

Now there was at that time in New York city a Mr.
Bell, great in railway matters—an uncle of the once
thriving but now departed Albany lawyer. He was a
rich man, but he liked his riches himself; or at any

rate had not found himself called upon to share them with the widow and daughters of his nephew. But when it chanced to come to pass that he had a hand in despatching Aaron Dunn to Saratoga, he took the young man aside and recommended him to lodge with the widow. 'There,' said he, 'show her my card.' So much the rich uncle thought he might vouchsafe to do for the nephew's widow.

Mrs. Bell and both her daughters were in the parlour when Aaron Dunn was shown in, snow and all. He told his story in a rough, shaky voice, for his teeth chattered; and he gave the card, almost wishing that he had gone to the empty big hotel, for the widow's welcome was not at first quite warm.

The widow listened to him as he gave his message, and then she took the card and looked at it. Hetta, who was sitting on the side of the fireplace facing the door, went on demurely with her work. Susan gave one glance round—her back was to the stranger—and then another; and then she moved her chair a little nearer to the wall, so as to give the young man room to come to the fire, if he would. He did not come, but his eyes glanced upon Susan Bell; and he thought that the old man in New York was right, and that the big hotel would be cold and dull. It was a pretty face to look on that cold evening as she turned it up from the stocking she was mending.

'Perhaps you don't wish to take winter boarders, ma'am?' said Aaron Dunn.

'We never have done so yet, sir,' said Mrs. Bell

timidly. 'Could she let this young wolf in among her lamb-fold? He might be a wolf;—who could tell?'

'Mr. Bell seemed to think it would suit,' said Aaron.

Had he acquiesced in her timidity and not pressed the point, it would have been all up with him. But the widow did not like to go against the big uncle; and so she said, 'Perhaps it may, sir.'

'I guess it will, finely,' said Aaron. And then the widow seeing that the matter was so far settled, put down her work and came round into the passage. Hetta followed her, for there would be house-work to do. Aaron gave himself another shake, settled the weekly number of dollars—with very little difficulty on his part, for he had caught another glance at Susan's face; and then went after his bag. 'Twas thus that Aaron Dunn obtained an entrance into Mrs. Bell's house. 'But what if he be a wolf?' she said to herself over and over again that night, though not exactly in those words. Ay, but there is another side to that question. What if he be a stalwart man, honest-minded, with clever eye, cunning hand, ready brain, broad back, and warm heart; in want of a wife mayhap; a man that can earn his own bread and another's;—half a dozen others, when the half-dozen come? Would not that be a good sort of lodger? Such a question as that too did flit, just flit, across the widow's sleepless mind. But then she thought so much more of the wolf! Wolves, she had taught herself to think, were more common than stalwart, honest-minded, wife-desirous men.

M

'I wonder mother consented to take him,' said Hetta when they were in the little room together.

'And why shouldn't she?' said Susan. 'It will be a help.'

'Yes, it will be a little help,' said Hetta. 'But we have done very well hitherto without winter lodgers.'

'But uncle Bell said she was to.'

'What is uncle Bell to us?' said Hetta, who had a spirit of her own. And she began to surmise within herself whether Aaron Dunn would join the Baptist congregation, and whether Phineas Beckard would approve of this new move.

He is a very well-behaved young man, at any rate,' said Susan, 'and he draws beautifully. Did you see those things he was doing?'

'He draws very well, I dare say,' said Hetta, who regarded this as but a poor warranty for good behaviour. Hetta also had some fear of wolves—not for herself, perhaps; but for her sister.

Aaron Dunn's work—the commencement of his work—lay at some distance from the Springs, and he left every morning with a lot of workmen by an early train—almost before daylight. And every morning, cold and wintry as the mornings were, the widow got nim his breakfast with her own hands. She took his dollars and would not leave him altogether to the awkward mercies of Kate O'Brien; nor would she trust her girls to attend upon the young man. Hetta she might have trusted; but then Susan would have asked why she was spared her share of such hardship.

In the evening, leaving his work when it was dark, Aaron always returned, and then the evening was passed together. But they were passed with the most demure propriety. These women would make the tea, cut the bread and butter, and then sew; while Aaron Dunn, when the cups were removed, would always go to his plans and drawings.

On Sundays they were more together; but even on this day there was cause of separation, for Aaron went to the Episcopalian church, rather to the disgust of Hetta. In the afternoon however they were together; and then Phineas Beckard came in to tea on Sundays, and he and Aaron got to talking on religion; and though they disagreed pretty much, and would not give an inch either one or the other, nevertheless the minister told the widow, and Hetta too probably, that the lad had good stuff in him, though he was so stiff-necked.

'But he should be more modest in talking on such matters with a minister,' said Hetta.

The Rev. Phineas acknowledged that perhaps he should; but he was honest enough to repeat that the lad had stuff in him. 'Perhaps after all he is not a wolf,' said the widow to herself.

Things went on in this way for above a month. Aaron had declared to himself over and over again that that face was sweet to look upon, and had unconsciously promised to himself certain delights in talking and perhaps walking with the owner of it. But the walkings had not been achieved—nor even the talkings as yet. The truth was that Dunn was bashful with young women, though he could be so stiff-necked with the minister.

And then he felt angry with himself, inasmuch as he had advanced no further; and as he lay in his bed—which perhaps those pretty hands had helped to make—he resolved that he would be a thought bolder in his bearing. He had no idea of making love to Susan Bell; of course not. But why should he not amuse himself by talking to a pretty girl when she sat so near him, evening after evening?

'What a very quiet young man he is,' said Susan to her sister.

'He has his bread to earn, and sticks to his work,' said Hetta. 'No doubt he has his amusement when he is in the city,' added the elder sister, not wishing to leave too strong an impression of the young man's virtue.

They had all now their settled places in the parlour. Hetta sat on one side of the fire, close to the table, having that side to herself. There she sat always busy. She must have made every dress and bit of linen worn in the house, and hemmed every sheet and towel, so busy was she always. Sometimes, once in a week or so, Phineas Beckard would come in, and then place was made for him between Hetta's usual seat and the table. For when there he would read out loud. On the other side, close also to the table, sat the widow, busy, but not savagely busy as her elder daughter. Between Mrs. Bell and the wall, with her feet ever on the fender, Susan used to sit; not absolutely idle, but doing work of some slender pretty sort, and talking ever and anon to her mother. Opposite to them all, at the other side of the table, far away from the fire, would Aaron Dunn place himself with his plans and drawings before him.

'Are you a judge of bridges, ma'am?' said Aaron, the evening after he had made his resolution. 'Twas thus he began his courtship.

'Of bridges!' said Mrs. Bell—'oh dear, no, sir.' But she put out her hand to take the little drawing which Aaron handed to her.

'Because that's one I've planned for our bit of a new branch from Moreau up to Lake George. I guess Miss Susan knows something about bridges.'

'I guess I don't,' said Susan—'only that they oughtn't to tumble down when the frost comes.'

'Ha, ha, ha; no more they ought. I'll tell McEvoy that.' McEvoy had been a former engineer on the line. 'Well, that won't burst with any frost, I guess.'

'Oh, my! how pretty!' said the widow, and then Susan of course jumped up to look over her mother's shoulder.

The artful dodger! He had drawn and coloured a beautiful little sketch of a bridge; not an engineer's plan with sections and measurements, vexatious to a woman's eye, but a graceful little bridge with a string of cars running under it. You could almost hear the bell going.

'Well; that is a pretty bridge,' said Susan. 'Isn't it, Hetta?'

'I don't know anything about bridges,' said Hetta, to whose clever eyes the dodge was quite apparent. But in spite of her cleverness Mrs. Bell and Susan had soon moved their chairs round to the table, and were looking through the contents of Aaron's portfolio. 'But yet he may be a wolf,' thought the poor widow, just as she was kneeling down to say her prayers.

That evening certainly made a commencement. Though Hetta went on pertinaciously with the body of a new dress, the other two ladies did not put in another stitch that night. From his drawings Aaron got to his instruments, and before bedtime was teaching Susan how to draw parallel lines. Susan found that she had quite an aptitude for parallel lines, and altogether had a good time of it that evening. It is dull to go on week after week, and month after month talking only to one's mother and sister. It is dull though one does not oneself recognize it to be so. A little change in such matters is so very pleasant. Susan had not the slightest idea of regarding Aaron as even a possible lover. But young ladies do like the conversation of young gentlemen. Oh, my exceedingly proper, prim, old lady, you who are so shocked at this as a general doctrine, has it never occurred to you that the Creator has so intended it?

Susan, understanding little of the how and why, knew that she had had a good time, and was rather in spirits as she went to bed. But Hetta had been frightened by the dodge.

'Oh, Hetta, you should have looked at those drawings. He is so clever!' said Susan.

'I don't know that they would have done me much good,' replied Hetta.

'Good! Well, they'd do me more good than a long sermon, I know,' said Susan; 'except on a Sunday, of course,' she added apologetically. This was an ill-tempered attack both on Hetta and Hetta's admirer. But then why had Hetta been so snappish?

'I'm sure he's a wolf,' thought Hetta as she went to bed.

'What a very clever young man he is!' thought Susan to herself as she pulled the warm clothes round about her shoulders and ears.

'Well; that certainly was an improvement,' thought Aaron as he went through the same operation, with a stronger feeling of self-approbation than he had enjoyed for some time past.

In the course of the next fortnight the family arrangements all altered themselves. Unless when Beckard was there Aaron would sit in the widow's place, the widow would take Susan's chair, and the two girls would be opposite. And then Dunn would read to them; not sermons, but passages from Shakspeare, and Byron, and Longfellow. 'He reads much better than Mr. Beckard,' Susan had said one night. 'Of course you're a competent judge!' had been Hetta's

retort. 'I mean that I like it better,' said Susan.
'It's well that all people don't think alike,' replied
Hetta.

And then there was a deal of talking. The widow
herself, as unconscious in this respect as her youngest
daughter, certainly did find that a little variety was
agreeable on those long winter nights; and talked herself with unaccustomed freedom. And Beckard came
there oftener and talked very much. When he was
there the two young men did all the talking, and they
pounded each other immensely. But still there grew
up a sort of friendship between them.

'Mr. Beckard seems quite to take to him,' said Mrs.
Bell to her eldest daughter.

'It is his great good nature, mother,' replied Hetta.

It was at the end of the second month when Aaron
took another step in advance—a perilous step. Sometimes on evenings he still went on with his drawing
for an hour or so; but during three or four evenings
he never asked any one to look at what he was doing.
On one Friday he sat over his work till late, without
any reading or talking at all; so late that at last Mrs.
Bell said, 'If you're going to sit much longer, Mr.
Dunn, I'll get you to put out the candles.' Thereby
showing, had he known it or had she, that the mother's
confidence in the young man was growing fast. Hetta
knew all about it, and dreaded that the growth was too
quick.

'I've finished now,' said Aaron; and he looked
carefully at the card-board on which he had been

washing in his water-colours. 'I've finished now.'
He then hesitated a moment; but ultimately he put
the card into his portfolio and carried it up to his bedroom. Who does not perceive that it was intended as
a present to Susan Bell?

The question which Aaron asked himself that night,
and which he hardly knew how to answer was this.
Should he offer the drawing to Susan in the presence
of her mother and sister, or on some occasion when
they two might be alone together? No such occasion
had ever yet occurred, but Aaron thought that it
might probably be brought about. But then he
wanted to make no fuss about it. His first intention
had been to chuck the drawing lightly across the table
when it was completed, and so make nothing of it.
But he had finished it with more care than he had at
first intended; and then he had hesitated when he had
finished it. It was too late now for that plan of
chucking it over the table.

On the Saturday evening when he came down from
his room, Mr. Beckard was there, and there was no
opportunity that night. On the Sunday, in conformity
with a previous engagement, he went to hear Mr.
Beckard preach, and walked to and from meeting with
the family. This pleased Mrs. Bell, and they were all
very gracious that afternoon. But Sunday was no day
for the picture.

On Monday the thing had become of importance to
him. Things always do when they are kept over.
Before tea that evening when he came down Mrs.

Bell and Susan only were in the room. He knew Hetta for his foe, and therefore determined to use this occasion.

'Miss Susan,' he said, stammering somewhat, and blushing too, poor fool! 'I have done a little drawing which I want you to accept,' and he put his portfolio down on the table.

'Oh! I don't know,' said Susan who had seen the blush.

Mrs. Bell had seen the blush also, and pursed her mouth up, and looked grave. Had there been no stammering and no blush, she might have thought nothing of it.

Aaron saw at once that his little gift was not to go down smoothly. He was however in for it now, so he picked it out from among the other papers in the case and brought it over to Susan. He endeavoured to hand it to her with an air of indifference, but I cannot say that he succeeded.

It was a very pretty well-finished, water-coloured drawing, representing still the same bridge, but with more adjuncts. In Susan's eyes it was a work of high art. Of pictures probably she had seen but little, and her liking for the artist no doubt added to her admiration. But the more she admired it and wished for it, the stronger was her feeling that she ought not to take it.

Poor Susan! she stood for a minute looking at the drawing, but she said nothing; not even a word of praise. She felt that she was red in the face, and uncourteous to their lodger; but her mother was looking at her and she did not know how to behave herself.

Mrs. Bell put out her hand for the sketch, trying to bethink herself as she did so in what least uncivil way she could refuse the present. She took a moment to look at it collecting her thoughts, and as she did so her woman's wit came to her aid.

'Oh dear, Mr. Dunn, it is very pretty; quite a beautiful picture. I cannot let Susan rob you of that. You must keep that for some of your own particular friends.'

'But I did it for her,' said Aaron innocently.

Susan looked down at the ground, half pleased at the declaration. The drawing would look very pretty in a small gilt frame put over her dressing-table. But the matter now was altogether in her mother's hands.

'I am afraid it is too valuable, sir, for Susan to accept.'

'It is not valuable at all,' said Aaron, declining to take it back from the widow's hand.

'Oh, I am quite sure it is. It is worth ten dollars at least—or twenty,' said poor Mrs. Bell, not in the very best taste. But she was perplexed and did not know how to get out of the scrape. The article in question now lay upon the table-cloth, appropriated by no one, and at this moment Hetta came into the room.

'It is not worth ten cents,' said Aaron, with something like a frown on his brow. 'But as we had been talking about the bridge, I thought Miss Susan would accept it.'

'Accept what?' said Hetta. And then her eye fell upon the drawing and she took it up.

'It is beautifully done,' said Mrs. Bell, wishing much to soften the matter; perhaps the more so, that Hetta the demure was now present. 'I am telling Mr. Dunn that we can't take a present of anything so valuable.'

'Oh dear, no,' said Hetta. 'It wouldn't be right.'

It was a cold frosty evening in March, and the fire was burning brightly on the hearth. Aaron Dunn took up the drawing quietly—very quietly—and rolling it up, as such drawings are rolled, put it between the blazing logs. It was the work of four evenings, and his chef-d'œuvre in the way of art.

Susan, when she saw what he had done, burst out into tears. The widow could very readily have done so also, but she was able to refrain herself, and merely exclaimed—'Oh, Mr. Dunn!'

'If Mr. Dunn chooses to burn his own picture, he has certainly a right to do so,' said Hetta.

Aaron immediately felt ashamed of what he had done; and he also could have cried, but for his manliness. He walked away to one of the parlour-windows, and looked out upon the frosty night. It was dark, but the stars were bright, and he thought that he should like to be walking fast by himself along the line of rails towards Balston. There he stood, perhaps for three minutes.   He thought it would be proper to give Susan time to recover from her tears.

'Will you please to come to your tea, sir?' said the soft voice of Mrs. Bell.

He turned round to do so, and found that Susan was gone.   It was not quite in her power to recover from her tears in three minutes.   And then the drawing had been so beautiful!   It had been done expressly for her too!   And there had been something, she knew not what, in his eye as he had so declared. She had watched him intently over those four evenings' work, wondering why he did not show it, till her feminine curiosity had become rather strong.   It was something very particular, she was sure, and she had learned that all that precious work had been for her. Now all that precious work was destroyed.   How was it possible that she should not cry for more than three minutes?

The others took their meal in perfect silence, and when it was over the two women sat down to their work.   Aaron had a book which he pretended to read, but instead of reading he was bethinking himself that he had behaved badly.   What right had he to throw them all into such confusion by indulging in his passion?   He was ashamed of what he had done, and fancied that Susan would hate him.   Fancying that, he began to find at the same time that he by no means hated her.

At last Hetta got up and left the room.   She knew that her sister was sitting alone in the cold, and

Hetta was affectionate. Susan had not been in fault, and therefore Hetta went up to console her.

'Mrs. Bell,' said Aaron, as soon as the door was closed, 'I beg your pardon for what I did just now.'

'Oh, sir, I'm so sorry that the picture is burnt,' said poor Mrs. Bell.

'The picture does not matter a straw,' said Aaron. 'But I see that I have disturbed you all,—and I am afraid I have made Miss Susan unhappy.'

'She was grieved because your picture was burnt,' said Mrs. Bell, putting some emphasis on the 'your,' intending to show that her daughter had not regarded the drawing as her own. But the emphasis bore another meaning; and so the widow perceived as soon as she had spoken.

'Oh, I can do twenty more of the same if anybody wanted them,' said Aaron. 'If I do another like it, will you let her take it, Mrs. Bell?—just to show that you have forgiven me, and that we are friends as we were before?'

Was he, or was he not a wolf? That was the question which Mrs. Bell scarcely knew how to answer. Hetta had given her voice, saying he was lupine. Mr. Beckard's opinion she had not liked to ask directly. Mr. Beckard she thought would probably propose to Hetta; but as yet he had not done so. And, as he was still a stranger in the family, she did not like in any way to compromise Susan's name. Indirectly she had asked the question, and, indirectly also, Mr. Beckard's answer had been favourable.

'But it mustn't mean anything, sir,' was the widow's weak answer, when she had paused on the question for a moment.

'Oh no, of course not,' said Aaron, joyously, and his face became radiant and happy. 'And I do beg your pardon for burning it; and the young ladies' pardon too.' And then he rapidly got out his card-board, and set himself to work about another bridge. The widow meditating many things in her heart, commenced the hemming of a handkerchief.

In about an hour the two girls came back to the room and silently took their accustomed places. Aaron hardly looked up, but went on diligently with his drawing. This bridge should be a better bridge than that other. Its acceptance was now assured. Of course it was to mean nothing. That was a matter of course. So he worked away diligently, and said nothing to anybody.

When they went off to bed the two girls went into the mother's room. 'Oh, mother, I hope he is not very angry,' said Susan.

'Angry!' said Hetta, 'if anybody should be angry, it is mother. He ought to have known that Susan could not accept it. He should never have offered it.'

'But he's doing another,' said Mrs. Bell.

'Not for her,' said Hetta.

'Yes he is,' said Mrs. Bell, 'and I have promised that she shall take it.' Susan as she heard this sank gently into the chair behind her, and her eyes became full of tears. The intimation was almost too much for her.

'Oh mother!' said Hetta.

'But I particularly said that it was to mean nothing.'

'Oh mother, that makes it worse.'

Why should Hetta interfere in this way, thought Susan to herself. Had she interfered when Mr. Beckard gave Hetta a testament bound in morocco? Had not she smiled, and looked gratified, and kissed her sister, and declared that Phineas Beckard was a nice dear man, and by far the most elegant preacher at the Springs? Why should Hetta be so cruel?

'I don't see that, my dear,' said the mother. Hetta would not explain before her sister, so they all went to bed.

On the Thursday evening the drawing was finished. Not a word had been said about it, at any rate in his presence, and he had gone on working in silence. 'There,' said he, late on the Thursday evening, 'I don't know that it will be any better if I go on daubing for another hour. There, Miss Susan; there's another bridge. I hope that will neither burst with the frost, nor yet be destroyed by fire,' and he gave it a light flip with his fingers and sent it skimming over the table.

Susan blushed and smiled, and took it up. 'Oh, it is beautiful,' she said. 'Isn't it beautifully done, mother?' and then all the three got up to look at it, and all confessed that it was excellently done.

'And I am sure we are very much obliged to you,' said Susan after a pause, remembering that she had not yet thanked him.

'Oh, it's nothing,' said he, not quite liking the word 'we.'

On the following day he returned from his work to Saratoga about noon. This he had never done before, and therefore no one expected that he would be seen in the house before the evening. On this occasion however he went straight thither, and as chance would have it, both the widow and her elder daughter were out. Susan was there alone in charge of the house.

He walked in and opened the parlour door. There she sat, with her feet on the fender, with her work unheeded on the table behind her, and the picture, Aaron's drawing, lying on her knees. She was gazing at it intently as he entered, thinking in her young heart that it possessed all the beauties which a picture could possess.

'Oh, Mr. Dunn,' she said getting up and holding the tell-tale sketch behind the skirt of her dress.

'Miss Susan, I have come here to tell your mother that I must start for New York this afternoon and be there for six weeks, or perhaps longer.'

'Mother is out,' said she ; 'I'm so sorry.'

'Is she?' said Aaron.

'And Hetta too. Dear me. And you'll be wanting dinner. I'll go and see about it.'

Aaron began to swear that he could not possibly eat any dinner. He had dined once, and was going to dine again ;—anything to keep her from going.

'But you must have something, Mr. Dunn,' and she walked towards the door.

N

But he put his back to it. 'Miss Susan,' said he, 'I guess I've been here nearly two months.'

'Yes, sir, I believe you have,' she replied, shaking in her shoes and not knowing which way to look.

'And I hope we have been good friends.'

'Yes, sir,' said Susan, almost beside herself as to what she was saying.

'I'm going away now, and it seems to be such a time before I'll be back.'

'Will it, sir?'

'Six weeks, Miss Susan!' and then he paused, looking into her eyes, to see what he could read there. She leant against the table, pulling to pieces a morsel of half ravelled muslin which she held in her hand; but her eyes were turned to the ground, and he could hardly see them.

'Miss Susan,' he continued, 'I may as well speak out now as at another time.' He too was looking towards the ground, and clearly did not know what to do with his hands. 'The truth is just this. I—I love you dearly, with all my heart. I never saw any one I ever thought so beautiful, so nice, and so good;—and what's more, I never shall. I'm not very good at this sort of thing, I know; but I couldn't go away from Saratoga for six weeks and not tell you.' And then he ceased. He did not ask for any love in return. His presumption had not got so far as that yet. He merely declared his passion, leaning against the door, and there he stood twiddling his thumbs.

Susan had not the slightest conception of the way in

which she ought to receive such a declaration. She had never had a lover before; nor had she ever thought of Aaron absolutely as a lover, though something very like love for him had been crossing over her spirit. Now, at this moment, she felt that he was the beau-idéal of manhood, though his boots were covered with the railway mud, and though his pantaloons were tucked up in rolls round his ankles. He was a fine, well-grown, open-faced fellow, whose eye was bold and yet tender, whose brow was full and broad, and all his bearing manly. Love him! Of course she loved him. Why else had her heart melted with pleasure when her mother said that that second picture was to be accepted?

But what was she to say? Anything but the open truth; she well knew that. The open truth would not do at all. What would her mother say and Hetta if she were rashly to say that? Hetta, she knew, would be dead against such a lover, and of her mother's approbation she had hardly more hope. Why they should disapprove of Aaron as a lover she had never asked herself. There are many nice things that seem to be wrong only because they are so nice. Maybe that Susan regarded a lover as one of them. 'Oh, Mr. Dunn, you shouldn't.' That in fact was all that she could say.

'Should not I?' said he. 'Well, perhaps not; but there's the truth, and no harm ever comes of that. Perhaps I'd better not ask you for an answer now, but I thought it better you should know it all. And

remember this—I only care for one thing now in the
world, and that is for your love.' And then he paused,
thinking possibly that in spite of what he had said he
might perhaps get some sort of an answer, some inkling
of the state of her heart's disposition towards him.

But Susan had at once resolved to take him at his
word when he suggested that an immediate reply was
not necessary. To say that she loved him was of
course impossible, and to say that she did not was
equally so. She determined therefore to close at once
with the offer of silence.

When he ceased speaking there was a moment's
pause, during which he strove hard to read what might
be written on her down-turned face. But he was not
good at such reading. 'Well, I guess I'll go and get
my things ready now,' he said, and then turned round
to open the door.

'Mother will be in before you are gone, I suppose,'
said Susan.

'I have only got twenty minutes,' said he, looking
at his watch. 'But, Susan, tell her what I have said
to you. Good-bye.' And he put out his hand. He
knew he should see her again, but this had been his
plan to get her hand in his.

'Good-bye, Mr. Dunn,' and she gave him her hand.

He held it tight for a moment, so that she could not
draw it away,—could not if she would. 'Will you tell
your mother?' he asked.

'Yes,' she answered, quite in a whisper. 'I guess
I'd better tell her.' And then she gave a long sigh.

He pressed her hand again and got it up to his lips.

'Mr. Dunn, don't,' she said.   But he did kiss it. 'God bless you, my own dearest, dearest girl! I'll just open the door as I come down.   Perhaps Mrs. Bell will be here.'   And then he rushed up stairs.

But Mrs. Bell did not come in.   She and Hetta were at a weekly service at Mr. Beckard's meeting-house, and Mr. Beckard it seemed had much to say.   Susan, when left alone, sat down and tried to think.   But she could not think; she could only love.   She could use her mind only in recounting to herself the perfections of that demigod whose heavy steps were so audible overhead, as he walked to and fro collecting his things and putting them into his bag.

And then, just when he had finished, she bethought herself that he must be hungry.   She flew to the kitchen, but she was too late.   Before she could even reach at the loaf of bread he descended the stairs with a clattering noise, and heard her voice as she spoke quickly to Kate O'Brien.

'Miss Susan,' he said, 'don't get anything for me, for I'm off.'

'Oh, Mr. Dunn, I am so sorry.   You'll be so hungry on your journey,' and she came out to him in the passage.

'I shall want nothing on the journey, dearest, if you'll say one kind word to me.'

Again her eyes went to the ground.   'What do you want me to say, Mr. Dunn?'

'Say, God bless you, Aaron

'God bless you, Aaron,' said she; and yet she was sure that she had not declared her love. He however thought otherwise, and went up to New York with a happy heart.

Things happened in the next fortnight rather quickly. Susan at once resolved to tell her mother, but she resolved also not to tell Hetta. That afternoon she got her mother to herself in Mrs. Bell's own room, and then she made a clean breast of it.

'And what did you say to him, Susan?'

'I said nothing, mother.'

'Nothing, dear!'

'No, mother; not a word. He told me he didn't want it.' She forgot how she had used his Christian name in bidding God bless him.

'Oh, dear!' said the widow.

'Was it very wrong?' asked Susan.

'But what do you think yourself, my child?' asked Mrs. Bell after a while. 'What are your own feelings?'

Mrs. Bell was sitting on a chair, and Susan was standing opposite to her against the post of the bed. She made no answer, but moving from her place, she threw herself into her mother's arms, and hid her face on her mother's shoulder. It was easy enough to guess what were her feelings.

'But, my darling,' said her mother, 'you must not think that it is an engagement.'

'No,' said Susan, sorrowfully.

'Young men say those things to amuse themselves.'

Wolves, she would have said, had she spoken out her mind freely.

'Oh, mother, he is not like that.'

The daughter contrived to extract a promise from the mother that Hetta should not be told just at present. Mrs. Bell calculated that she had six weeks before her; as yet Mr. Beckard had not spoken out, but there was reason to suppose that he would do so before those six weeks would be over, and then she would be able to seek counsel from him.

Mr. Beckard spoke out at the end of six days, and Hetta frankly accepted him. 'I hope you'll love your brother-in-law,' said she to Susan.

'Oh, I will indeed,' said Susan; and in the softness of her heart at the moment she almost made up her mind to tell; but Hetta was full of her own affairs, and thus it passed off.

It was then arranged that Hetta should go and spend a week with Mr. Beckard's parents. Old Mr. Beckard was a farmer living near Utica, and now that the match was declared and approved, it was thought well that Hetta should know her future husband's family. So she went for a week, and Mr. Beckard went with her. 'He will be back in plenty of time for me to speak to him before Aaron Dunn's six weeks are over,' said Mrs. Bell to herself.

But things did not go exactly as she expected. On the very morning after the departure of the engaged couple, there came a letter from Aaron, saying that he would be at Saratoga that very evening. The railway people had ordered him down again for some days' special work; then he was to go elsewhere, and not to return to Saratoga till June. 'But he hoped,' so said the letter, 'that Mrs. Bell would not turn him into the street even then, though the summer might have come, and her regular lodgers might be expected.'

'Oh dear, oh dear!' said Mrs. Bell to herself, reflecting that she had no one of whom she could ask advice, and that she must decide that very day. Why had she let Mr. Beckard go without telling him? Then she told Susan, and Susan spent the day trembling. Perhaps, thought Mrs. Bell, he will say nothing about it. In such case, however, would it not be her duty to say something? Poor mother! She trembled nearly as much as Susan.

It was dark when the fatal knock came at the door. The tea-things were already laid, and the tea-cake was already baked; for it would at any rate be necessary to give Mr. Dunn his tea. Susan, when she heard the knock, rushed from her chair and took refuge up stairs. The widow gave a long sigh, and settled her dress. Kate O'Brien with willing step opened the door, and bade her old friend welcome.

'How are the ladies?' asked Aaron, trying to gather something from the face and voice of the domestic.

'Miss Hetta and Mr. Beckard be gone off to Utica, just man-and-wife like; and so they are, more power to them.'

'Oh indeed; I'm very glad,' said Aaron—and so

he was; very glad to have Hetta the demure out of the way. And then he made his way into the parlour, doubting much, and hoping much.

Mrs. Bell rose from her chair, and tried to look grave. Aaron glancing round the room saw that Susan was not there. He walked straight up to the widow, and offered her his hand, which she took. It might be that Susan had not thought fit to tell, and in such case it would not be right for him to compromise her; so he said never a word.

But the subject was too important to the mother to allow of her being silent when the young man stood before her. 'Oh, Mr. Dunn,' said she, 'what is this you have been saying to Susan?'

'I have asked her to be my wife,' said he, drawing himself up and looking her full in the face. Mrs. Bell's heart was almost as soft as her daughter's, and it was nearly gone; but at the moment she had nothing to say but, 'oh dear, oh dear!'

'May I not call you mother?' said he, taking both her hands in his.

'Oh dear—oh dear! But will you be good to her? Oh, Aaron Dunn, if you deceive my child!'

In another quarter of an hour, Susan was kneeling at her mother's knee, with her face on her mother's lap; the mother was wiping tears out of her eyes; and Aaron was standing by holding one of the widow's hands.

'You are my mother too, now,' said he. What would Hetta and Mr. Beckard say, when they came back? But then he surely was not a wolf!

There were four or five days left for courtship before
Hetta and Mr. Beckard would return ; four or five
days during which Susan might be happy, Aaron
triumphant, and Mrs. Bell nervous. Days I have said,
but after all it was only the evenings that were so left.
Every morning Susan got up to give Aaron his breakfast, but Mrs. Bell got up also. Susan boldly declared
her right to do so, and Mrs. Bell found no objection
which she could urge. But after that Aaron was
always absent till seven or eight in the evening, when
he would return to his tea.   Then came the hour or
two of lovers' intercourse.

But they were very tame, those hours. The widow
still felt an undefined fear that she was wrong, and
though her heart yearned to know that her daughter
was happy in the sweet happiness of accepted love,
yet she dreaded to be too confident.   Not a word had
been said about money matters ; not a word of Aaron
Dunn's relatives. So she did not leave them by themselves, but waited with what patience she could for the
return of her wise counsellors.

And then Susan hardly knew how to behave herself
with her accepted suitor.   She felt that she was very
happy ; but perhaps she was most happy when she was
thinking about him through the long day, assisting in
fixing little things for his comfort, and waiting for his
evening return.   And as he sat there in the parlour,
she could be happy then too, if she were but allowed to
sit still and look at him,—not stare at him but raise her
eyes every now and again to his face for the shortest

possible glance, as she had been used to do ever since
he came there.

But he, unconsciable lover, wanted to hear her speak,
was desirous of being talked to, and perhaps thought that
he should by rights be allowed to sit by her, and hold
her hand. No such privileges were accorded to him. If
they had been alone together, walking side by side on
the green turf, as lovers should walk, she would soon have
found the use of her tongue,—have talked fast enough
no doubt. Under such circumstances, when a girl's
shyness has given way to real intimacy, there is in
general no end to her power of chatting. But though
there was much love between Aaron and Susan, there
was as yet but little intimacy. And then, let a mother
be ever so motherly—and no mother could have more
of a mother's tenderness than Mrs. Bell—still her
presence must be a restraint. Aaron was very fond of
Mrs. Bell; but nevertheless he did sometimes wish
that some domestic duty would take her out of the
parlour for a few happy minutes. Susan went out very
often, but Mrs. Bell seemed to be a fixture.

Once for a moment he did find his love alone, immediately as he came into the house. 'My own Susan,
you do love me? do say so to me once.' And he contrived to slip his arm round her waist. 'Yes,' she
whispered; but she slipped, like an eel, from his hands,
and left him only preparing himself for a kiss. And
then when she got to her room, half frightened, she
clasped her hands together, and bethought herself that
she did really love him with a strength and depth of

love which filled her whole existence. Why could she
not have told him something of all this?

And so the few days of his second sojourn at Saratoga
passed away, not altogether satisfactorily. It was
settled that he should return to New York on Saturday
night, leaving Saratoga on that evening; and as the
Beckards—Hetta was already regarded quite as a
Beckard—were to be back to dinner on that day, Mrs.
Bell would have an opportunity of telling her wondrous
tale. It might be well that Mr. Beckard should see
Aaron before his departure.

On that Saturday the Beckards did arrive just in
time for dinner. It may be imagined that Susan's
appetite was not very keen, nor her manner very
collected. But all this passed by unobserved in the
importance attached to the various Beckard arrangements which came under discussion. Ladies and
gentlemen circumstanced as were Hetta and Mr.
Beckard are perhaps a little too apt to think that their
own affairs are paramount. But after dinner Susan
vanished at once, and when Hetta prepared to follow
her, desirous of further talk about matrimonial arrangements, her mother stopped her, and the disclosure was
made.

'Proposed to her!' said Hetta, who perhaps thought
that one marriage in a family was enough at a
time.

'Yes, my love—and he did it, I must say, in a very
honourable way, telling her not to make any answer till
she had spoken to me;—now that was very nice; was it

not, Phineas?' Mrs. Bell had become very anxious
that Aaron should not be voted a wolf.

'And what has been said to him since?' asked the
discreet Phineas.

'Why—nothing absolutely decisive.' Oh, Mrs. Bell!
'You see I know nothing as to his means.'

'Nothing at all,' said Hetta.

'He is a man that will always earn his bread,' said
Mr. Beckard; and Mrs. Bell blessed him in her heart
for saying it.

'But has he been encouraged?' asked Hetta.

'Well; yes, he has,' said the widow.

'Then Susan I suppose likes him?' asked Phineas.

'Well; yes, she does,' said the widow. And the
conference ended in a resolution that Phineas Beckard
should have a conversation with Aaron Dunn, as to his
worldly means and position; and that he, Phineas,
should decide whether Aaron might, or might not be
at once accepted as a lover, according to the tenor of
that conversation. Poor Susan was not told anything of all this. 'Better not,' said Hetta the demure.
'It will only flurry her the more.' How would she
have liked it, if without consulting her, they had left it
to Aaron to decide whether or no she might marry
Phineas?

They knew where on the works Aaron was to be
found, and thither Mr. Beckard rode after dinner.
We need not narrate at length the conference between
the young men. Aaron at once declared that he had
nothing but what he made as an engineer, and ex-

plained that he held no permanent situation on the line. He was well paid at that present moment, but at the end of summer he would have to look for employment.

'Then you can hardly marry quite at present,' said the discreet minister.

'Perhaps not quite immediately.'

'And long engagements are never wise,' said the other.

'Three or four months,' suggested Aaron. But Mr. Beckard shook his head.

The afternoon at Mrs. Bell's house was melancholy. The final decision of the three judges was as follows. There was to be no engagement; of course no correspondence. Aaron was to be told that it would be better that he should get lodgings elsewhere when he returned; but that he would be allowed to visit at Mrs. Bell's house,—and at Mrs. Beckard's, which was very considerate. If he should succeed in getting a permanent appointment, and if he and Susan still held the same mind, why then——&c. &c. Such was Susan's fate, as communicated to her by Mrs. Bell and Hetta. She sat still añd wept when she heard it; but she did not complain. She had always felt that Hetta would be against her.

'Mayn't I see him, then?' she said through her tears.

Hetta thought she had better not. Mrs. Bell thought she might. Phineas decided that they might shake hands, but only in full conclave. There was to be no lovers' farewell.   Aaron was to leave the house at half-past five ; but before he went Susan should be called down. Poor Susan! She sat down and bemoaned herself ; uncomplaining, but very sad.

Susan was soft, feminine, and manageable.   But Aaron Dunn was not very soft, was especially masculine, and in some matters not easily manageable.   When Mr. Beckard in the widow's presence—Hetta had retired in obedience to her lover—informed him of the court's decision, there came over his face the look which he had worn when he burned the picture. 'Mrs. Bell,' he said, 'had encouraged his engagement; and he did not understand why other people should now come and disturb it.'

'Not an engagement, Aaron,' said Mrs. Bell piteously.

'He was able and willing to work,' he said, 'and knew his profession.   What young man of his age had done better than he had?' and he glanced round at them with perhaps more pride than was quite becoming.

Then Mr. Beckard spoke out, very wisely no doubt, but perhaps a little too much at length. Sons and daughters as well as fathers and mothers will know very well what he said; so I need not repeat his words. I cannot say that Aaron listened with much attention, but he understood perfectly what the upshot of it was. Many a man understands the purport of many a sermon without listening to one word in ten. Mr. Beckard meant to be kind in his manner ; indeed was so, only that Aaron could not accept as kindness any interference on his part.

'I'll tell you what, Mrs. Bell,' said he. 'I look upon myself as engaged to her. And I look on her as engaged to me. I tell you so fairly; and I believe that's her mind as well as mine.'

'But, Aaron, you won't try to see her—or to write to her,—not in secret; will you?

'When I try to see her, I'll come and knock at this door; and if I write to her, I'll write to her full address by the post. I never did and never will do anything in secret.'

'I know you're good and honest,' said the widow with her handkerchief to her eyes.

'Then why do you separate us?' asked he, almost roughly. 'I suppose I may see her at any rate before I go. My time's nearly up now, I guess.'

And then Susan was called for, and she and Hetta came down together. Susan crept in behind her sister. Her eyes were red with weeping, and her appearance was altogether disconsolate. She had had a lover for a week, and now she was to be robbed of him.

'Good-bye, Susan,' said Aaron, and he walked up to her without bashfulness or embarrassment. Had they all been compliant and gracious to him he would have been as bashful as his love; but now his temper was hot. 'Good-bye, Susan,' and she took his hand, and he held hers till he had finished. 'And remember this, I look upon you as my promised wife, and I don't fear that you'll deceive me. At any rate I sha'n't deceive you.'

'Good-bye, Aaron,' she sobbed.

'Good-bye, and God bless you, my own darling!' And then without saying a word to any one else, he turned his back upon them and went his way.

There had been something very consolatory, very sweet, to the poor girl in her lover's last words. And yet they had almost made her tremble. He had been so bold, and stern, and confident. He had seemed so utterly to defy the impregnable discretion of Mr. Beckard, so to despise the demure propriety of Hetta. But of this she felt sure, when she came to question her heart, that she could never, never, never cease to love him better than all the world beside. She would wait—patiently if she could find patience—and then, if he deserted her, she would die.

In another month Hetta became Mrs. Beckard. Susan brisked up a little for the occasion, and looked very pretty as bridesmaid. She was serviceable too in arranging household matters, hemming linen and sewing table-cloths; though of course in these matters she did not do a tenth of what Hetta did.

Then the summer came, the Saratoga summer of July, August, and September, during which the widow's house was full; and Susan's hands saved the pain of her heart, for she was forced into occupation. Now that Hetta was gone to her own duties, it was necessary that Susan's part in the household should be more prominent.   o

Aaron did not come back to his work at Saratoga.
Why he did not, they could not then learn. During
the whole long summer they heard not a word of him
nor from him; and then when the cold winter months
came and their boarders had left them, Mrs. Beckard
congratulated her sister in that she had given no
further encouragement to a lover who cared so little for
her. This was very hard to bear. But Susan did
bear it.

That winter was very sad. They learned nothing
of Aaron Dunn till about January; and then they
heard that he was doing very well. He was engaged
on the Erie trunk line, was paid highly, and was much
esteemed. And yet he neither came nor sent! ' He
has an excellent situation,' their informant told them.
' And a permanent one?' asked the widow. 'Oh, yes,
no doubt,' said the gentleman, ' for I happen to know
that they count greatly on him.' And yet he sent no
word of love.

After that the winter became very sad indeed.
Mrs. Bell thought it to be her duty now to teach her
daughter that in all probability she would see Aaror
Dunn no more. It was open to him to leave her
without being absolutely a wolf. He had been driven
from the house when he was poor, and they had no
right to expect that he would return, now that he
had made some rise in the world. 'Men do amuse
themselves in that way,' the widow tried to teach
her.

' He is not like that, mother,' she said again.

'But they do not think so much of these things as we do,' urged the mother.

'Don't they?' said Susan, oh, so sorrowfully; and so through the whole long winter months she became paler and paler, and thinner and thinner.

And then Hetta tried to console her with religion, and that perhaps did not make things any better. Religious consolation is the best cure for all griefs; but it must not be looked for specially with regard to any individual sorrow. A religious man, should he become bankrupt through the misfortunes of the world, will find true consolation in his religion even for that sorrow. But a bankrupt, who has not thought much of such things, will hardly find solace by taking up religion for that special occasion.

And Hetta perhaps was hardly prudent in her attempts. She thought that it was wicked in Susan to grow thin and pale for love of Aaron Dunn, and she hardly hid her thoughts. Susan was not sure but that it might be wicked, but this doubt in no way tended to make her plump or rosy. So that in those days she found no comfort in her sister.

But her mother's pity and soft love did ease her sufferings, though it could not make them cease. Her mother did not tell her that she was wicked, or bid her read long sermons, or force her to go oftener to the meeting-house.

'He will never come again, I think,' she said one day, as with a shawl wrapped around her shoulders, she leant with her head upon her mother's bosom.

'My own darling,' said the mother, pressing her child closely to her side.

'You think he never will, eh, mother?' What could Mrs. Bell say? In her heart of hearts she did not think he ever would come again.

'No, my child. I do not think he will.' And then the hot tears ran down, and the sobs came thick and frequent.

'My darling, my darling!' exclaimed the mother; and they wept together.

'Was I wicked to love him at the first?' she asked that night.

'No, my child; you were not wicked at all. At least I think not.'

'Then why——' Why was he sent away? It was on her tongue to ask that question; but she paused and spared her mother. This was as they were going to bed. The next morning Susan did not get up. She was not ill, she said; but weak and weary. Would her mother let her lie that day? And then Mrs. Bell went down alone to her room, and sorrowed with all her heart for the sorrow of her child. Why, oh why, had she driven away from her door-sill the love of an honest man?

On the next morning Susan again did not get up;—nor did she hear, or if she heard she did not recognize, the step of the postman who brought a letter to the door. Early, before the widow's breakfast the postman came, and the letter which he brought was as follows:—

'My dear Mrs. Bell,

'I have now got a permanent situation on the Erie line, and the salary is enough for myself and a wife. At least I think so, and I hope you will too. I shall be down at Saratoga to-morrow evening, and I hope neither Susan nor you will refuse to receive me.

'Yours affectionately,

'Aaron Dunn.'

That was all. It was very short, and did not contain one word of love; but it made the widow's heart leap for joy. She was rather afraid that Aaron was angry, he wrote so curtly and with such a brusque business-like attention to mere facts; but surely he could have but one object in coming there. And then he alluded specially to a wife. So the widow's heart leapt with joy.

But how was she to tell Susan? She ran up stairs almost breathless with haste, to the bedroom door: but then she stopped: too much joy she had heard was as dangerous as too much sorrow; she must think it over for a while, and so she crept back again.

But after breakfast—that is, when she had sat for a while over her teacup—she returned to the room, and this time she entered it. The letter was in her hand, but held so as to be hidden;—in her left hand as she sat down with her right arm towards the invalid.

'Susan dear,' she said, and smiled at her child, 'you'll be able to get up this morning? eh, dear?'

'Yes, mother,' said Susan, thinking that her mother

objected to this idleness of her lying in bed. And so
she began to bestir herself.

'I don't mean this very moment, love. Indeed, I
want to sit with you for a little while,' and she put her
right arm affectionately round her daughter's waist.

'Dearest mother,' said Susan.

'Ah! there's one dearer than me, I guess,' and Mrs.
Bell smiled sweetly, as she made the maternal charge
against her daughter.

Susan raised herself quickly in the bed, and looked
straight into her mother's face. 'Mother, mother,' she
said, 'What is it? You've something to tell. Oh,
mother!' And stretching herself over, she struck her
hand against the corner of Aaron's letter. 'Mother,
you've a letter. Is he coming, mother?' and with eager
eyes and open lips, she sat up, holding tight to her
mother's arm.

'Yes, love. I have got a letter.'

'Is he—is he coming?'

How the mother answered, I can hardly tell; but
she did answer, and they were soon lying in each other's
arms, warm with each other's tears. It was almost hard
to say which was the happier.

Aaron was to be there that evening—that very evening. 'Oh, mother, let me get up,' said Susan.

But Mrs. Bell said no, not yet ; her darling was pale
and thin, and she almost wished that Aaron was not
coming for another week. What if he should come and
look at her, and finding her beauty gone, vanish again
and seek a wife elsewhere!

So Susan lay in bed, thinking of her happiness, dozing now and again, and fearing as she waked that it was a dream, looking constantly at that drawing of his, which she kept outside upon the bed, nursing her love and thinking of it, and endeavouring, vainly endeavouring, to arrange what she would say to him.

'Mother,' she said, when Mrs. Bell once went up to her, 'you won't tell Hetta and Phineas, will you? Not to-day, I mean?' Mrs. Bell agreed that it would be better not to tell them. Perhaps she thought that she had already depended too much on Hetta and Phineas in the matter.

Susan's finery in the way of dress had never been extensive, and now lately, in these last sad winter days, she had thought but little of the fashion of her clothes. But when she began to dress herself for the evening, she did ask her mother with some anxiety what she had better wear. 'If he loves you he will hardly see what you have on,' said the mother. But not the less was she careful to smooth her daughter's hair, and make the most that might be made of those faded roses.

How Susan's heart beat,—how both their hearts beat as the hands of the clock came round to seven! And then, sharp at seven, came the knock; that same short bold ringing knock which Susan had so soon learned to know as belonging to Aaron Dunn. 'Oh mother, I had better go up stairs,' she cried, starting from her chair.

'No dear; you would only be more nervous.'

'I will, mother.'

'No, no dear; you have not time;' and then Aaron Dunn was in the room.

She had thought much what she would say to him, but had not yet quite made up her mind. It mattered however but very little. On whatever she might have resolved, her resolution would have vanished to the wind. Aaron Dunn came into the room, and in one second she found herself in the centre of a whirlwind, and his arms were the storms that enveloped her on every side.

'My own, own darling girl,' he said over and over again, as he pressed her to his heart, quite regardless of Mrs. Bell, who stood by, sobbing with joy. 'My own Susan.'

'Aaron, dear Aaron,' she whispered. But she had already recognized the fact that for the present meeting a passive part would become her well, and save her a deal of trouble. She had her lover there quite safe, safe beyond anything that Mr. or Mrs. Beckard might have to say to the contrary. She was quite happy; only that there were symptoms now and again that the whirlwind was about to engulf her yet once more.

'Dear Aaron, I am so glad you are come,' said the innocent-minded widow, as she went up stairs with him, to show him his room; and then he embraced her also. 'Dear, dear mother,' he said.

On the next day there was, as a matter of course, a family conclave. Hetta and Phineas came down, and discussed the whole subject of the coming marriage with Mrs. Bell. Hetta at first was not quite certain;—ought they not to inquire whether the situation was permanent?

'I won't inquire at all,' said Mrs. Bell, with an energy that startled both the daughter and son-in-law. 'I would not part them now; no, not if——' and the widow shuddered as she thought of her daughters sunken eyes, and pale cheeks.

'He is a good lad,' said Phineas, 'and I trust she will make him a sober steady wife;' and so the matter was settled.

During this time, Susan and Aaron were walking along the Balston road; and they also had settled the matter—quite as satisfactorily.

Such was the courtship of Susan Dunn.

RELICS OF GENERAL CHASSÉ.

A TALE OF ANTWERP.

THAT Belgium is now one of the European kingdoms, living by its own laws, resting on its own bottom, with a king and court, palaces and parliament of its own, is known to all the world. And a very nice little kingdom it is; full of old towns, fine Flemish pictures, and interesting Gothic churches. But in the memory of very many of us who do not think ourselves old men, Belgium, as it is now called—in those days it used to be Flanders and Brabant—was a part of Holland; and it obtained its own independence by a revolution. In that revolution the most important military step was the siege of Antwerp, which was defended on the part of the Dutch by General Chassé, with the utmost gallantry, but nevertheless ineffectually.

After the siege Antwerp became quite a show place; and among the visitors who flocked there to talk of the gallant general, and to see what remained of the great effort which he had made to defend the place, were two Englishmen. One¹ was the hero of this little history;

and the other was a young man of considerably less weight in the world. The less I say of the latter the better; but it is necessary that I should give some description of the former.

The Rev. Augustus Horne was, at the time of my narrative, a beneficed clergyman of the Church of England. The profession which he had graced sat easily on him. Its external marks and signs were as pleasing to his friends as were its internal comforts to himself. He was a man of much quiet mirth, full of polished wit, and on some rare occasions he could descend to the more noisy hilarity of a joke. Loved by his friends he loved all the world. He had known no care and seen no sorrow. Always intended for holy orders he had entered them without a scruple, and remained within their pale without a regret. At twenty-four he had been a deacon, at twenty-seven a priest, at thirty a rector, and at thirty-five a prebendary; and as his rectory was rich and his prebendal stall well paid, the Rev. Augustus Horne was called by all, and called himself, a happy man. His stature was about six feet two, and his corpulence exceeded even those bounds which symmetry would have preferred as being most perfectly compatible even with such a height. But nevertheless Mr. Horne was a well-made man; his hands and feet were small; his face was handsome, frank, and full of expression; his bright eyes twinkled with humour; his finely-cut mouth disclosed two marvellous rows of well-preserved ivory; and his slightly aquiline nose was just such a projection as one would wish to see on the face of a well-fed, good-natured dignitary of the Church of England. When I add to all this that the reverend gentleman was as generous as he was rich—and the kind mother in whose arms he had been nurtured had taken care that he should never want—I need hardly say that I was blessed with a very pleasant travelling companion.

I must mention one more interesting particular. Mr. Horne was rather inclined to dandyism, in an innocent way. His clerical starched neckcloth was always of the whitest, his cambric handkerchief of the finest, his bands adorned with the broadest border; his sable suit never degenerated to a rusty brown; it not only gave on all occasions glossy evidence of freshness, but also of the talent which the artisan had displayed in turning out a well-dressed clergyman of the Church of England. His hair was ever brushed with scrupulous attention, and showed in its regular waves the guardian care of each separate bristle. And all this was done with that ease and grace which should be the characteristics of a dignitary of the established English Church.

I had accompanied Mr. Horne to the Rhine; and we had reached Brussels on our return, just at the close of that revolution which ended in affording a throne to the son-in-law of George the Fourth. At that moment General Chassé's name and fame were in every man's mouth, and, like other curious admirers of the brave, Mr. Horne determined to devote two days to the scene of the late events at Antwerp. Antwerp, moreover, possesses perhaps the finest spire, and certainly one of the three or four finest pictures, in the world. Of General Chassé, of the cathedral, and of the Rubens, I had heard much, and was therefore well pleased that such should be his resolution. This accomplished we were to return to Brussels; and thence, *viâ* Ghent, Ostend, and Dover, I to complete my legal studies in London, and Mr. Horne to enjoy once more the peaceful retirement of Ollerton rectory. As we were to be absent from Brussels but one night we were enabled to indulge in the gratification of travelling without our luggage. A small *sac-de-nuit* was prepared; brushes, combs, razors, strops, a change of linen, etc., etc., were carefully put up; but our heavy baggage, our coats, waistcoats, and other wearing apparel were unnecessary. It was delightful to feel oneself so light-handed. The reverend gentleman, with my humble self by his side, left the portal of the Hôtel de Belle Vue at 7 A. M., in good humour with all the world. There were no railroads in those days; but a cabriolet, big enough to hold six persons, with rope traces and corresponding appendages, deposited us at the Golden Fleece in something less than six hours. The inward man was duly fortified, and we started for the castle.

It boots not here to describe the effects which gunpowder and grape-shot had had on the walls of Antwerp. Let the curious in these matters read the horrors of the siege of Troy, or the history of Jerusalem taken by Titus. The one may be found in Homer, and the other in Josephus. Or if they prefer doings of a later date there is the taking of Sebastopol, as narrated in

the columns of the *Times* newspaper. The accounts
are equally true, instructive, and intelligible. In the
mean time allow the Rev. Augustus Horne and myself
to enter the private chambers of the renowned though
defeated general.

We rambled for a while through the covered way,
over the glacis and along the counterscarp, and listened
to the guide as he detailed to us, in already accustomed
words, how the siege had gone. Then we got into the
private apartments of the general, and, having dex-
terously shaken off our attendant, wandered at large
among the deserted rooms.

'It is clear that no one ever comes here,' said I.

'No,' said the Rev. Augustus; 'it seems not: and
to tell the truth, I don't know why any one should come.
The chambers in themselves are not attractive.'

What he said was true. They were plain, ugly,
square, unfurnished rooms, here a big one and there a
little one, as is usual in most houses;—unfurnished, that
is, for the most part. In one place we did find a table
and a few chairs, in another a bedstead, and so on.
But to me it was pleasant to indulge in those rumina-
tions which any traces of the great or unfortunate
create in softly sympathizing minds. For a time we
communicated our thoughts to each other as we roamed
free as air through the apartments; and then I lingered
for a few moments behind, while Mr. Horne moved on
with a quicker step.

At last I entered the bedchamber of the general,
and there I overtook my friend. He was inspecting,

with much attention, an article of the great man's wardrobe which he held in his hand. It was precisely that virile habiliment to which a well-known gallant captain alludes in his conversation with the posthumous appearance of Miss Bailey, as containing a Bank of England 5*l.* note.

'The general must have been a large man, George, or he would hardly have filled these,' said Mr. Horne, holding up to the light the respectable leathern articles in question. 'He must have been a very large man,—the largest man in Antwerp, I should think; or else his tailor has done him more than justice.'

They were certainly large, and had about them a charming regimental military appearance. They were made of white leather, with bright metal buttons at the knees and bright metal buttons at the top. They owned no pockets, and were, with the exception of the legitimate outlet, continuous in the circumference of the waistband. No dangling strings gave them an appearance of senile imbecility. Were it not for a certain rigidity, sternness, and mental inflexibility,—we will call it military ardour,—with which they were imbued, they would have created envy in the bosom of a fox-hunter.

Mr. Horne was no fox-hunter, but still he seemed to be irresistibly taken with the lady-like propensity of wishing to wear them. 'Surely, George,' he said, 'the general must have been a stouter man than I am'—and he contemplated his own proportions with complacency—'these what's-the-names are quite big enough for me.'

I differed in opinion, and was obliged to explain that I thought he did the good living of Ollerton insufficient justice.

' I am sure they are large enough for me,' he repeated, with considerable obstinacy. I smiled incredulously ; and then to settle the matter he resolved that he would try them on. Nobody had been in these rooms for the last hour, and it appeared as though they were never visited. Even the guide had not come on with us, but was employed in showing other parties about the fortifications. It was clear that this portion of the building was left desolate, and that the experiment might be safely made. So the sportive rector declared that he would for a short time wear the regimentals which had once contained the valorous heart of General Chassé.

With all decorum the Rev. Mr. Horne divested himself of the work of the London artist's needle, and, carefully placing his own garments beyond the reach of dust, essayed to fit himself in military garb.

At that important moment—at the critical instant of the attempt—the clatter of female voices was heard approaching the chamber. They must have suddenly come round some passage corner, for it was evident by the sound that they were close upon us before we had any warning of their advent. At this very minute Mr. Horne was somewhat embarrassed in his attempts, and was not fully in possession of his usual active powers of movement, nor of his usual presence of mind. He only looked for escape ; and seeing a door partly open he with difficulty retreated through it, and I followed him.

P

We found that we were in a small dressing-room; and as by good luck the door was defended by an inner bolt, my friend was able to protect himself.

'There shall be another siege, at any rate as stout as the last, before I surrender,' said he.

As the ladies seemed inclined to linger in the room it became a matter of importance that the above-named articles should fit, not only for ornament but for use. It was very cold, and Mr. Horne was altogether unused to move in a Highland sphere of life. But alas, alas! General Chassé had not been nurtured in the classical retirement of Ollerton. The ungiving leather would stretch no point to accommodate the divine, though it had been willing to minister to the convenience of the soldier. Mr. Horne was vexed and chilled; and throwing the now hateful garments into a corner, and protecting himself from the cold as best he might by standing with his knees together and his body somewhat bent so as to give the skirts of his coat an opportunity of doing extra duty, he begged me to see if those jabbering females were not going to leave him in peace to recover his own property. I accordingly went to the door, and opening it to a small extent I peeped through.

Who shall describe my horror at the sight which I then saw? The scene, which had hitherto been tinted with comic effect, was now becoming so decidedly tragic that I did not dare at once to acquaint my worthy pastor with that which was occurring,—and, alas! had already occurred.

Five country-women of our own—it was easy to know
them by their dress and general aspect—were standing
in the middle of the room; and one of them, the centre
of the group, the senior harpy of the lot, a maiden
lady—I could have sworn to that—with a red nose,
held in one hand a huge pair of scissors and in the
other—the already devoted goods of my most unfortunate companion! Down from the waistband, through
that goodly expanse, a fell gash had already gone
through and through; and in useless, unbecoming disorder the broadcloth fell pendant from her arm on this
side and on that. At that moment I confess that I had
not the courage to speak to Mr. Horne,—not even to
look at him.

I must describe that group. Of the figure next to
me I could only see the back. It was a broad back
done up in black silk not of the newest. The whole
figure, one may say, was dumpy. The black silk was
not long, as dresses now are worn, nor wide in its skirts.
In every way it was skimpy, considering the breadth it
had to cover; and below the silk I saw the heels of two
thick shoes, and enough to swear by of two woollen
stockings. Above the silk was a red-and-blue shawl;
and above that a ponderous, elaborate brown bonnet, as
to the materials of which I should not wish to undergo
an examination. Over and beyond this I could only
see the backs of her two hands. They were held up as
though in wonder at that which the red-nosed holder
of the scissors had dared to do.

Opposite to this lady, and with her face fully turned

to me, was a kindly-looking, fat motherly woman, with
light-coloured hair, not in the best order. She was
hot and scarlet with exercise, being perhaps too stout
for the steep steps of the fortress; and in one hand she
held a handkerchief, with which from time to time she
wiped her brow. In the other hand she held one of the
extremities of my friend's property, feeling—good, careful soul!—what was the texture of the cloth. As she
did so, I could see a glance of approbation pass across
her warm features. I liked that lady's face, in spite
of her untidy hair, and felt that had she been alone my
friend would not have been injured.

On either side of her there stood a flaxen-haired
maiden, with long curls, large blue eyes, fresh red
cheeks, an undefined lumpy nose, and large good-humoured mouth. They were as like as two peas, only that
one was half an inch taller than the other; and there
was no difficulty in discovering, at a moment's glance,
that they were the children of that overheated matron
who was feeling the web of my friend's cloth.

But the principal figure was she who held the centre
place in the group. She was tall and thin, with fierce-
looking eyes, rendered more fierce by the spectacles
which she wore; with a red nose as I said before; and
about her an undescribable something which quite convinced me that she had never known—could never
know—aught of the comforts of married life. It was
she who held the scissors and the black garments. It
was she who had given that unkind cut. As I looked
at her she whisked herself quickly round from one com-

panion to the other, triumphing in what she had done, and ready to triumph further in what she was about to do. I immediately conceived a deep hatred for that Queen of the Harpies.

'Well, I suppose they can't be wanted again,' said the mother, rubbing her forehead.

'Oh dear no!' said she of the red nose. 'They are relics!'

I thought to leap forth; but for what purpose should I have leaped? The accursed scissors had already done their work; and the symmetry, nay, even the utility of the vestment was destroyed.

'General Chassé wore a very good article;—I will say that for him,' continued the mother.

'Of course he did!' said the Queen Harpy. 'Why should he not, seeing that the country paid for it for him? Well, ladies, who's for having a bit?'

'Oh my! you won't go for to cut them up,' said the stout back.

'Won't I?' said the scissors; and she immediately made another incision. 'Who's for having a bit? Don't all speak at once.'

'I should like a morsel for a pincushion,' said flaxen haired Miss No. 1, a young lady about nineteen, actuated by a general affection for all sword-bearing, fire-eating heroes. 'I should like to have something to make me think of the poor general!'

Snip, snip went the scissors with professional rapidity, and a round piece was extracted from the back of the calf of the left leg. I shuddered with horror; and so did the Rev. Augustus Horne with cold.

'I hardly think it's proper to cut them up,' said Miss No. 2.

'Oh isn't it?' said the harpy. 'Then I'll do what's improper!' And she got her finger and thumb well through the holes in the scissors' handles. As she spoke resolution was plainly marked on her brow.

'Well; if they are to be cut up, I should certainly like a bit for a pen-wiper,' said No. 2. No. 2 was a literary young lady with a periodical correspondence, a journal, and an album. Snip, snip went the scissors again, and the broad part of the upper right division afforded ample materials for a pen-wiper.

Then the lady with the back, seeing that the desecration of the article had been completed, plucked up heart of courage and put in her little request: 'I think I might have a needle-case out of it,' said she, 'just as a *suvneer* of the poor general'—and a long fragment cut rapidly out of the waistband afforded her unqualified delight.

Mamma, with the hot face and untidy hair, came next. 'Well, girls,' she said, 'as you are all served, I don't see why I'm to be left out. Perhaps, Miss Grogram'—she was an old maid, you see—'perhaps, Miss Grogram, you could get me as much as would make a decent-sized reticule.'

There was not the slightest difficulty in doing this. The harpy in the centre again went to work, snip, snip, and extracting from that portion of the affairs which usually sustained the greater portion of Mr. Horne's weight two large round pieces of cloth, presented them to the well-pleased matron. 'The general knew well where to get a bit of good broadcloth, certainly,' said she, again feeling the pieces.

'And now for No. 1,' said she whom I so absolutely hated; 'I think there is still enough for a pair of slippers. There's nothing so nice for the house as good black cloth slippers that are warm to the feet and don't show the dirt.' And so saying, she spread out on the floor the lacerated remainders.

'There's a nice bit there,' said young lady No. 2, poking at one of the pockets with the end of her parasol.

'Yes,' said the harpy, contemplating her plunder. 'But I'm thinking whether I couldn't get leggings as well. I always wear leggings in the thick of the winter.' And so she concluded her operations, and there was nothing left but a melancholy skeleton of seams and buttons.

All this having been achieved, they pocketed their plunder and prepared to depart. There are people who have a wonderful appetite for relics. A stone with which Washington had broken a window when a boy— with which he had done so or had not, for there is little difference; a button that was on a coat of Napoleon's, or on that of one of his lackeys; a bullet said to have been picked up at Waterloo or Bunker's Hill; these, and suchlike things are great treasures. And their most desirable characteristic is the ease with which

they are attained. Any bullet or any button does the
work. Faith alone is necessary. And now these
ladies had made themselves happy and glorious with
'Relics' of General Chassé cut from the ill-used habiliments of an elderly English gentleman!

They departed at last, and Mr. Horne, for once in
an ill humour, followed me into the bedroom. Here I
must be excused if I draw a veil over his manly sorrow
at discovering what fate had done for him. Remember
what was his position, unclothed in the castle of Antwerp! The nearest suitable change for those which
had been destroyed was locked up in his portmanteau
at the Hôtel de Belle Vue in Brussels! He had
nothing left to him—literally nothing, in that Antwerp
world. There was no other wretched being wandering
then in that Dutch town so utterly denuded of the goods
of life. For what is a man fit,—for what can he be
fit,—when left in such a position? There are some evils
which seem utterly to crush a man; and if there be any
misfortune to which a man may be allowed to succumb
without imputation on his manliness, surely it is such as
this. How was Mr. Horne to return to his hotel without incurring the displeasure of the municipality?
That was my first thought.

He had a cloak, but it was at the inn; and I found
that my friend was oppressed with a great horror at
the idea of being left alone; so that I could not go in
search of it. There is an old saying, that no man is a
hero to his *valet de chambre*,—the reason doubtless
being this, that it is customary for his valet to see the

hero divested of those trappings in which so much of the heroic consists. Who reverences a clergyman without his gown, or a warrior without his sword and sabre-tasche? What would even Minerva be without her helmet?

I do not wish it to be understood that I no longer reverenced Mr. Horne because he was in an undress; but he himself certainly lost much of his composed, well-sustained dignity of demeanour. He was fearful and querulous, cold, and rather cross. When, forgetting his size, I offered him my own he thought that I was laughing at him. He began to be afraid that the story would get abroad, and he then and there exacted a promise that I would never tell it during his lifetime. I have kept my word; but now my old friend has been gathered to his fathers, full of years.

At last I got him to the hotel. It was long before he would leave the castle, cloaked though he was;—not, indeed, till the shades of evening had dimmed the outlines of men and things, and made indistinct the outward garniture of those who passed to and fro in the streets. Then, wrapped in his cloak, Mr. Horne followed me along the quays and through the narrowest of the streets; and at length, without venturing to return the gaze of any one in the hotel court, he made his way up to his own bedroom.

Dinnerless and supperless he went to his couch. But when there he did consent to receive some consolation in the shape of mutton cutlets and fried potatoes, a savory omelet, and a bottle of claret. The mutton cutlets and fried potatoes at the Golden Fleece at Antwerp are—or were then, for I am speaking now of wellnigh thirty years since—remarkably good ; the claret, also, was of the best ; and so, by degrees, the look of despairing dismay passed from his face, and some scintillations of the old fire returned to his eyes.

'I wonder whether they find themselves much happier for what they have got ?' said he.

'A great deal happier,' said I. 'They'll boast of those things to all their friends at home, and we shall doubtless see some account of their success in the newspapers.'

'It would be delightful to expose their blunder,—to show them up. Would it not, George ? To turn the tables on them ?'

'Yes,' said I, 'I should like to have the laugh against them.'

'So would I, only that I should compromise myself by telling the story. It wouldn't do at all to have it told at Oxford with my name attached to it.'

To this also I assented. To what would I not have assented in my anxiety to make him happy after his misery ?

But all was not over yet. He was in bed now, but it was necessary that he should rise again on the morrow. At home, in England, what was required might perhaps have been made during the night ; but here, among the slow Flemings, any such exertion would have been impossible. Mr. Horne, moreover, had no desire to be troubled in his retirement by a tailor.

Now the landlord of the Golden Fleece was a very stout man,—a very stout man indeed. Looking at him as he stood with his hands in his pockets at the portal of his own establishment, I could not but think that he was stouter even than Mr. Horne. But then he was certainly much shorter, and the want of due proportion probably added to his unwieldy appearance. I walked round him once or twice wishfully, measuring him in my eye, and thinking of what texture might be the Sunday best of such a man. The clothes which he then had on were certainly not exactly suited to Mr. Horne's tastes.

He saw that I was observing him, and appeared uneasy and offended. I had already ascertained that he spoke a little English. Of Flemish I knew literally nothing, and in French, with which probably he was also acquainted, I was by no means voluble. The business which I had to transact was intricate, and I required the use of my mother-tongue.

It was intricate and delicate, and difficult withal. I began by remarking on the weather, but he did not take my remarks kindly. I am inclined to fancy that he thought I was desirous of borrowing money from him. At any rate he gave me no encouragement in my first advances.

'Vat misfortune?' at last he asked, when I had succeeded in making him understand that a gentleman up stairs required his assistance.

'He has lost these things,' and I took hold of my own garments. 'It's a long story, or I'd tell you how;

but he has not a pair in the world till he gets back to
Brussels,—unless you can lend him one.'

'Lost hees br——?' and he opened his eyes wide,
and looked at me with astonishment.

'Yes, yes, exactly so,' said I, interrupting him.
'Most astonishing thing, isn't it? But it's quite true.'

'Vas hees money in de pocket?' asked my suspicious
landlord.

'No, no, no. It's not so bad as that. His money
is all right. I had the money, luckily.'

'Ah! dat is better. But he have lost hees b——?'

'Yes, yes;' I was now getting rather impatient.
'There is no mistake about it. He has lost them as
sure as you stand there.' And then I proceeded to
explain that as the gentleman in question was very
stout, and as he, the landlord, was stout also, he might
assist us in this great calamity by a loan from his own
wardrobe.

When he found that the money was not in the
pocket, and that his bill therefore would be paid, he
was not indisposed to be gracious. He would, he
said, desire his servant to take up what was required
to Mr. Horne's chamber. I endeavoured to make
him understand that a sombre colour would be prefer-
able; but he only answered that he would put the best
that he had at the gentleman's disposal. He could not
think of offering anything less than his best on such an
occasion. And then he turned his back and went his
way, muttering as he went something in Flemish,
which I believed to be an exclamation of astonishment

that any man should, under any circumstances, lose such an article.

It was now getting late; so when I had taken a short stroll by myself, I went to bed without disturbing Mr. Horne again that night. On the following morning I thought it best not to go to him unless he sent for me; so I desired the boots to let him know that I had ordered breakfast in a private room, and that I would await him there unless he wished to see me. He sent me word back to say that he would be with me very shortly.

He did not keep me waiting above half an hour, but I confess that that half-hour was not pleasantly spent. I feared that his temper would be tried in dressing, and that he would not be able to eat his breakfast in a happy state of mind. So that when I heard his heavy footstep advancing along the passage my heart did misgive me, and I felt that I was trembling.

That step was certainly slower and more ponderous than usual. There was always a certain dignity in the very sound of his movements, but now this seemed to have been enhanced. To judge merely by the step one would have said that a bishop was coming that way instead of a prebendary.

And then he entered. In the upper half of his august person no alteration was perceptible. The hair was as regular and as graceful as ever, the handkerchief as white, the coat as immaculate; but below his well-filled waistcoat a pair of red plush began to shine in unmitigated splendour, and continued from thence down to within an inch above his knee; nor, as it appeared, could any pulling induce them to descend lower. Mr. Horne always wore black silk stockings,— at least so the world supposed,—but it was now apparent that the world had been wrong in presuming him to be guilty of such extravagance. Those, at any rate, which he exhibited on the present occasion were more economical. They were silk to the calf, but thence upwards they continued their career in white cotton. These then followed the plush; first two snowy, full-sized pillars of white, and then two jet columns of flossy silk. Such was the appearance, on that well-remembered morning, of the Reverend Augustus Horne, as he entered the room in which his breakfast was prepared.

I could see at a glance that a dark frown contracted his eyebrows, and that the compressed muscles of his upper lip gave a strange degree of austerity to his open face. He carried his head proudly on high, determined to be dignified in spite of his misfortunes, and advanced two steps into the room without a remark, as though he were able to show that neither red plush nor black cloth could disarrange the equal poise of his mighty mind!

And after all what are a man's garments but tne outward husks in which the fruit is kept, duly tempered from the wind?

'The rank is but the guinea stamp,
    The man's the gowd for a' that.'

And is not the tailor's art as little worthy, as insignificant as that of the king who makes

'A marquis, duke and a' that?'

Who would be content to think that his manly dignity depended on his coat and waistcoat, or his hold on the world's esteem on any other garment of usual wear? That no such weakness soiled his mind Mr. Horne was determined to prove; and thus he entered the room with measured tread, and stern dignified demeanour.

Having advanced two steps his eye caught mine. I do not know whether he was moved by some unconscious smile on my part;—for in truth I endeavoured to seem as indifferent as himself to the nature of his dress;—or whether he was invincibly tickled by some inward fancy of his own, but suddenly his advancing step ceased, a broad flash of comic humour spread itself over his features, he retreated with his back against the wall, and then burst out into an immoderate roar of loud laughter.

And I—what else could I then do but laugh? He laughed, and I laughed. He roared, and I roared. He lifted up his vast legs to view till the rays of the morning sun shone through the window on the bright hues which he displayed; and he did not sit down to his breakfast till he had in every fantastic attitude shown off to the best advantage the red plush of which he had so recently become proud.

An Antwerp private cabriolet on that day reached the yard of the Hôtel de Belle Vue at about 4 P.M., and four waiters, in a frenzy of astonishment, saw the Reverend Augustus Horne descend from the vehicle and seek his chamber dressed in the garments which I have described. But I am inclined to think that he never again favoured any of his friends with such a sight.

It was on the next evening after this that I went out to drink tea with two maiden ladies, relatives of mine, who kept a seminary for English girls at Brussels. The Misses Macmanus were very worthy women, and earned their bread in an upright, painstaking manner. I would not for worlds have passed through Brussels without paying them this compliment. They were, however, perhaps a little dull, and I was aware that I should not probably meet in their drawing-room many of the fashionable inhabitants of the city. Mr. Horne had declined to accompany me; but in doing so he was good enough to express a warm admiration for the character of my worthy cousins.

The elder Miss Macmanus, in her little note, had informed me that she would have the pleasure of introducing me to a few of my 'compatriots.' I presumed she meant Englishmen; and as I was in the habit of meeting such every day of my life at home, I cannot say that I was peculiarly elevated by the promise. When, however, I entered the room, there was no Englishman there;—there was no man of any kind. There were twelve ladies collected together with the view of making the evening pass agreeably to me, the single virile being among them all. I felt as though I were a sort of Mohammed in Paradise; but I certainly felt also that the Paradise was none of my own choosing.

In the centre of the amphitheatre which the ladies formed sat the two Misses Macmanus;—there, at least, they sat when they had completed the process of shaking hands with me. To the left of them, making one wing of the semicircle, were arranged the five pupils by attending to whom the Misses Macmanus earned their living; and the other wing consisted of the five ladies who had furnished themselves with relics of General Chassé. They were my ' compatriots.'

I was introduced to them all, one after the other : but their names did not abide in my memory one moment. I was thinking too much of the singularity of the adventure, and could not attend to such minutiæ. That the red-nosed harpy was Miss Grogram, that I remembered;—that, I may say, I shall never forget. But whether the motherly lady with the somewhat blowsy hair was Mrs. Jones or Mrs. Green, or Mrs. Walker, I cannot now say. The dumpy female with the broad back was always called Aunt Sally by the young ladies.

Too much sugar spoils one's tea; I think I have heard that even prosperity will cloy when it comes in overdoses; and a schoolboy has been known to be overdone with jam. I myself have always been peculiarly attached to ladies' society, and have avoided bachelor parties as things execrable in their very nature. But on this special occasion I felt myself to be that schoolboy ;—I was literally overdone with jam. My tea

Q

was all sugar, so that I could not drink it. I was one
among twelve. What could I do or say? The proportion of alloy was too small to have any effect in
changing the nature of the virgin silver, and the
conversation became absolutely feminine.

I must confess also that my previous experience as to
these compatriots of mine had not prejudiced me in
their favour. I regarded them with,—I am ashamed to
say so, seeing that they were ladies,—but almost with
loathing. When last I had seen them their occupation
had reminded me of some obscene feast of harpies, or
almost of ghouls. They had brought down to the
verge of desperation the man whom of all men I most
venerated. On these accounts I was inclined to be
taciturn with reference to them;—and then what could
I have to say to the Misses Macmanus's five
pupils?

My cousin at first made an effort or two in my
favour, but these efforts were fruitless. I soon died
away into utter unrecognized insignificance; and the
conversation, as I have before said, became feminine.
And indeed that horrid Miss Grogram, who was, as it
were, the princess of the ghouls, nearly monopolized
the whole of it. Mamma Jones—we will call her
Jones for the occasion—put in a word now and then, as
did also the elder and more energetic Miss Macmanus.
The dumpy lady with the broad back ate tea-cake
incessantly; the two daughters looked scornful, as
though they were above their company with reference
to the five pupils; and the five pupils themselves sat in

a row with the utmost propriety, each with her hands crossed on her lap before her.

Of what they were talking at last I became utterly oblivious. They had ignored me, going into realms of muslin, questions of maid-servants, female rights, and cheap under-clothing; and I therefore had ignored them. My mind had gone back to Mr. Horne and his garments. While they spoke of their rights, I was thinking of his wrongs; when they mentioned the price of flannel I thought of that of broadcloth.

But of a sudden my attention was arrested. Miss Macmanus had said something of the black silks of Antwerp, when Miss Grogram replied that she had just returned from that city and had there enjoyed a great success. My cousin had again asked something about the black silks, thinking, no doubt, that Miss Grogram had achieved some bargain; but that lady had soon undeceived her.

'Oh no,' said Miss Grogram, 'it was at the castle. We got such beautiful relics of General Chassé! Didn't we, Mrs. Jones?'

'Indeed we did,' said Mrs. Jones, bringing out from beneath the skirts of her dress and ostensibly displaying a large black bag.

'And I've got such a beautiful needle-case,' said the broad-back, displaying her prize. 'I've been making it up all the morning.' And she handed over the article to Miss Macmanus.

'And only look at this duck of a pen-wiper, simpered flaxen-hair No. 2. 'Only think of wiping

one's pens with relics of General Chassé!' and she
handed it over to the other Miss Macmanus.

'And mine's a pin-cushion,' said No. 1, exhibiting
the trophy.

'But that's nothing to what I've got,' said Miss
Grogram. 'In the first place, there's a pair of slippers,
—a beautiful pair;—they're not made up yet, of course;
and then—'

The two Misses Macmanus and their five pupils were
sitting open-eared, open-eyed, and open-mouthed.
How all these sombre-looking articles could be relics
of General Chassé did not at first appear clear to
them.

'What are they, Miss Grogram?' said the elder
Miss Macmanus, holding the needle-case in one hand
and Mrs. Jones's bag in the other. Miss Macmanus
was a strong-minded female, and I reverenced my
cousin when I saw the decided way in which she
intended to put down the greedy arrogance of Miss
Grogram.

'They are relics.'

'But where do they come from, Miss Grogram?'

'Why, from the castle, to be sure;—from General
Chassé's own rooms.'

'Did anybody sell them to you?'

'No.'

'Or give them to you?'

'Why, no;—at least not exactly give.'

'There they were, and she took 'em,' said the
broad-back.

Oh, what a look Miss Grogram gave her! 'Took them! of course I took them. That is, you took them as much as I did. They were things that we found lying about.'

'What things?' asked Miss Macmanus, in a peculiarly strong-minded tone.

Miss Grogram seemed to be for a moment silenced. I had been ignored, as I have said, and my existence forgotten; but now I observed that the eyes of the culprits were turned towards me,—the eyes, that is, of four of them. Mrs. Jones looked at me from beneath her fan; the two girls glanced at me furtively, and then their eyes fell to the lowest flounces of their frocks. Miss Grogram turned her spectacles right upon me, and I fancied that she nodded her head at me as a sort of answer to Miss Macmanus. The five pupils opened their mouths and eyes wider; but she of the broad-back was nothing abashed. It would have been nothing to her had there been a dozen gentlemen in the room. 'We just found a pair of black ——.' The whole truth was told in the plainest possible language.

'Oh, Aunt Sally!' 'Aunt Sally, how can you?' 'Hold your tongue, Aunt Sally!'

'And then Miss Grogram just cut them up with her scissors,' continued Aunt Sally, not a whit abashed, 'and gave us each a bit, only she took more than half for herself.' It was clear to me that there had been some quarrel, some delicious quarrel, between Aunt Sally and Miss Grogram. Through the whole adventure I had rather respected Aunt Sally. 'She took more than half for herself,' continued Aunt Sally. 'She kept all the ——.'

'Jemima,' said the elder Miss Macmanus, interrupting the speaker and addressing her sister, 'it is time, I think, for the young ladies to retire. Will you be kind enough to see them to their rooms?' The five pupils thereupon rose from their seats and courtesied. They then left the room in file, the younger Miss Macmanus showing them the way.

'But we haven't done any harm, have we?' asked Mrs. Jones, with some tremulousness in her voice.

'Well, I don't know,' said Miss Macmanus. 'What I'm thinking of now is this;—to whom, I wonder, did the garments properly belong? Who had been the owner and wearer of them?'

'Why General Chassé, of course,' said Miss Grogram.

'They were the general's,' repeated the two young ladies; blushing, however, as they alluded to the subject.

'Well, we thought they were the general's, certainly; and a very excellent article they were,' said Mrs. Jones.

'Perhaps they were the butler's?' said Aunt Sally. I certainly had not given her credit for so much sarcasm.

'Butler's!' exclaimed Miss Grogram, with a toss of her head.

'Oh! Aunt Sally, Aunt Sally! how can you?' shrieked the two young ladies.

'Oh laws!' ejaculated Mrs. Jones.

'I don't think that they could have belonged to the butler,' said Miss Macmanus, with much authority, 'seeing that domestics in this country are never clad in garments of that description; so far my own observation enables me to speak with certainty. But it is equally sure that they were never the property of the general lately in command at Antwerp. Generals, when they are in full dress, wear ornamental lace upon their—their regimentals; and when—' So much she said, and something more, which it may be unnecessary that I should repeat; but such were her eloquence and logic that no doubt would have been left on the mind of any impartial hearer. If an argumentative speaker ever proved anything, Miss Macmanus proved that General Chassé had never been the wearer of the article in question.

'But I know very well they were his!' said Miss Grogram, who was not an impartial hearer. 'Of course they were; whose else's should they be?'

'I'm sure I hope they were his,' said one of the young ladies, almost crying.

'I wish I'd never taken it,' said the other.

'Dear, dear, dear!' said Mrs. Jones.

'I'll give you my needle-case, Miss Grogram,' said Aunt Sally.

I had sat hitherto silent during the whole scene, meditating how best I might confound the red-nosed harpy. Now, I thought, was the time for me to strike in.

'I really think, ladies, that there has been some mistake,' said I.

'There has been no mistake at all, sir!' said Miss Grogram.

'Perhaps not,' I answered, very mildly; 'very likely not. But some affair of a similar nature was very much talked about in Antwerp yesterday.'

'Oh laws!' again ejaculated Mrs. Jones.

'The affair I allude to has been talked about a good deal, certainly,' I continued. 'But perhaps it may be altogether a different circumstance.'

'And what may be the circumstance to which you allude?' asked Miss Macmanus, in the same authoritative tone.

'I dare say it has nothing to do with these ladies,' said I; 'but an article of dress, of the nature they have described, was cut up in the Castle of Antwerp on the day before yesterday. It belonged to a gentleman who was visiting the place; and I was given to understand that he is determined to punish the people who have wronged him.'

'It can't be the same,' said Miss Grogram; but I could see that she was trembling.

'Oh laws! what will become of us?' said Mrs. Jones.

'You can all prove that I didn't touch them, and that I warned her not,' said Aunt Sally. In the mean time the two young ladies had almost fainted behind their fans.

'But how had it come to pass,' asked Miss Macmanus, 'that the gentleman had—'

'I know nothing more about it, cousin,' said I ; 'only it does seem that there is an odd coincidence.'

Immediately after this I took my leave. I saw that I had avenged my friend, and spread dismay in the hearts of those who had injured him. I had learned in the course of the evening at what hotel the five ladies were staying; and in the course of the next morning I sauntered into the hall, and finding one of the porters alone, asked if they were still there. The man told me that they had started by the earliest diligence. 'And,' said he, 'if you are a friend of theirs, perhaps you will take charge of these things, which they have left behind them ?' So saying, he pointed to a table at the back of the hall, on which were lying the black bag, the black needle-case, the black pin-cushion, and the black pen-wiper. There was also a heap of fragments of cloth which I well knew had been intended by Miss Grogram for the comfort of her feet and ankles.

I declined the commission, however. 'They were no special friends of mine,' I said ; and I left all the relics still lying on the little table in the back hall.

'Upon the whole, I am satisfied !' said the Rev. Augustus Horne, when I told him the finale of the story.

AN UNPROTECTED FEMALE AT THE PYRAMIDS.

In the happy days when we were young, no description conveyed to us so complete an idea of mysterious reality as that of an Oriental city. We knew it was actually there, but had such vague notions of its ways and looks! Let any one remember his early impressions as to Bagdad or Grand Cairo, and then say if this was not so. It was probably taken from the 'Arabian Nights,' and the picture produced was one of strange, fantastic, luxurious houses; of women who were either very young and very beautiful, or else very old and very cunning; but in either state exercising much more influence in life than women in the East do now; of good-natured, capricious, though sometimes tyrannical monarchs; and of life full of quaint mysteries, quite unintelligible in every phasis, and on that account the more picturesque.

And perhaps Grand Cairo has thus filled us with more wonder even than Bagdad. We have been in a certain manner at home at Bagdad, but have only visited Grand Cairo occasionally. I know no place which was to me, in early years, so delightfully mysterious as Grand Cairo.

But the route to India and Australia has changed all this. Men from all countries going to the East, now pass through Cairo, and its streets and costumes are no longer strange to us. It has become also a resort for invalids, or rather for those who fear that they may become invalids if they remain in a cold climate during the winter months. And thus at Cairo there is always to be found a considerable population of French, Americans, and of English. Oriental life is brought home to us, dreadfully diluted by western customs, and the delights of the 'Arabian Nights' are shorn of half their value. When we have seen a thing it is never so magnificent to us as when it was half unknown.

It is not much that we deign to learn from these Orientals,—we who glory in our civilization. We do not copy their silence or their abstemiousness, nor that invariable mindfulness of his own personal dignity which always adheres to a Turk or to an Arab. We chatter as much at Cairo as elsewhere, and eat as much and drink as much, and dress ourselves generally in the same old, ugly costume. But we do usually take upon ourselves to wear red caps, and we do ride on donkeys.

Nor are the visitors from the West to Cairo by any means confined to the male sex. Ladies are to be seen in the streets, quite regardless of the Mahommedan custom which presumes a veil to be necessary for an appearance in public; and, to tell the truth, the Mahommedans in general do not appear to be much shocked by their effrontery.

A quarter of the town has in this way become inhabited by men wearing coats and waistcoats, and by women who are without veils; but the English tongue in Egypt finds its centre at Shepheard's Hotel. It is here that people congregate who are looking out for parties to visit with them the Upper Nile, and who are generally all smiles and courtesy; and here also are to be found they who have just returned from this journey, and who are often in a frame of mind towards their companions that is much less amiable. From hence, during the winter, a *cortége* proceeds almost daily to the Pyramids, or to Memphis, or to the petrified forest, or to the City of the Sun. And then, again, four or five times a month the house is filled with young aspirants going out to India, male and female, full of valour and bloom; or with others coming home, no longer young, no longer aspiring, but laden with children and grievances.

The party with whom we are at present concerned is not about to proceed further than the Pyramids, and we shall be able to go with them and return in one and the same day.

It consisted chiefly of an English family, Mr. and Mrs. Damer, their daughter, and two young sons;—of these chiefly, because they were the nucleus to which the others had attached themselves as adherents;

they had originated the journey, and in the whole management of it Mr. Damer regarded himself as the master.

The adherents were, firstly, M. Delabordeau, a Frenchman, now resident in Cairo, who had given out that he was in some way concerned in the canal about to be made between the Mediterranean and the Red Sea. In discussion on this subject he had become acquainted with Mr. Damer; and although the latter gentleman, true to English interests, perpetually declared that the canal would never be made, and thus irritated M. Delabordeau not a little—nevertheless, some measure of friendship had grown up between them.

There was also an American gentleman, Mr. Jefferson Ingram, who was comprising all countries and all nations in one grand tour, as American gentlemen so often do. He was young and good-looking, and had made himself especially agreeable to Mr. Damer, who had declared, more than once, that Mr. Ingram was by far the most rational American he had ever met. Mr. Ingram would listen to Mr. Damer by the half-hour as to the virtue of the British Constitution, and had even sat by almost with patience when Mr. Damer had expressed a doubt as to the good working of the United States' scheme of policy,—which, in an American, was most wonderful. But some of the sojourners at Shepheard's had observed that Mr. Ingram was in the habit of talking with Miss Damer almost as much as with her father, and argued from that, that fond as the young man was of politics, he did sometimes turn his mind to other things also.

And then there was Miss Dawkins. Now Miss Dawkins was an important person, both as to herself and as to her line of life, and she must be described. She was, in the first place, an unprotected female of about thirty years of age. As this is becoming an established profession, setting itself up as it were in opposition to the old-world idea that women, like green peas, cannot come to perfection without supporting-sticks, it will be understood at once what were Miss Dawkins' sentiments. She considered—or at any rate so expressed herself—that peas could grow very well without sticks, and could not only grow thus unsupported, but could also make their way about the world without any incumbrance of sticks whatsoever. She did not intend, she said, to rival Ida Pfeiffer, seeing that she was attached in a moderate way to bed and oard, and was attached to society in a manner almost more than moderate; but she had no idea of being prevented from seeing anything she wished to see because she had neither father, nor husband, nor brother available for the purpose of escort. She was a human creature, with arms and legs, she said; and she intended to use them. And this was all very well; but nevertheless she had a strong inclination to use the arms and legs of other people when she could make them serviceable.

In person Miss Dawkins was not without attraction. I should exaggerate if I were to say that she was

beautiful and elegant; but she was good looking, and
not usually ill mannered. She was tall, and gifted
with features rather sharp and with eyes very bright.
Her hair was of the darkest shade of brown, and was
always worn in *bandeaux*, very neatly. She appeared
generally in black, though other circumstances did not
lead one to suppose that she was in mourning; and
then, no other travelling costume is so convenient! She
always wore a dark broad-brimmed straw hat, as to the
ribbons on which she was rather particular. She was
very neat about her gloves and boots; and though it
cannot be said that her dress was got up without
reference to expense, there can be no doubt that it was
not effected without considerable outlay,—and more
considerable thought.

Miss Dawkins—Sabrina Dawkins was her name, but
she seldom had friends about her intimate enough to
use the word Sabrina,—was certainly a clever young
woman. She could talk on most subjects, if not well,
at least well enough to amuse. If she had not read
much, she never showed any lamentable deficiency;
she was good-humoured, as a rule, and could on
occasions be very soft and winning. People who had
known her long would sometimes say that she was
selfish; but with new acquaintance she was forbearing
and self-denying.

With what income Miss Dawkins was blessed no
one seemed to know. She lived like a gentlewoman,
as far as outward appearance went, and never seemed
to be in want; but some people would say that she

knew very well how many sides there were to a shilling, and some enemy had once declared that she was an ' old soldier.' Such was Miss Dawkins.

She also, as well as Mr. Ingram and M. Delabordeau, had laid herself out to find the weak side of Mr. Damer. Mr. Damer, with all his family, was going up the Nile, and it was known that he had room for two in his boat over and above his own family. Miss Dawkins had told him that she had not quite made up her mind to undergo so great a fatigue, but that, nevertheless, she had a longing of the soul to see something of Nubia. To this Mr. Damer had answered nothing but ' Oh !' which Miss Dawkins had not found to be encouraging.

But she had not on that account despaired. To a married man there are always two sides, and in this instance there was Mrs. Damer as well as Mr. Damer. When Mr. Damer said ' Oh !' Miss Dawkins sighed, and said, ' Yes, indeed !' then smiled, and betook herself to Mrs. Damer.

Now Mrs. Damer was soft-hearted, and also somewhat old-fashioned. She did not conceive any violent affection for Miss Dawkins, but she told her daughter that ' the single lady by herself was a very nice young woman, and that it was a thousand pities she should have to go about so much alone like '

Miss Damer had turned up her pretty nose, thinking, perhaps, how small was the chance that it ever should be her own lot to be an unprotected female. But

R

Miss Dawkins carried her point at any rate as regarded the expedition to the Pyramids.

Miss Damer, I have said, had a pretty nose. I may also say that she had pretty eyes, mouth, and chin, with other necessary appendages, all pretty. As to the two Master Damers, who were respectively of the ages of fifteen and sixteen, it may be sufficient to say that they were conspicuous for red caps and for the constancy with which they raced their donkeys.

And now the donkeys, and the donkey-boys, and the dragomen were all standing at the steps of Shepheard's Hotel. To each donkey there was a donkey-boy, and to each gentleman there was a dragoman, so that a goodly *cortége* was assembled, and a goodly noise was made. It may here be remarked, perhaps with some little pride, that not half the noise is given in Egypt to persons speaking any other language that is bestowed on those whose vocabulary is English.

This lasted for half an hour. Had the party been French the donkeys would have arrived only fifteen minutes before the appointed time. And then out came Damer père and Damer mère, Damer fille and Damer fils. Damer mère was leaning on her husband, as was her wont. She was not an unprotected female, and had no desire to make any attempts in that line. Damer fille was attended sedulously by Mr. Ingram, for whose demolishment, however, Mr. Damer still brought up, in a loud voice, the fag ends of certain political arguments which he would fain have poured

direct into the ears of his opponent, had not his wife
been so persistent in claiming her privileges. M. Delabordeau should have followed with Miss Dawkins,
but his French politeness, or else his fear of the unprotected female, taught him to walk on the other side of
the mistress of the party.

Miss Dawkins left the house with an eager young
Damer yelling on each side of her; but nevertheless,
though thus neglected by the gentlemen of the party,
she was all smiles and prettiness, and looked so sweetly
on Mr. Ingram when that gentleman stayed a moment
to help her on to her donkey, that his heart almost misgave him for leaving her as soon as she was in her seat.

And then they were off. In going from the hotel to
the Pyramids our party had not to pass through any
of the queer old narrow streets of the true Cairo—
Cairo the Oriental. They all lay behind them as they
went down by the back of the hotel, by the barracks of
the Pasha and the College of the Dervishes, to the village of old Cairo and the banks of the Nile.

Here they were kept half an hour while their dragomans made a bargain with the ferryman, a stately reis,
or captain of a boat, who declared with much dignity
that he could not carry them over for a sum less than
six times the amount to which he was justly entitled;
while the dragomans, with great energy on behalf of
their masters, offered him only five times that sum. As
far as the reis was concerned, the contest might soon
have been at an end, for the man was not without a
conscience; and would have been content with five

times and a half; but then the three dragomans quarrelled among themselves as to which should have the paying of the money, and the affair became very tedious.

'What horrid, odious men!' said Miss Dawkins, appealing to Mr. Damer. 'Do you think they will let us go over at all?'

'Well, I suppose they will; people do get over generally, I believe. Abdallah! Abdallah! why don't you pay the man? That fellow is always striving to save half a piastre for me.'

'I wish he wasn't quite so particular,' said Mrs. Damer, who was already becoming rather tired; 'but I'm sure he's a very honest man in trying to protect us from being robbed.'

'That he is,' said Miss Dawkins. 'What a delightful trait of national character it is to see these men so faithful to their employers!' And then at last they got over the ferry, Mr. Ingram having descended among the combatants, and settled the matter in dispute by threats and shouts, and an uplifted stick.

They crossed the broad Nile exactly at the spot where the nilometer, or river gauge, measures from day to day, and from year to year, the increasing or decreasing treasures of the stream, and landed at a village where thousands of eggs are made into chickens by the process of artificial incubation.

Mrs. Damer thought that it was very hard upon the maternal hens—the hens which should have been maternal—that they should be thus robbed of the delights of motherhood.

'So unnatural, you know,' said Miss Dawkins; 'so opposed to the fostering principles of creation. Don't you think so, Mr. Ingram?'

Mr. Ingram said he didn't know. He was again seating Miss Damer on her donkey, and it must be presumed that he performed this feat clumsily; for Fanny Damer could jump on and off the animal with hardly a finger to help her, when her brother or her father was her escort; but now, under the hands of Mr. Ingram, this work of mounting was one which required considerable time and care. All which Miss Dawkins observed with precision.

'It's all very well talking,' said Mr. Damer, bringing up his donkey nearly alongside of that of Mr. Ingram, and ignoring his daughter's presence, just as he would have done that of his dog; 'but you must admit that political power is more equally distributed in England than it is in America.'

'Perhaps it is,' said Mr. Ingram; 'equally distributed among, we will say, three dozen families,' and he made a feint as though to hold in his impetuous donkey, using the spur, however, at the same time on the side that was unseen by Mr. Damer. As he did so, Fanny's donkey became equally impetuous, and the two cantered on in advance of the whole party. It was quite in vain that Mr. Damer, at the top of his voice, shouted out something about 'three dozen corruptible demagogues.' Mr. Ingram found it quite impossible to restrain his donkey so as to listen to the sarcasm.

'I do believe papa would talk politics,' said Fanny,

' if he were at the top of Mont Blanc, or under the Falls
of Niagara. I do hate politics, Mr. Ingram.'

' I am sorry for that, very,' said Mr. Ingram, almost
sadly.

' Sorry, why? You don't want me to talk politics,
do you?'

' In America we are all politicians, more or less ;
and, therefore, I suppose you will hate us all.'

' Well, I rather think I should,' said Fanny ; 'you
would be such bores.' But there was something in her
eye, as she spoke, which atoned for the harshness of her
words.

' A very nice young man is Mr. Ingram ; don't you
think so?' said Miss Dawkins to Mrs. Damer. Mrs.
Damer was going along upon her donkey, not altogether
comfortably. She much wished to have her lord and
legitimate protector by her side, but he had left her to
the care of a dragoman whose English was not intelligible to her, and she was rather cross.

' Indeed, Miss Dawkins, I don't know who are nice
and who are not. This nasty donkey stumbles at
every step. There! I know I shall be down directly.'

' You need not be at all afraid of that; they are
perfectly safe, I believe, always,' said Miss Dawkins
rising in her stirrup, and handling her reins quite
triumphantly. ' A very little practice will make you
quite at home.'

' I don't know what you mean by a very little
practice. I have been here six weeks. Why did you

put me on such a bad donkey as this?' and she turned to Abdallah, the dragoman.

'Him berry good donkey, my lady; berry good,— best of all. Call him Jack in Cairo. Him go to Pyramid and back, and mind noting.'

'What does he say, Miss Dawkins?'

'He says that that donkey is one called Jack. If so I've had him myself many times, and Jack is a very good donkey.'

'I wish you had him now with all my heart,' said Mrs. Damer. Upon which Miss Dawkins offered to change; but those perils of mounting and dismounting were to Mrs. Damer a great deal too severe to admit of this.

'Seven miles of canal to be carried out into the sea, at a minimum depth of twenty-three feet, and the stone to be fetched from Heaven knows where! All the money in France wouldn't do it.' This was addressed by Mr. Damer to M. Delabordeau, whom he had caught after the abrupt flight of Mr. Ingram.

'Den we will borrow a leetle from England,' said M. Delabordeau.

'Precious little, I can tell you. Such stock would not hold its price in our markets for twenty-four hours. If it were made, the freights would be too heavy to allow of merchandise passing through. The heavy goods would all go round; and as for passengers and mails, you don't expect to get them, I suppose, while there is a railroad ready made to their hand?'

'Ve vill carry all your ships through vidout any transportation. Think of that, my friend.'

'Pshaw! You are worse than Ingram. Of all the plans I ever heard of it is the most monstrous, the most impracticable, the most——' But here he was interrupted by the entreaties of his wife, who had, in absolute deed and fact, slipped from her donkey, and was now calling lustily for her husband's aid. Whereupon Miss Dawkins allied herself to the Frenchman, and listened with an air of strong conviction to those arguments which were so weak in the ears of Mr. Damer. M, Delabordeau was about to ride across the Great Desert to Jerusalem, and it might perhaps be quite as well to do that with him, as to go up the Nile as far as the second cataract with the Damers.

'And so, M. Delabordeau, you intend really to start for Mount Sinai ?'

'Yes, mees; ve intend to make one start on Monday week.'

'And so on to Jerusalem. You are quite right. It would be a thousand pities to be in these countries, and to return without going over such ground as that. I shall certainly go to Jerusalem myself by that route.'

'Vot, mees! you? Vould you not find it too much fatigante ?'

'I care nothing for fatigue, if I like the party I am with,—nothing at all, literally. You will hardly understand me, perhaps, M. Delabordeau ; but I do not see any reason why I, as a young woman, should not make any journey that is practicable for a young man.'

'Ah! dat is great resolution for you, mees.'

'I mean as far as fatigue is concerned. You are a

Frenchman, and belong to the nation that is at the head of all human civilization ——'

M. Delabordeau took off his hat and bowed low, to the peak of his donkey saddle. He dearly loved to hear his country praised, as Miss Dawkins was aware.

' And I am sure you must agree with me,' continued Miss Dawkins, ' that the time is gone by for women to consider themselves helpless animals, or to be so considered by others.'

' Mees Dawkins vould never be considered, not in any times at all, to be one helpless animal,' said M. Delabordeau, civilly.

' I do not, at any rate, intend to be so regarded,' said she. ' It suits me to travel alone; not that I am averse to society; quite the contrary; if I meet pleasant people I am always ready to join them. But it suits me to travel without any permanent party, and I do not see why false shame should prevent my seeing the world as thoroughly as though I belonged to the other sex. Why should it, M. Delabordeau?'

M Delabordeau declared that he did not see any reason why it should.

' I am passionately anxious to stand upon Mount Sinai,' continued Miss Dawkins; ' to press with my feet the earliest spot in sacred history, of the identity of which we are certain; to feel within me the awe-inspiring thrill of that thrice sacred hour !'

The Frenchman looked as though he did not quite understand her, but he said that it would be magnifique.

'You have already made up your party, I suppose, M. Delabordeau?'

M. Delabordeau gave the names of two Frenchmen and one Englishman who were going with him.

'Upon my word it is a great temptation to join you,' said Miss Dawkins, 'only for that horrid Englishman.'

'Vat, Mr. Stanley?'

'Oh, I don't mean any disrespect to Mr. Stanley. The horridness I speak of does not attach to him personally, but to his stiff, respectable, ungainly, well-behaved, irrational, and uncivilized country. You see I am not very patriotic.'

'Not quite so moch as my dear friend Mr. Damer.'

'Ha! ha! ha! an excellent creature, isn't he? And so they all are; dear creatures. But then they are so backward. They are most anxious that I should join them up the Nile, but——,' and then Miss Dawkins shrugged her shoulders gracefully, and, as she flattered herself, like a Frenchwoman. After that they rode on in silence for a few moments.

'Yes, I must see Mount Sinai,' said Miss Dawkins, and then sighed deeply. M. Delabordeau, notwithstanding that his country does stand at the head of all human civilization, was not courteous enough to declare that if Miss Dawkins would join his party across the desert, nothing would be wanting to make his beatitude in this world perfect.

Their road from the village of the chicken-hatching ovens lay up along the left bank of the Nile, through

an immense grove of lofty palm-trees, looking out from
among which our visitors could ever and anon see the
heads of the two great pyramids;—that is, such of them
could see it as felt any solicitude in the matter.

It is astonishing how such things lose their great
charm as men find themselves in their close neighbourhood. To one living in New York or London,
how ecstatic is the interest inspired by these huge
structures. One feels that no price would be too high
to pay for seeing them as long as time and distance,
and the world's inexorable task-work forbid such a
visit. How intense would be the delight of climbing
over the wondrous handiwork of those wondrous architects so long since dead; how thrilling the awe with
which one would penetrate down into their interior
caves—those caves in which lay buried the bones of
ancient kings, whose very names seem to have come to
us almost from another world!

But all these feelings become strangely dim, their
acute edges wonderfully worn, as the subjects which
inspired them are brought near to us. 'Ah! so those
are the Pyramids, are they?' says the traveller, when
the first glimpse of them is shown to him from the
window of a railway carriage. 'Dear me; they don't
look so very high, do they? For Heaven's sake put
the blind down, or we shall be destroyed by the dust.'
And then the ecstasy and keen delight of the Pyramids
has vanished, and for ever.

Our friends, therefore, who for weeks past had seen
them from a distance, though they had not yet visited

them, did not seem to have any strong feeling on the
subject as they trotted through the grove of palm-trees.
Mr. Damer had not yet escaped from his wife, who was
still fretful from the result of her little accident.

'It was all the chattering of that Miss Dawkins,'
said Mrs. Damer. 'She would not let me attend to
what I was doing.'

'Miss Dawkins is an ass,' said her husband.

'It is a pity she has no one to look after her,' said
Mrs. Damer.

M. Delabordeau was still listening to Miss Dawkins's raptures about Mount Sinai. 'I wonder whether
she has got any money,' said M. Delabordeau to
himself. 'It can't be much,' he went on thinking, 'or
she would not be left in this way by herself.' And the
result of his thoughts was that Miss Dawkins, if undertaken, might probably become more plague than profit.
As to Miss Dawkins herself, though she was ecstatic
about Mount Sinai—which was not present—she seemed
to have forgotten the poor Pyramids, which were then
before her nose.

The two lads were riding races along the dusty path,
much to the disgust of their donkey-boys. Their time
for enjoyment was to come. There were hampers to
be opened; and then the absolute climbing of the
Pyramids would actually be a delight to them.

As for Miss Damer and Mr. Ingram, it was clear
that they had forgotten palm-trees, Pyramids, the Nile,
and all Egypt. They had escaped to a much fairer
paradise.

'Could I bear to live among Republicans?' said Fanny, repeating the last words of her American lover, and looking down from her donkey to the ground as she did so. 'I hardly know what Republicans are, Mr. Ingram.'

'Let me teach you,' said he.

'You do talk such nonsense. I declare there is that Miss Dawkins looking at us as though she had twenty eyes. Could you not teach her, Mr. Ingram?'

And so they emerged from the palm-tree grove, through a village crowded with dirty, straggling Arab children, on to the cultivated plain, beyond which the Pyramids stood, now full before them; the two large Pyramids, a smaller one, and the huge sphinx's head all in a group together.

'Fanny,' said Bob Damer, riding up to her, 'mamma wants you; so toddle back.'

'Mamma wants me! What can she want me for now?' said Fanny, with a look of anything but filial duty in her face.

'To protect her from Miss Dawkins, I think. She wants you to ride at her side, so that Dawkins mayn't get at her. Now, Mr. Ingram, I'll bet you half a crown I'm at the top of the big Pyramid before you.'

Poor Fanny! She obeyed, however; doubtless feeling that it would not do as yet to show too plainly that she preferred Mr. Ingram to her mother. She arrested her donkey, therefore, till Mrs. Damer overtook her; and Mr. Ingram, as he paused for a moment with her while she did so, fell into the hands of Miss Dawkins.

'I cannot think, Fanny, how you get on so quick,' said Mrs. Damer. 'I'm always last; but then my donkey is such a very nasty one. Look there, now; he's always trying to get me off.'

'We shall soon be at the Pyramids now, mamma.'

'How on earth I am ever to get back again I cannot think. I am so tired now that I can hardly sit.'

'You'll be better, mamma, when you get your luncheon and a glass of wine.'

'How on earth we are to eat and drink with those nasty Arab people around us, I can't conceive. They tell me we shall be eaten up by them. But, Fanny, what has Mr. Ingram been saying to you all the day?'

'What has he been saying, mamma? Oh! I don't know;—a hundred things, I dare say. But he has not been talking to me all the time.'

'I think he has, Fanny, nearly, since we crossed the river. Oh, dear! oh, dear! this animal does hurt me so! Every time he moves he flings his head about, and that gives me such a bump.' And then Fanny commiserated her mother's sufferings, and in her commiseration contrived to elude any further questionings as to Mr. Ingram's conversation.

'Majestic piles, are they not?' said Miss Dawkins, who, having changed her companion, allowed her mind to revert from Mount Sinai to the Pyramids. They were now riding through cultivated ground, with the vast extent of the sands of Libya before them. The two Pyramids were standing on the margin of the sand, with the head of the recumbent sphynx plainly visible between them. But no idea can be formed of the size of this immense figure till it is visited much more closely. The body is covered with sand, and the head and neck alone stand above the surface of the ground. They were still two miles distant, and the sphynx as yet was but an obscure mound between the two vast Pyramids.

'Immense piles!' said Miss Dawkins, repeating her own words.

' Yes, they are large,' said Mr. Ingram, who did not choose to indulge in enthusiasm in the presence of Miss Dawkins.

' Enormous! What a grand idea!—eh, Mr. Ingram? The human race does not create such things as those nowadays!'

' No, indeed,' he answered; 'but perhaps we create better things.'

'Better! You do not mean to say, Mr. Ingram, that you are an utilitarian. I do, in truth, hope better things of you than that. Yes! steam mills are better, no doubt, and mechanics' institutes, and penny newspapers. But is nothing to be valued but what is useful?' And Miss Dawkins, in the height of her enthusiasm, switched her donkey severely over the shoulder.

' I might, perhaps, have said also that we create more beautiful things,' said Mr. Ingram.

'But we cannot create older things.'

'No, certainly; we cannot do that.'

' Nor can we imbue what we do create with the

grand associations which environ those piles with so intense an interest. Think of the mighty dead, Mr.
Ingram, and of their great homes when living. Think
of the hands which it took to raise those huge blocks—'

'And of the lives which it cost.'

'Doubtless. The tyranny and invincible power of
the royal architects add to the grandeur of the idea.
One would not wish to have back the kings of Egypt.'

'Well, no; they would be neither useful nor beautiful.'

'Perhaps not; and I do not wish to be picturesque
at the expense of my fellow-creatures.'

'I doubt, even, whether they would be picturesque.'

'You know what I mean, Mr. Ingram. But the
associations of such names, and the presence of the
stupendous works with which they are connected, fill
the soul with awe. Such, at least, is the effect with mine.'

'I fear that my tendencies, Miss Dawkins, are more
realistic than your own.'

'You belong to a young country, Mr. Ingram, and
are naturally prone to think of material life. The
necessity of living looms large before you.'

'Very large, indeed, Miss Dawkins.'

'Whereas with us, with some of us at least, the
material aspect has given place to one in which poetry
and enthusiasm prevail. To such among us the associations of past times are very dear. Cheops, to me,
is more than Napoleon Bonaparte.'

'That is more than most of your countrymen can
say, at any rate, just at present.'

'I am a woman,' continued Miss Dawkins.

Mr. Ingram took off his hat in acknowledgment both of the announcement and of the fact.

'And to us it is not given—not given as yet—to share in the great deeds of the present. The envy of your sex has driven us from the paths which lead to honour. But the deeds of the past are as much ours as yours.'

'Oh, quite as much.'

' 'Tis to your country that we look for enfranchisement from this thraldom. Yes, Mr. Ingram, the women of America have that strength of mind which has been wanting to those of Europe. In the United States woman will at last learn to exercise her proper mission.'

Mr. Ingram expressed a sincere wish that such might be the case; and then wondering at the ingenuity with which Miss Dawkins had travelled round from Cheops and his Pyramid to the rights of women in America, he contrived to fall back, under the pretence of asking after the ailments of Mrs. Damer.

And now at last they were on the sand, in the absolute desert, making their way up to the very foot of the most northern of the two Pyramids. They were by this time surrounded by a crowd of Arab guides, or Arabs professing to be guides, who had already ascertained that Mr. Damer was the chief of the party, and were accordingly driving him almost to madness by the offers of their services, and their assurance that he could not possibly see the outside or the inside of either structure, or even remain alive upon the ground, unless he at once accepted their offers made at their own prices.

'Get away, will you?' said he. 'I don't want any of you, and I won't have you! If you take hold of me I'll shoot you!' This was said to one specially energetic Arab, who, in his efforts to secure his prey, had caught hold of Mr. Damer by the leg.

'Yes, yes, I say! Englishmen always take me;—me—me, and then no break him leg. Yes—yes—yes;—I go. Master say, yes. Only one leetle ten shilling!'

'Abdallah!' shouted Mr. Damer, 'why don't you take this man away? Why don't you make him understand that if all the Pyramids depended on it, I would not give him sixpence!'

And then Abdallah, thus invoked, came up, and explained to the man in Arabic that he would gain his object more surely if he would behave himself a little more quietly; a hint which the man took for one minute, and for one minute only.

And then poor Mrs. Damer replied to an application for backsheish by the gift of a sixpence. Unfortunate woman! The word backsheish means, I believe, a gift; but it has come in Egypt to signify money, and is eternally dinned into the ears of strangers by Arab suppliants. Mrs. Damer ought to have known better, as, during the last six weeks she had never shown her face out of Shepheard's Hotel without being pestered for backsheish; but she was tired and weak, and foolishly thought to rid herself of the man who was annoying her.

No sooner had the coin dropped from her hand into that of the Arab, than she was surrounded by a cluster of beggars, who loudly made their petitions as though they would, each of them, individually be injured if treated with less liberality than that first comer. They took hold of her donkey, her bridle, her saddle, her legs, and at last her arms and hands, screaming for backsheish in voices that were neither sweet nor mild.

In her dismay she did give away sundry small coins—all, probably, that she had about her; but this only made the matter worse. Money was going, and each man, by sufficient energy, might hope to get some of it. They were very energetic, and so frightened the poor lady that she would certainly have fallen, had she not been kept on her seat by their pressure around her.

'Oh, dear! oh, dear! get away,' she cried. 'I haven't got any more; indeed, I haven't. Go. away, I tell you! Mr. Damer! oh, Mr. Damer!' and then, in the excess of her agony, she uttered one loud, long, and continuous shriek.

Up came Mr. Damer; up came Abdallah; up came M. Delabordeau; up came Mr. Ingram, and at last she was rescued. 'You shouldn't go away, and leave me to the mercy of these nasty people. As to that Abdallah, he is of no use to anybody.'

'Why you bodder de good lady, you dem black-guard?' said Abdallah, raising his stick, as though he were going to lay them all low with a blow. 'Now you get noting, you tief!

The Arabs for a moment retired to a little distance, like flies driven from a sugar-bowl; but it was easy to see that, like the flies, they would return at the first vacant moment.

And now they had reached the very foot of the Pyramids and proceeded to dismount from their donkeys. Their intention was first to ascend to the top, then to come down to their banquet, and after that to penetrate into the interior. And all this would seem to be easy of performance. The Pyramid is undoubtedly high, but it is so constructed as to admit of climbing without difficulty. A lady mounting it would undoubtedly need some assistance, but any man possessed of moderate activity would require no aid at all.

But our friends were at once imbued with the tremendous nature of the task before them. A sheikh of the Arabs came forth, who communicated with them through Abdallah. The work could be done, no doubt, he said; but a great many men would be wanted to assist. Each lady must have four Arabs, and each gentleman three; and then, seeing that the work would be peculiarly severe on this special day, each of these numerous Arabs must be remunerated by some very large number of piastres.

Mr. Damer, who was by no means a close man in his money dealings, opened his eyes with surprise, and mildly expostulated; M. Delabordeau, who was rather a close man in his reckonings, immediately buttoned up his breeches-pocket and declared that he should decline to mount the Pyramid at all at that price; and then Mr. Ingram descended to the combat.

The protestations of the men were fearful. They declared, with loud voices, eager actions, and manifold English oaths, that an attempt was being made to rob them. They had a right to demand the sums which they were charging, and it was a shame that English gentlemen should come and take the bread out of their mouths. And so they screeched, gesticulated, and swore, and frightened poor Mrs. Damer almost into fits.

But at last it was settled and away they started, the sheikh declaring that the bargain had been made at so low a rate as to leave him not one piastre for himself. Each man had an Arab on each side of him, and Miss Dawkins and Miss Damer had each, in addition, one behind. Mrs. Damer was so frightened as altogether to have lost all ambition to ascend. She sat below on a fragment of stone, with the three dragomans standing around her as guards; but even with the three dragomans the attacks on her were so frequent, and as she declared afterwards she was so bewildered, that she never had time to remember that she had come there from England to see the Pyramids, and that she was now immediately under them.

The boys, utterly ignoring their guides, scrambled up quicker than the Arabs could follow them. Mr. Damer started off at a pace which soon brought him to the end of his tether, and from that point was dragged up by the sheer strength of his assistants;

thereby accomplishing the wishes of the men, who
induce their victims to start as rapidly as possible,
in order that they may soon find themselves helpless
from want of wind.   Mr. Ingram endeavoured to
attach himself to Fanny, and she would have been
nothing loth to have him at her right hand instead
of the hideous brown, shrieking, one-eyed Arab who
took hold of her.   But it was soon found that any
such arrangement was impossible.   Each guide felt
that if he lost his own peculiar hold he would lose his
prey, and held on, therefore, with invincible tenacity.
Miss Dawkins looked, too, as though she had thought
to be attended to by some Christian cavalier, but no
Christian cavalier was forthcoming.   M. Delabordeau
was the wisest, for he took the matter quietly, did as
he was bid, and allowed the guides nearly to carry him
to the top of the edifice.

'Ha! So this is the top of the Pyramid, is it?' said
Mr. Damer, bringing out his words one by one, being
terribly out of breath.   'Very wonderful, very wonderful indeed!'

'It is wonderful,' said Miss Dawkins, whose breath
had not failed her in the least, 'very wonderful indeed!
Only think, Mr. Damer, you might travel on for days
and days, till days became months, through those inter-
minable sands, and yet you would never come to the
end of them.   Is it not quite stupendous?'

'Ah, yes, quite,—puff, puff'—said Mr. Damer,
striving to regain his breath.

Mr. Damer was now at her disposal; weak and

worn with toil and travel, out of breath, and with half his manhood gone ; if ever she might prevail over him so as to procure from his mouth an assent to that Nile proposition, it would be now. And after all, that Nile proposition was the best one now before her. She did not quite like the idea of starting off across the Great Desert without any lady, and was not sure that she was prepared to be fallen in love with by M. Dela-bordeau, even if there should ultimately be any readiness on the part of that gentleman to perform the rôle of lover. With Mr. Ingram the matter was different, nor was she so diffident of her own charms as to think it altogether impossible that she might succeed, in the teeth of that little chit, Fanny Damer. That Mr. Ingram would join the party up the Nile she had very little doubt ; and then there would be one place left for her. She would thus, at any rate, become com-mingled with a most respectable family, who might be of material service to her.

Thus actuated she commenced an earnest attack upon Mr. Damer.

'Stupendous!' she said again, for she was fond of repeating favourite words. 'What a wondrous race must have been those Egyptian kings of old !'

'I dare say they were,' said Mr. Damer, wiping his brow as he sat upon a large loose stone, a fragment lying on the flat top of the Pyramid, one of those stones with which the complete apex was once made, or was once about to be made.

'A magnificent race! so gigantic in their conceptions! Their ideas altogether overwhelm us poor, insignificant, latter-day mortals. They built these vast Pyramids; but for us, it is task enough to climb to their top.'

'Quite enough,' ejaculated Mr. Damer.

But Mr. Damer would not always remain weak and out of breath, and it was absolutely necessary for Miss Dawkins to hurry away from Cheops and his tomb, to Thebes and Karnac.

'After seeing this it is impossible for any one with a spark of imagination to leave Egypt without going further a-field.'

Mr. Damer merely wiped his brow and grunted. This Miss Dawkins took as a signal of weakness, and went on with her task perseveringly.

'For myself, I have resolved to go up, at any rate as far as Asouan and the first cataract. I had thought of acceding to the wishes of a party who are going across the Great Desert by Mount Sinai to Jerusalem; but the kindness of yourself and Mrs. Damer is so great, and the prospect of joining in your boat is so pleasurable, that I have made up my mind to accept your very kind offer.'

This, it will be acknowledged, was bold on the part of Miss Dawkins; but what will not audacity effect? To use the slang of modern language, cheek carries everything nowadays. And whatever may have been Miss Dawkins's deficiencies, in this virtue she was not deficient.

'I have made up my mind to accept your very kind

offer,' she said, shining on Mr. Damer with her blandest smile.

What was a stout, breathless, perspiring, middle-aged gentleman to do under such circumstances? Mr. Damer was a man who, in most matters, had his own way. That his wife should have given such an invitation without consulting him, was, he knew, quite impossible. She would as soon have thought of asking all those Arab guides to accompany them. Nor was it to be thought of that he should allow himself to be kidnapped into such an arrangement by the impudence of any Miss Dawkins. But there was, he felt, a difficulty in answering such a proposition from a young lady with a direct negative, especially while he was so scant of breath. So he wiped his brow again, and looked at her.

'But I can only agree to this on one understanding,' continued Miss Dawkins, 'and that is, that I am allowed to defray my own full share of the expense of the journey.'

Upon hearing this Mr. Damer thought that he saw his way out of the wood. 'Wherever I go, Miss Dawkins, I am always the paymaster myself,' and this he contrived to say with some sternness, palpitating though he still was; and the sternness which was deficient in his voice he endeavoured to put into his countenance.

But he did not know Miss Dawkins. 'Oh, Mr. Damer,' she said, and as she spoke her smile became almost blander than it was before; 'oh, Mr. Damer, I could not think of suffering you to be so liberal; I could not, indeed. But I shall be quite content that you should pay everything, and let me settle with you in one sum afterwards.'

Mr. Damer's breath was now rather more under his own command. 'I am afraid, Miss Dawkins,' he said, ' that Mrs. Damer's weak state of health will not admit of such an arrangement.'

' What, about the paying?'

' Not only as to that, but we are a family party, Miss Dawkins; and great as would be the benefit of your society to all of us, in Mrs. Damer's present state of health, I am afraid—in short, you would not find it agreeable.—And therefore—' this he added, seeing that she was still about to persevere—' I fear that we must forego the advantage you offer.'

And then, looking into his face, Miss Dawkins did perceive that even her audacity would not prevail.

' Oh, very well,' she said, and moving from the stone on which she had been sitting, she walked off, carrying her head very high, to a corner of the Pyramid from which she could look forth alone towards the sands of Libya.

In the mean time another little overture was being made on the top of the same Pyramid,—an overture which was not received quite in the same spirit. While Mr. Damer was recovering his breath for the sake of answering Miss Dawkins, Miss Damer had walked to the further corner of the square platform on which they were placed, and there sat herself down with her face turned towards Cairo. Perhaps it was not singular that Mr. Ingram should have followed her.

This would have been very well if a dozen Arabs had not also followed them. But as this was the case, Mr. Ingram had to play his game under some difficulty. He had no sooner seated himself beside her than they came and stood directly in front of the seat, shutting out the view, and by no means improving the fragrance of the air around them.

'And this, then, Miss Damer, will be our last excursion together,' he said, in his tenderest, softest tone.

'De good Englishman will gib de poor Arab one little backsheish,' said an Arab, putting out his hand and shaking Mr. Ingram's shoulder.

'Yes, yes, yes; him gib backsheish,' said another.

'Him berry good man,' said a third, putting up his filthy hand, and touching Mr. Ingram's face.

'And young lady berry good, too; she give backsheish to poor Arab.'

'Yes,' said a fourth, preparing to take a similar liberty with Miss Damer.

This was too much for Mr. Ingram. He had already used very positive language in his endeavour to assure his tormentors that they would not get a piastre from him. But this only changed their soft persuasions into threats. Upon hearing which, and upon seeing what the man attempted to do in his endeavour to get money from Miss Damer, he raised his stick, and struck first one and then the other as violently as he could upon their heads.

Any ordinary civilized men would have been stunned by such blows, for they fell on the bare foreheads of the Arabs; but the objects of the American's wrath merely skulked away; and the others, convinced by the only arguments which they understood, followed in pursuit of victims who might be less pugnacious.

It is hard for a man to be at once tender and pugnacious—to be sentimental, while he is putting forth his physical strength with all the violence in his power. It is difficult, also, for him to be gentle instantly after having been in a rage. So he changed his tactics at the moment, and came to the point at once in a manner befitting his present state of mind.

'Those vile wretches have put me in such a heat,' he said, 'that I hardly know what I am saying. But the fact is this, Miss Damer, I cannot leave Cairo without knowing——. You understand what I mean, Miss Damer.'

'Indeed I do not, Mr. Ingram; except that I am afraid you mean nonsense.'

'Yes, you do; you know that I love you. I am sure you must know it. At any rate you know it now.'

'Mr. Ingram, you should not talk in such a way.'

'Why should I not? But the truth is, Fanny, I can talk in no other way. I do love you dearly. Can you love me well enough to go and be my wife in a country far away from your own?'

Before she left the top of the Pyramid Fanny Damer had said that she would try.

Mr. Ingram was now a proud and happy man, and seemed to think the steps of the Pyramid too small for his elastic energy. But Fanny feared that her troubles were to come. There was papa—that terrible bugbear on all such occasions. What would papa say? She was sure her papa would not allow her to marry and go so far away from her own family and country. For herself, she liked the Americans—always had liked them; so she said;—would desire nothing better than to live among them. But papa! And Fanny sighed as she felt that all the recognized miseries of a young lady in love were about to fall upon her.

Nevertheless, at her lover's instance, she promised, and declared, in twenty different loving phrases, that nothing on earth should ever make her false to her love or to her lover.

'Fanny, where are you? Why are you not ready to come down?' shouted Mr. Damer, not in the best of tempers. He felt that he had almost been unkind to an unprotected female, and his heart misgave him. And yet it would have misgiven him more had he allowed himself to be entrapped by Miss Dawkins.

'I am quite ready, papa,' said Fanny, running up to him—for it may be understood that there is quite room enough for a young lady to run on the top of the Pyramid.

'I am sure I don't know where you have been all the time,' said Mr. Damer; 'and where are those two boys?'

Fanny pointed to the top of the other Pyramid, and there they were, conspicuous with their red caps.

'And M. Delabordeau?'

'Oh! he has gone down, I think;—no, he is there with Miss Dawkins.' And in truth Miss Dawkins was leaning on his arm most affectionately, as she stooped over and looked down upon the ruins below her.

'And where is that fellow, Ingram?' said Mr. Damer, looking about him. 'He is always out of the way when he's wanted.'

To this Fanny said nothing. Why should she? She was not Mr. Ingram's keeper.

And then they all descended, each again with his proper number of Arabs to hurry and embarrass him; and they found Mrs. Damer at the bottom, like a piece of sugar covered with flies. She was heard to declare afterwards that she would not go to the Pyramids again, not if they were to be given to her for herself, as ornaments for her garden.

The picnic lunch among the big stones at the foot of the Pyramid was not a very gay affair. Miss Dawkins talked more than any one else, being determined to show that she bore her defeat gallantly. Her conversation, however, was chiefly addressed to M. Delabordeau, and he seemed to think more of his cold chicken and ham than he did of her wit and attention.

Fanny hardly spoke a word. There was her father before her, and she could not eat, much less talk, as she thought of all that she would have to go through. What would he say to the idea of having an American for a son-in-law?

Nor was Mr. Ingram very lively. A young man when he has been just accepted, never is so. His happiness under the present circumstances was, no doubt, intense, but it was of a silent nature.

And then the interior of the building had to be visited. To tell the truth none of the party would have cared to perform this feat had it not been for the honour of the thing. To have come from Paris, New York, or London, to the Pyramids, and then not to have visited the very tomb of Cheops, would have shown on the part of all of them an indifference to subjects of interest which would have been altogether fatal to their character as travellers. And so a party for the interior was made up.

Miss Damer when she saw the aperture through which it was expected that she should descend, at once declared for staying with her mother. Miss Dawkins, however, was enthusiastic for the journey. 'Persons with so very little command over their nerves might really as well stay at home,' she said to Mr. Ingram, who glowered at her dreadfully for expressing such an opinion about his Fanny.

This entrance into the Pyramids is a terrible task, which should be undertaken by no lady. Those who perform it have to creep down, and then to be dragged up, through infinite dirt, foul smells, and bad air; and when they have done it, they see nothing. But they do earn the gratification of saying that they have been inside a Pyramid.

'Well, I've done that once,' said Mr. Damer, coming out, 'and I do not think that any one will catch me doing it again. I never was in such a filthy place in my life.'

'Oh, Fanny! I am so glad you did not go; I am

sure it is not fit for ladies,' said poor Mrs. Damer, forgetful of her friend Miss Dawkins.

'I should have been ashamed of myself,' said Miss Dawkins, bristling up, and throwing back her head as she stood, 'if I had allowed any consideration to have prevented my visiting such a spot. If it be not improper for men to go there, how can it be improper for women?'

'I did not say improper, my dear,' said Mrs. Damer, apologetically.

'And as for the fatigue, what can a woman be worth who is afraid to encounter as much as I have now gone through for the sake of visiting the last resting-place of such a king as Cheops?' And Miss Dawkins, as she pronounced the last words, looked round her with disdain upon poor Fanny Damer.

'But I meant the dirt,' said Mrs. Damer.

'Dirt!' ejaculated Miss Dawkins, and then walked away. Why should she now submit her high tone of feeling to the Damers, or why care longer for their good opinion? Therefore she scattered contempt around her as she ejaculated the last word, 'dirt.'

And then the return home! 'I know I shall never get there,' said Mrs. Damer, looking piteously up into her husband's face.

'Nonsense, my dear; nonsense; you must get there.' Mrs. Damer groaned, and acknowledged in her heart that she must,—either dead or alive.

'And, Jefferson,' said Fanny, whispering—for there had been a moment since their descent in which she

had been instructed to call him by his Christian name—
'never mind talking to me going home. I will ride by
mamma. Do you go with papa and put him in good
humour; and if he says anything about the lords and
the bishops, don't you contradict him, you know.'

What will not a man do for love? Mr. Ingram
promised. And in this way they started; the two boys
led the van; then came Mr. Damer and Mr. Ingram,
unusually and unpatriotically acquiescent as to England's aristocratic propensities; then Miss Dawkins
riding, alas! alone; after her, M. Delabordeau, also
alone,—the ungallant Frenchman! And the rear was
brought up by Mrs. Damer and her daughter, flanked
on each side by a dragoman, with a third dragoman
behind them.

And in this order they went back to Cairo, riding
their donkeys, and crossing the ferry solemnly, and, for
the most part, silently. Mr. Ingram did talk, as he
had an important object in view,—that of putting Mr.
Damer into a good humour.

In this he succeeded so well that by the time they
had remounted, after crossing the Nile, Mr. Damer
opened his heart to his companion on the subject that
was troubling him, and told him all about Miss
Dawkins.

'I don't see why we should have a companion that
we don't like for eight or ten weeks, merely because it
seems rude to refuse a lady.'

'Indeed, I agree with you,' said Mr. Ingram; 'I
should call it weak-minded to give way in such a case.'

T

'My daughter does not like her at all,' continued Mr. Damer.

'Nor would she be a nice companion for Miss Damer; not according to my way of thinking,' said Mr. Ingram.

'And as to my having asked her, or Mrs. Damer having asked her! Why God bless my soul, it is pure invention on the woman's part!'

'Ha! ha! ha!' laughed Mr. Ingram; 'I must say she plays her game well; but then she is an old soldier, and has the benefit of experience.' What would Miss Dawkins have said had she known that Mr. Ingram called her an old soldier?

'I don't like the kind of thing at all,' said Mr. Damer, who was very serious upon the subject. 'You see the position in which I am placed. I am forced to be very rude, or——'

'I don't call it rude at all.'

'Disobliging, then; or else I must have all my comfort invaded and pleasure destroyed by, by, by——' And Mr. Damer paused, being at a loss for an appropriate name for Miss Dawkins.

'By an unprotected female,' suggested Mr. Ingram.

'Yes; just so. I am as fond of pleasant company as anybody; but then I like to choose it myself.'

'So do I,' said Mr. Ingram, thinking of his own choice.

'Now, Ingram, if you would join us, we should be delighted.'

'Upon my word, sir, the offer is too flattering,' said

Ingram, hesitatingly; for he felt that he could not undertake such a journey until Mr. Damer knew on what terms he stood with Fanny.

'You are a terrible democrat,' said Mr. Damer, laughing; 'but then, on that matter, you know, we could agree to differ.'

'Exactly so,' said Mr. Ingram, who had not collected his thoughts or made up his mind as to what he had better say and do, on the spur of the moment.

'Well what do you say to it?' said Mr. Damer, encouragingly. But Ingram paused before he answered.

'For Heaven's sake, my dear fellow, don't have the slightest hesitation in refusing, if you don't like the plan.'

'The fact is, Mr. Damer, I should like too well.'

'Like it too well?'

'Yes, sir, and I may as well tell you now as later. I had intended this evening to have asked for your permission to address your daughter.'

'God bless my soul!' said Mr. Damer, looking as though a totally new idea had now been opened to him.

'And under these circumstances, I will now wait and see whether or no you will renew your offer.'

'God bless my soul!' said Mr. Damer again. It often does strike an old gentleman as very odd that any man should fall in love with his daughter, whom he has not ceased to look upon as a child. The case is generally quite different with mothers. They seem to think that every young man must fall in love with their girls.

'And have you said anything to Fanny about this?' asked Mr. Damer.

'Yes, sir, I have her permission to speak to you.'

'God bless my soul!' said Mr. Damer; and by this time they had arrived at Shepheard's Hotel.

'Oh, mamma,' said Fanny, as soon as she found herself alone with her mother that evening, 'I have something that I must tell you.'

'Oh, Fanny, don't tell me anything to-night, for I am a great deal too tired to listen.'

'But oh, mamma, pray;—you must listen to this; indeed you must.' And Fanny knelt down at her mother's knee, and looked beseechingly up into her face.

'What is it, Fanny? You know that all my bones are sore, and that I am so tired that I am almost dead.'

'Mamma, Mr. Ingram has—'

'Has what, my dear? has he done anything wrong?'

'No, mamma: but he has;—he has proposed to me.' And Fanny bursting into tears hid her face in her mother's lap.

And thus the story was told on both sides of the house. On the next day, as a matter of course, all the difficulties and dangers of such a marriage as that which was now projected were insisted on by both father and mother It was improper; it would cause a severing of the family not to be thought of; it would be an alliance of a dangerous nature, and not at all calculated to insure happiness; and, in short, it was impossible.

On that day, therefore, they all went to bed very unhappy. But on the next day, as was also a matter of
course, seeing that there were no pecuniary difficulties,
the mother and father were talked over, and Mr. Ingram
was accepted as a son-in-law. It need hardly be said
that the offer of a place in Mr. Damer's boat was again
made, and that on this occasion it was accepted without
hesitation.

There was an American Protestant clergyman resident in Cairo, with whom, among other persons, Miss
Dawkins had become acquainted. Upon this gentleman or upon his wife Miss Dawkins called a few days
after the journey to the Pyramid, and finding him in
his study, thus performed her duty to her neighbour:

'You know your countryman Mr. Ingram, I think?'
said she.

'Oh, yes; very intimately.'

'If you have any regard for him, Mr. Burton,' such
was the gentleman's name, ' I think you should put him
on his guard.'

'On his guard against what?' said Mr. Burton with
a serious air, for there was something serious in the
threat of impending misfortune as conveyed by Miss
Dawkins.

'Why,' said she, 'those Damers, I fear, are dangerous people.'

'Do you mean that they will borrow money of him?'

'Oh, no; not that exactly; but they are clearly setting their cap at him.'

' Setting their cap at him ?'

' Yes ; there is a daughter, you know ; a little chit of a thing ; and I fear Mr. Ingram may be caught before he knows where he is. It would be such a pity, you know. He is going up the river with them, I hear. That, in his place, is very foolish. They asked me, but I positively refused.'

Mr. Burton remarked that ' in such a matter as that Mr. Ingram would be perfectly able to take care of himself.'

' Well, perhaps so ; but seeing what was going on, I thought it my duty to tell you.' And so Miss Dawkins took her leave.

Mr. Ingram did go up the Nile with the Damers, as did an old friend of the Damers who arrived from England. And a very pleasant trip they had of it. And, as far as the present historian knows, the two lovers were shortly afterwards married in England.

Poor Miss Dawkins was left in Cairo for some time on her beam ends. But she was one of those who are not easily vanquished. After an interval of ten days she made acquaintance with an Irish family—having utterly failed in moving the hard heart of M. Delabordeau—and with these she proceeded to Constantinople. They consisted of two brothers and a sister, and were, therefore, very convenient for matrimonial purposes. But nevertheless, when I last heard of Miss Dawkins, she was still an unprotected female.

THE CHÂTEAU OF PRINCE POLIGNAC.

FEW Englishmen or Englishwomen are intimately acquainted with the little town of Le Puy. It is the capital of the old province of Le Velay, which also is now but little known, even to French ears, for it is in these days called by the imperial name of the Department of the Haute Loire. It is to the south-east of Auvergne, and is nearly in the centre of the southern half of France.

But few towns, merely as towns, can be better worth visiting. In the first place, the volcanic formation of the ground on which it stands is not only singular in the extreme, so as to be interesting to the geologist but it is so picturesque as to be equally gratifying to the general tourist. Within a narrow valley there stand several rocks, rising up from the ground with absolute abruptness. Round two of these the town clusters, and a third stands but a mile distant, forming the centre of a faubourg, or suburb. These rocks appear to be, and I believe are, the harder particles of volcanic matter, which have not been carried away

through successive ages by the joint agency of water
and air. When the tide of lava ran down between the
hills the surface left was no doubt on a level with the
heads of these rocks ; but here and there the deposit
became harder than elsewhere, and these harder points
have remained, lifting up their steep heads in a line
through the valley.

The highest of these is called the Rocher de Corneille. Round this and up its steep sides the town
stands. On its highest summit there was an old castle ;
and there now is, or will be before these pages are
printed, a colossal figure in bronze of the Virgin Mary,
made from the cannon taken at Sebastopol. Half-way
down the hill the cathedral is built, a singularly gloomy
edifice,—Romanesque, as it is called, in its style, but
extremely similar in its mode of architecture to what we
know of Byzantine structures. But there has been no
surface on the rock side large enough to form a resting-
place for the church, which has therefore been built out
on huge supporting piles, which form a porch below the
west front ; so that the approach is by numerous steps
laid along the side of the wall below the church, forming
a wondrous flight of stairs. Let all men who may find
themselves stopping at Le Puy visit the top of these
stairs at the time of the setting sun, and look down
from thence through the framework of the porch on the
town beneath, and at the hill-side beyond.

Behind the church is the seminary of the priests, with
its beautiful walks stretching round the Rocher de
Corneille, and overlooking the town and valley below.

Next to this rock, and within a quarter of a mile of
it, is the second peak, called the Rock of the Needle.
It rises narrow, sharp, and abrupt from the valley,
allowing of no buildings on its sides. But on its very
point has been erected a church sacred to St. Michael,
that lover of rock summits, accessible by stairs cut
from the stone. This, perhaps—this rock, I mean—is
the most wonderful of the wonders which Nature has
formed at Le Puy.

Above this, at a mile's distance, is the rock of
Espailly, formed in the same way, and almost equally
precipitous. On its summit is a castle, having its own
legend, and professing to have been the residence of
Charles VII., when little of France belonged to its
kings but the provinces of Berry, Auvergne, and Le
Velay. Some three miles further up there is another
volcanic rock, larger, indeed, but equally sudden in its
spring,—equally remarkable as rising abruptly from the
valley—on which stands the castle and old family
residence of the house of Polignac. It was lost by
them at the time of the Revolution, but was repurchased
by the minister of Charles X., and is still the property
of the head of the race.

Le Puy itself is a small, moderate, pleasant French
town, in which the language of the people has not the
pure Parisian aroma, nor is the glory of the boulevards
of the capital emulated in its streets. These are
crooked, narrow, steep, and intricate, forming here
and there excellent sketches for a lover of street
picturesque beauty; but hurtful to the feet with their

small round-topped paving stones, and not always as
clean as pedestrian ladies might desire.

And now I would ask my readers to join me at the
morning table d'hôte at the Hôtel des Ambassadeurs.
It will of course be understood that this does not mean
a breakfast in the ordinary fashion of England, con-
sisting of tea or coffee, bread and butter, and perhaps
a boiled egg. It comprises all the requisites for a
composite dinner, excepting soup; and as one gets
further south in France, this meal is called dinner. It
is, however, eaten without any prejudice to another
similar and somewhat longer meal at six or seven
o'clock, which, when the above name is taken up by
the earlier enterprise, is styled supper.

The *déjeuner*, or dinner, at the Hôtel des Ambassadeurs, on the morning in question, though very elaborate, was not a very gay affair. There were some
fourteen persons present, of whom half were residents
in the town, men employed in some official capacity,
who found this to be the cheapest, the most luxurious,
and to them the most comfortable mode of living.
They clustered together at the head of the table, and
as they were customary guests at the house they talked
their little talk together—it was very little—and made
the most of the good things before them. Then there
were two or three *commis-voyageurs*, a chance traveller
or two, and an English lady with a young daughter.
The English lady sat next to one of the accustomed
guests; but he, unlike the others, held converse with
her rather than with them. Our story at present

has reference only to that lady and to that gentleman.

Place aux dames. We will speak first of the lady, whose name was Mrs. Thompson. She was, shall I say, a young woman, of about thirty-six. In so saying, I am perhaps creating a prejudice against her in the minds of some readers, as they will, not unnaturally, suppose her, after such an announcement, to be in truth over forty. Any such prejudice will be unjust. I would have it believed that thirty-six was the outside, not the inside of her age. She was good-looking, lady-like, and considering that she was an English-woman, fairly well dressed. She was inclined to be rather full in her person, but perhaps not more so than is becoming to ladies at her time of life. She had rings on her fingers and a brooch on her bosom which were of some value, and on the back of her head she wore a jaunty small lace cap, which seemed to tell, in conjunction with her other appointments, that her circumstances were comfortable.

The little girl who sat next to her was the youngest of her two daughters, and might be about thirteen years of age. Her name was Matilda, but infantine circumstances had invested her with the nickname of Mimmy, by which her mother always called her. A nice, pretty, playful little girl was Mimmy Thompson, wearing two long tails of plaited hair hanging behind her head, and inclined occasionally to be rather loud in her sport.

Mrs. Thompson had another and an elder daughter,

now some fifteen years old, who was at school in Le
Puy; and it was with reference to her tuition that
Mrs. Thompson had taken up a temporary residence at
the Hôtel des Ambassadeurs in that town. Lilian
Thompson was occasionally invited down to dine or
breakfast at the inn, and was visited daily at her school
by her mother.

'When I'm sure that she'll do, I shall leave her
there and go back to England,' Mrs. Thompson had
said, not in the purest French, to the neighbour who
always sat next to her at the table d'hôte, the gentleman, namely, to whom we have above alluded. But
still she had remained at Le Puy a month, and did not
go; a circumstance which was considered singular, but
by no means unpleasant, both by the innkeeper and by
the gentleman in question.

The facts, as regarded Mrs. Thompson, were as
follows:—She was the widow of a gentleman who
had served for many years in the civil service of the
East Indies, and who, on dying, had left her a comfortable income of—it matters not how many pounds,
but constituting quite a sufficiency to enable her to live
at her ease and educate her daughters.

Her children had been sent home to England before
her husband's death, and after that event she had
followed them; but there, though she was possessed of
moderate wealth, she had no friends and few acquaint-
ances, and after a little while she had found life to be
rather dull. Her customs were not those of England,
nor were her propensities English; therefore she had

gone abroad, and having received some recommendation
of this school at Le Puy, had made her way thither.
As it appeared to her that she really enjoyed more
consideration at Le Puy than had been accorded to her
either at Torquay or Leamington, there she remained
from day to day. The total payment required at the
Hôtel des Ambassadeurs was but six francs daily for
herself and three and a half for her little girl; and
where else could she live with a better junction of
economy and comfort? And then the gentleman who
always sat next to her was so exceedingly civil!

The gentleman's name was M. Lacordaire. So
much she knew, and had learned to call him by his
name very frequently. Mimmy, too, was quite intimate
with M. Lacordaire; but nothing more than his name
was known of him. But M. Lacordaire carried a
general letter of recommendation in his face, manner,
gait, dress, and tone of voice. In all these respects
there was nothing left to be desired; and, in addition
to this, he was decorated, and wore the little red ribbon
of the Legion of Honour, ingeniously twisted into the
shape of a small flower.

M. Lacordaire might be senior in age to Mrs.
Thompson by about ten years, nor had he about him
any of the airs and graces of a would-be young man.
His hair, which he wore very short, was grizzled, as
was also the small pretence of a whisker which came
down about as far as the middle of his ear; but the
tuft on his chin was still brown, without a gray hair.
His eyes were bright and tender, his voice was low and

soft, his hands were very white, his clothes were always new and well-fitting, and a better-brushed hat could not be seen out of Paris, nor perhaps in it.

Now, during the weeks which Mrs. Thompson had passed at Le Puy, the acquaintance which she had formed with M. Lacordaire had progressed beyond the prolonged meals in the salle à manger. He had occasionally sat beside her evening table as she took her English cup of tea in her own room, her bed being duly screened off in its distinct niche by becoming curtains; and then he had occasionally walked beside her, as he civilly escorted her to the lions of the place; and he had once accompanied her, sitting on the back seat of a French voiture, when she had gone forth to see something of the surrounding country.

On all such occasions she had been accompanied by one of her daughters, and the world of Le Puy had had nothing material to say against her. But still the world of Le Puy had whispered a little, suggesting that M. Lacordaire knew very well what he was about. But might not Mrs. Thompson also know as well what she was about? At any rate, everything had gone on very pleasantly since the acquaintance had been made; and now, so much having been explained, we will go back to the elaborate breakfast at the Hôtel des Ambassadeurs.

Mrs. Thompson, holding Mimmy by the hand, walked into the room some few minutes after the last bell had been rung, and took the place which was now hers by custom. The gentlemen who constantly frequented the house all bowed to her, but M. Lacordaire rose from his seat and offered her his hand.

'And how is Mees Meemy this morning?' said he; for 'twas thus he always pronounced her name.

Miss Mimmy, answering for herself, declared that she was very well, and suggested that M. Lacordaire should give her a fig from off a dish that was placed immediately before him on the table. This M. Lacordaire did, presenting it very elegantly between his two fingers, and making a little bow to the little lady as he did so.

'Fie, Mimmy!' said her mother; 'why do you ask for the things before the waiter brings them round?'

'But, mamma,' said Mimmy, speaking English, 'M. Lacordaire always gives me a fig every morning.'

'M. Lacordaire always spoils you, I think,' answered Mrs. Thompson, in French. And then they went thoroughly to work at their breakfast. During the whole meal M. Lacordaire attended assiduously to his neighbour; and did so without any evil result, except that one Frenchman with a black moustache, at the head of the table trod on the toe of another Frenchman with another black moustache—winking as he made the sign—just as M. Lacordaire, having selected a bunch of grapes, put it on Mrs. Thompson's plate with infinite grace. But who among us all is free from such impertinences as these?

'But madame really must see the château of Prince Polignac before she leaves Le Puy,' said M. Lacordaire.

'The château of who?' asked Mimmy, to whose young ears the French words were already becoming familiar.

'Prince Polignac, my dear. Well I really don't know, M. Lacordaire;—I have seen a great deal of the place already, and I shall be going now very soon; probably in a day or two,' said Mrs. Thompson.

'But madame must positively see the château,' said M. Lacordaire, very impressively; and then after a pause he added, 'if madame will have the complaisance to commission me to procure a carriage for this afternoon, and will allow me the honour to be her guide, I shall consider myself one of the most fortunate of men.'

'Oh, yes, mamma, do go,' said Mimmy, clapping her hands. 'And it is Thursday, and Lilian can go with us.'

'Be quiet, Mimmy, do. Thank you, no, M. Lacordaire. I could not go to-day; but I am extremely obliged by your politeness.'

M. Lacordaire still pressed the matter, and Mrs. Thompson still declined, till it was time to rise from the table. She then declared that she did not think it possible that she should visit the château before she left Le Puy; but that she would give him an answer at dinner.

The most tedious time in the day to Mrs. Thompson were the two hours after breakfast. At one o'clock she daily went to the school, taking Mimmy, who for an hour or two shared her sister's lessons. This and her little excursions about the place, and her shopping, managed to make away with her afternoon. Then in the evening, she generally saw something of M. Lacordaire. But those two hours after breakfast were hard of killing.

On this occasion, when she gained her own room, she as usual placed Mimmy on the sofa with a needle. Her custom then was to take up a novel; but on this morning she sat herself down in her arm-chair, and resting her head upon her hand and elbow, began to turn over certain circumstances in her mind.

'Mamma,' said Mimmy, 'why won't you go with M. Lacordaire to that place belonging to the prince? Prince—Polly something, wasn't it?'

'Mind your work, my dear,' said Mrs. Thompson.

'But I do so wish you'd go, mamma. What was the prince's name?'

'Polignac.'

'Mamma, ain't princes very great people?'

'Yes, my dear; sometimes.'

'Is Prince Polly-nac like our Prince Alfred?'

'No, my dear; not at all. At least, I suppose not.'

'Is his mother a queen?'

'No, my dear.'

'Then his father must be a king?'

'No, my dear. It is quite a different thing here. Here in France they have a great many princes.'

'Well, at any rate I should like to see a prince's château; so I do hope you'll go.' And then there was a pause. 'Mamma, could it come to pass, here in France, that M. Lacordaire should ever be a prince?'

U

' M. Lacordaire a prince!   No; don't talk such
nonsense, but mind your work.'

' Isn't M. Lacordaire a very nice man? Ain't you
very fond of him?'

To this question Mrs. Thompson made no answer.

'Mamma,' continued Mimmy, after a moment's
pause, 'won't you tell me whether you are fond of
M. Lacordaire?   I'm quite sure of this,—that he's very
fond of you.'

' What makes you think that?' asked Mrs. Thompson,
who could not bring herself to refrain from the question.

' Because he looks at you in that way, mamma, and
squeezes your hand.'

' Nonsense, child,' said Mrs. Thompson; 'hold your
tongue. I don't know what can have put such stuff
into your head.'

' But he does, mamma,' said Mimmy, who rarely
allowed her mother to put her down.

Mrs. Thompson made no further answer, but again
sat with her head resting on her hand. She also, if
the truth must be told, was thinking of M. Lacordaire
and his fondness for herself. He had squeezed her
hand and he had looked into her face. However much
it may have been nonsense on Mimmy's part to talk of
such things, they had not the less absolutely occurred.
Was it really the fact that M. Lacordaire was in love
with her?

And if so, what return should she, or could she make
to such a passion? He had looked at her yesterday,
and squeezed her hand to-day. Might it not be pro-

bable that he would advance a step further to-morrow?
If so, what answer would she be prepared to make to
him?

She did not think—so she said to herself—that she
had any particular objection to marrying again.
Thompson had been dead now for four years, and
neither his friends, nor her friends, nor the world could
say she was wrong on that score. And as to marrying a Frenchman, she could not say that she felt
within herself any absolute repugnance to doing that.
Of her own country, speaking of England as such, she,
in truth, knew but little—and perhaps cared less.
She had gone to India almost as a child, and England
had not been specially kind to her on her return. She
had found it dull and cold, stiff, and almost ill-natured.
People there had not smiled on her and been civil as
M. Lacordaire had done. As far as England and
Englishmen were considered she saw no reason why
she should not marry M. Lacordaire.

And then, as regarded the man; could she in her
heart say that she was prepared to love, honour, and
obey M. Lacordaire? She certainly knew no reason
why she should not do so. She did not know much of
him, she said to herself at first; but she knew as much,
she said afterwards, as she had known personally of
Mr. Thompson before their marriage. She had known,
to be sure, what was Mr. Thompson's profession and
what his income; or, if not, some one else had known
for her. As to both these points she was quite in the
dark as regarded M. Lacordaire.

Personally, she certainly did like him, as she said to herself more than once. There was a courtesy and softness about him which were very gratifying to her; and then, his appearance was so much in his favour. He was not very young, she acknowledged; but neither was she young herself. It was quite evident that he was fond of her children, and that he would be a kind and affectionate father to them. Indeed, there was kindness in all that he did.

Should she marry again,—and she put it to herself quite hypothetically,—she would look for no romance in such a second marriage. She would be content to sit down in a quiet home, to the tame dull realities of life, satisfied with the companionship of a man who would be kind and gentle to her, and whom she could respect and esteem. Where could she find a companion with whom this could be more safely anticipated than with M. Lacordaire?

And so she argued the question within her own breast in a manner not unfriendly to that gentleman. That there was as yet one great hindrance she at once saw; but then that might be remedied by a word. She did not know what was his income or his profession. The chambermaid, whom she had interrogated, had told her that he was a 'marchand.' To merchants, generally, she felt that she had no objection. The Barings and the Rothscnilds were merchants, as was also that wonderful man at Bombay, Sir Hommajee Bommajee, who was worth she did not know how many thousand lacs of rupees.

That it would behove her, on her own account and that of her daughters, to take care of her own little fortune in contracting any such connection, that she felt strongly. She would never so commit herself as to put security in that respect out of her power. But then she did not think that M. Lacordaire would ever ask her to do so; at any rate, she was determined on this, that there should never be any doubt on that matter; and as she firmly resolved on this, she again took up her book, and for a minute or two made an attempt to read.

'Mamma,' said Mimmy, 'will M. Lacordaire go up to the school to see Lilian when you go away from this?'

'Indeed, I cannot say, my dear. If Lilian is a good girl, perhaps he may do so now and then.'

'And will he write to you and tell you how she is?'

'Lilian can write for herself; can she not?'

'Oh! yes; I suppose she can; but I hope M. Lacordaire will write too. We shall come back here some day; sha'n't we, mamma?'

'I cannot say, my dear.'

'I do so hope we shall see M. Lacordaire again. Do you know what I was thinking, mamma?'

'Little girls like you ought not to think,' said Mrs. Thompson, walking slowly out of the room to the top of the stairs and back again; for she had felt the necessity of preventing Mimmy from disclosing any more of her thoughts. 'And now, my dear, get yourself ready, and we will go up to the school.'

Mrs. Thompson always dressed herself with care, though not in especially fine clothes, before she went down to dinner at the table d'hôte; but on this occasion she was more than usually particular. She hardly explained to herself why she did this; but, nevertheless, as she stood before the glass, she did in a certain manner feel that the circumstances of her future life might perhaps depend on what might be said and done that evening. She had not absolutely decided whether or no she would go to the Prince's château; but if she did go——. Well, if she did; what then? She had sense enough, as she assured herself more than once, to regulate her own conduct with propriety in any such emergency.

During the dinner, M. Lacordaire conversed in his usual manner, but said nothing whatever about the visit to Polignac. He was very kind to Mimmy, and very courteous to her mother, but did not appear to be at all more particular than usual. Indeed, it might be a question whether he was not less so. As she had entered the room Mrs. Thompson had said to herself that, perhaps, after all, it would be better that there should be nothing more thought about it; but before the four or five courses were over, she was beginning to feel a little disappointed.

And now the fruit was on the table, after the consumption of which it was her practice to retire. It was certainly open to her to ask M. Lacordaire to take tea with her that evening, as she had done on former occasions; but she felt that she must not do

this now, considering the immediate circumstances of
the case. If any further steps were to be taken, they
must be taken by him, and not by her;—or else by
Mimmy, who, just as her mother was slowly consuming
her last grapes, ran round to the back of M. Lacordaire's chair, and whispered something into his ear.
It may be presumed that Mrs. Thompson did not see
the intention of the movement in time to arrest it, for
she did nothing till the whispering had been whispered;
and then she rebuked the child, bade her not to be
troublesome, and with more than usual austerity in her
voice, desired her to get herself ready to go up stairs to
their chamber.

As she spoke she herself rose from her chair, and
made her final little bow to the table, and her other
final little bow and smile to M. Lacordaire; but this
was certain to all who saw it, that the smile was not
as gracious as usual.

As she walked forth, M. Lacordaire rose from his
chair—such being his constant practice when she left
the table; but on this occasion he accompanied her to
the door.

'And has madame decided,' he asked, 'whether she
will permit me to accompany her to the château?'

'Well, I really don't know,' said Mrs. Thompson.

'Mees Meemy,' continued M. Lacordaire, 'is very
anxious to see the rock, and I may perhaps hope that
Mees Leelian would be pleased with such a little excursion. As for myself——' and then M. Lacordaire

put his hand upon his heart in a manner that seemed to speak more plainly than he had ever spoken.

'Well, if the children would really like it, and—as you are so very kind,' said Mrs. Thompson; and so the matter was conceded.

'To-morrow afternoon?' suggested M. Lacordaire. But Mrs. Thompson fixed on Saturday, thereby showing that she herself was in no hurry for the expedition.

'Oh, I am so glad!' said Mimmy, when they had re-entered their own room. 'Mamma, do let me tell Lilian myself when I go up to the school to-morrow!'

But mamma was in no humour to say much to her child on this subject at the present moment. She threw herself back on her sofa in perfect silence, and began to reflect whether she would like to sign her name in future as Fanny Lacordaire, instead of Fanny Thompson. It certainly seemed as though things were verging towards such a necessity. A marchand! But a marchand of what? She had an instinctive feeling that the people in the hotel were talking about her and M. Lacordaire, and was therefore more than ever averse to asking any one a question.

As she went up to the school the next afternoon, she walked through more of the streets of Le Puy than was necessary, and in every street she looked at the names which she saw over the doors of the more respectable houses of business. But she looked in vain. It might be that M. Lacordaire was a marchand of so specially high a quality as to be under no necessity to put up his name at all. Sir Hommajee Bommajee's name did not appear over any door in Bombay;—at least, she thought not.

And then came the Saturday morning. 'We shall be ready at two,' she said, as she left the breakfast-table; 'and perhaps you would not mind calling for Lilian on the way.'

M. Lacordaire would be delighted to call anywhere for anybody on behalf of Mrs. Thompson; and then, as he got to the door of the salon, he offered her his hand. He did so with so much French courtesy that she could not refuse it, and then she felt that his purpose was more tender than ever it had been. And why not, if this was the destiny which Fate had prepared for her?

Mrs. Thompson would rather have got into the carriage at any other spot in Le Puy than at that at which she was forced to do so—the chief entrance, namely, of the Hôtel des Ambassadeurs. And what made it worse was this, that an appearance of a special fête was given to the occasion. M. Lacordaire was dressed in more than his Sunday best. He had on new yellow kid gloves. His coat, if not new, was newer than any Mrs. Thompson had yet observed, and was lined with silk up to the very collar. He had on patent leather boots, which glittered, as Mrs. Thompson thought, much too conspicuously. And as for his hat, it was quite evident that it was fresh that morning from the maker's block.

In this costume, with his hat in his hand, he stood under the great gateway of the hotel, ready to hand Mrs. Thompson into the carriage. This would have been nothing if the landlord and landlady had not been there also, as well as the man-cook, and the four waiters, and the fille de chambre. Two or three other pair of eyes Mrs. Thompson also saw, as she glanced round, and then Mimmy walked across the yard in her best clothes with a fête-day air about her for which her mother would have liked to have whipped her.

But what did it matter? If it was written in the book that she should become Madame Lacordaire, of course the world would know that there must have been some preparatory love-making. Let them have their laugh ; a good husband would not be dearly purchased at so trifling an expense. And so they sallied forth with already half the ceremony of a wedding.

Mimmy seated herself opposite to her mother, and M. Lacordaire also sat with his back to the horses, leaving the second place of honour for Lilian. 'Pray make yourself comfortable, M. Lacordaire, and don't mind her,' said Mrs. Thompson. But he was firm in his purpose of civility, perhaps making up his mind that when he should in truth stand in the place of papa to the young lady, then would be his time for having the back seat in the carriage.

Lilian, also in her best frock, came down the school steps, and three of the school teachers came with her. It would have added to Mrs. Thompson's happiness at that moment if M. Lacordaire would have kept his polished boots out of sight, and put his yellow gloves into his pocket.

And then they started. The road from Le Puy to

Polignac is nearly all up hill; and a very steep hill it is, so that there was plenty of time for conversation. But the girls had it nearly all to themselves. Mimmy thought that she had never found M. Lacordaire so stupid; and Lilian told her sister on the first safe opportunity that occurred, that it seemed very much as though they were all going to church.

'And do any of the Polignac people ever live at this place?' asked Mrs. Thompson, by way of making conversation; in answer to which M. Lacordaire informed madame that the place was at present only a ruin; and then there was again silence till they found themselves under the rock, and were informed by the driver that the rest of the ascent must be made on foot.

The rock now stood abrupt and precipitous above their heads. It was larger in its circumference and with much larger space on its summit than those other volcanic rocks in and close to the town; but then at the same time it was higher from the ground, and quite as inaccessible except by the single path which led up to the château.

M. Lacordaire, with conspicuous gallantry, first assisted Mrs. Thompson from the carriage, and then handed down the two young ladies. No lady could have been so difficult to please as to complain of him, and yet Mrs. Thompson thought that he was not as agreeable as usual. Those horrid boots and those horrid gloves gave him such an air of holiday finery that neither could he be at his ease wearing them, nor could she, in seeing them worn.

They were soon taken in hand by the poor woman whose privilege it was to show the ruins. For a little distance they walked up the path in single file; not that it was too narrow to accommodate two, but M. Lacordaire's courage had not yet been screwed to a point which admitted of his offering his arm to the widow. For in France, it must be remembered, that this means more than it does in some other countries.

Mrs. Thompson felt that all this was silly and useless. If they were not to be dear friends this coming out fêteing together, those boots and gloves and new hat were all very foolish; and if they were, the sooner that they understood each other the better. So Mrs. Thompson, finding that the path was steep and the weather warm, stood still for a while leaning against the wall, with a look of considerable fatigue in her face.

'Will madame permit me the honour of offering her my arm?' said M. Lacordaire. 'The road is so extraordinarily steep for madame to climb.'

Mrs. Thompson did permit him the honour, and so they went on till they reached the top.

The view from the summit was both extensive and grand, but neither Lilian nor Mimmy were much pleased with the place. The elder sister, who had talked over the matter with her school companions, expected a fine castle with turrets, battlements, and romance; and the other expected a pretty smiling house, such as princes, in her mind, ought to inhabit.

Instead of this they found an old turret, with steps so broken that M. Lacordaire, did not care to ascend them, and the ruined walls of a mansion, in which nothing was to be seen but the remains of an enormous kitchen chimney.

'It was the kitchen of the family,' said the guide.

'Oh,' said Mrs. Thompson.

'And this,' said the woman, taking them into the next ruined compartment, 'was the kitchen of *monsieur et madame.*'

'What! two kitchens?' exclaimed Lilian, upon which M. Lacordaire explained that the ancestors of the Prince de Polignac had been very great people, and had therefore required culinary performances on a great scale.

And then the woman began to chatter something about an oracle of Apollo. There was, she said, a hole in the rock, from which in past times, perhaps more than a hundred years ago, the oracle used to speak forth mysterious words.

'There,' she said, pointing to a part of the rock at some distance, 'was the hole. And if the ladies would follow her to a little outhouse which was just beyond, she would show them the huge stone mouth out of which the oracle used to speak.'

Lilian and Mimmy both declared at once for seeing the oracle, but Mrs. Thompson expressed her determination to remain sitting where she was upon the turf. So the guide started off with the young ladies; and will it be thought surprising that M. Lacordaire should have remained alone by the side of Mrs. Thompson?

It must be now or never, Mrs. Thompson felt; and

as regarded M. Lacordaire, he probably entertained
some idea of the same kind. Mrs. Thompson's inclinations, though they had never been very strong in
the matter, were certainly in favour of the 'now.' M.
Lacordaire's inclinations were stronger. He had fully
and firmly made up his mind in favour of matrimony;
but then he was not so absolutely in favour of the 'now.'
Mrs. Thompson's mind, if one could have read it, would
have shown a great objection to shilly-shallying, as she
was accustomed to call it. But M. Lacordaire, were it
not for the danger which might thence arise, would
have seen no objection to some slight further procrasti-
nation. His courage was beginning, perhaps, to ooze
out from his fingers' ends.

'I declare that those girls have scampered away ever
so far,' said Mrs. Thompson.

'Would madame wish that I should call them back?'
said M. Lacordaire, innocently.

'Oh, no, dear children! let them enjoy themselves;
it will be a pleasure to them to run about the rock, and
I suppose they will be safe with that woman?'

'Oh, yes, quite safe,' said M. Lacordaire; and then
there was another little pause.

Mrs. Thompson was sitting on a broken fragment of
a stone just outside the entrance to the old family
kitchen, and M. Lacordaire was standing immediately
before her. He had in his hand a little cane with
which he sometimes slapped his boots and sometimes
poked about among the rubbish. His hat was not
quite straight on his head, having a little jaunty twist

to one side, with reference to which, by-the-by, Mrs. Thompson then resolved that she would make a change, should ever the gentleman become her own property. He still wore his gloves, and was very smart ; but it was clear to see that he was not at his ease.

' I hope the heat does not incommode you,' he said after a few moments' silence. Mrs. Thompson declared that it did not, that she liked a good deal of heat, and that, on the whole, she was very well where she was. She was afraid, however, that she was detaining M. Lacordaire, who might probably wish to be moving about upon the rock. In answer to which M. Lacordaire declared that he never could be so happy anywhere as in her close vicinity.

' You are too good to me,' said Mrs. Thompson, almost sighing. 'I don't know what my stay here would have been without your great kindness.'

' It is madame that has been kind to me,' said M. Lacordaire, pressing the handle of his cane against his heart.

There was then another pause, after which Mrs. Thompson said that that was all his French politeness ; that she knew that she had been very troublesome to him, but that she would now soon be gone ; and that then, in her own country, she would never forget his great goodness.

' Ah, madame !' said M. Lacordaire ; and, as he said it, much more was expressed in his face than in his words. But, then, you can neither accept nor reject a gentleman by what he says in his face. He blushed, too, up to his grizzled hair, and, turning round, walked a step or two away from the widow's seat, and back again.

Mrs. Thompson the while sat quite still. The displaced fragment, lying, as it did, near a corner of the building, made not an uncomfortable chair. She had only to be careful that she did not injure her hat or crush her clothes, and throw in a word here and there to assist the gentleman, should occasion permit it.

'Madame!' said M. Lacordaire, on his return from a second little walk.

'Monsieur!' replied Mrs. Thompson, perceiving that M. Lacordaire paused in his speech.

'Madame,' he began again, and then, as he again paused, Mrs. Thompson looked up to him very sweetly; 'madame, what I am going to say will, I am afraid, seem to evince by far too great audacity on my part.'

Mrs. Thompson may, perhaps, have thought that, at the present moment, audacity was not his fault. She replied, however, that she was quite sure that monsieur would say nothing that was in any way unbecoming either for him to speak or for her to hear.

'Madame, may I have ground to hope that such may be your sentiments after I have spoken! Madame'— and now he went down, absolutely on his knees, on the hard stones; and Mrs. Thompson, looking about into the distance, almost thought that she saw the top of the guide's cap—'Madame, I have looked forward to this opportunity as one in which I may declare for you the greatest passion that I have ever yet felt. Madame, with all my heart and soul I love you. Madame, I offer to you the homage of my heart, my hand, the happiness of my life, and all that I possess in this world;' and then, taking her hand gracefully between his gloves, he pressed his lips against the tips of her fingers.

If the thing was to be done this way of doing it was, perhaps, as good as any other. It was one, at any rate, which left no doubt whatever as to the gentleman's intentions. Mrs. Thompson, could she have had her own way, would not have allowed her lover of fifty to go down upon his knees, and would have spared him much of the romance of his declaration. So also would she have spared him his yellow gloves and his polished boots. But these were a part of the necessity of the situation, and therefore she wisely took them as matters to be passed over with indifference. Seeing, however, that M. Lacordaire still remained on his knees, it was necessary that she should take some step toward raising him, especially as her two children and the guide would infallibly be upon them before long.

'M. Lacordaire,' she said, 'you surprise me greatly; but pray get up.'

'But will madame vouchsafe to give me some small ground for hope?'

'The girls will be here directly, M. Lacordaire; pray get up. I can talk to you much better if you will stand up, or sit down on one of these stones.'

M. Lacordaire did as he was bid; he got up, wiped

the knees of his pantaloons with his handkerchief, sat down beside her, and then pressed the handle of his cane to his heart.

'You really have so surprised me that I hardly know how to answer you,' said Mrs. Thompson. 'Indeed, I cannot bring myself to imagine that you are in earnest.'

'Ah, madame, do not be so cruel! How can I have lived with you so long, sat beside you for so many days, without having received your image into my heart? I am in earnest! Alas! I fear too much in earnest!' And then he looked at her with all his eyes, and sighed with all his strength.

Mrs. Thompson's prudence told her that it would be well to settle the matter, in one way or the other, as soon as possible. Long periods of love-making were fit for younger people than herself and her future possible husband. Her object would be to make him comfortable if she could, and that he should do the same for her, if that also were possible. As for lookings and sighings and pressings of the hand, she had gone through all that some twenty years since in India, when Thompson had been young, and she was still in her teens.

'But, M. Lacordaire, there are so many things to be considered. There! I hear the children coming! Let us walk this way for a minute.' And they turned behind a wall which placed them out of sight, and walked on a few paces till they reached a parapet, which stood on the uttermost edge of the high rock.

Leaning upon this they continued their conversation.

'There are so many things to be considered,' said Mrs. Thompson again.

'Yes, of course,' said M. Lacordaire. 'But my one great consideration is this;—that I love madame to distraction.'

'I am very much flattered : of course, any lady would so feel. But, M. Lacordaire ——'

'Madame, I am all attention. But, if you would deign to make me happy, say that one word, "I love you!"' M. Lacordaire, as he uttered these words, did not look, as the saying is, at his best. But Mrs. Thompson forgave him. She knew that elderly gentlemen under such circumstances do not look at their best.

'But if I consented to—to—to such an arrangement, I could only do so on seeing that it would be beneficial —or, at any rate, not injurious ;—to my children ; and that it would offer to ourselves a fair promise of future happiness.'

'Ah, madame ! it would be the dearest wish of my heart to be a second father to those two young ladies ; except, indeed ——' and then M. Lacordaire stopped the flow of his speech.

'In such matters it is so much the best to be explicit at once,' said Mrs. Thompson.

'Oh, yes ; certainly ! Nothing can be more wise than madame.'

'And the happiness of a household depends so much on money.'

'Madame!'

'Let me say a word or two, Monsieur Lacordaire.
I have enough for myself and my children; and, should
I ever marry again, I should not, I hope, be felt as a
burden by my husband; but it would, of course, be my
duty to know what were his circumstances, before I
accepted him. Of yourself, personally, I have seen
nothing that I do not like.'

'Oh, madame!'

'But as yet I know nothing of your circumstances.'

M. Lacordaire, perhaps, did feel that Mrs. Thompson's prudence was of a strong, masculine description;
but he hardly liked her the less on this account. To
give him his due he was not desirous of marrying her
solely for her money's sake. He also wished for a
comfortable home, and proposed to give as much as he
got; only he had been anxious to wrap up the solid
cake of this business in a casing of sugar of romance.
Mrs. Thompson would not have the sugar; but the
cake might not be the worse on that account.

'No, madame; not as yet: but they shall all be
made open and at your disposal,' said M. Lacordaire;
and Mrs. Thompson bowed approvingly.

'I am in business,' continued M. Lacordaire:
'and my business gives me eight thousand francs a
year.'

'Four times eight are thirty-two,' said Mrs. Thompson to herself; putting the francs into pounds sterling,
in the manner that she had always found to be the
readiest. Well, so far the statement was satisfactory

An income of three hundred and twenty pounds a year from business, joined to her own, might do very well. She did not in the least suspect M. Lacordaire of being false, and so far the matter sounded well.

' And what is the business?' she asked, in a tone of voice intended to be indifferent, but which nevertheless showed that she listened anxiously for an answer to her question.

They were both standing with their arms upon the wall, looking down upon the town of Le Puy; but they had so stood that each could see the other's countenance as they talked. Mrs. Thompson could now perceive that M. Lacordaire became red in the face, as he paused before answering her. She was near to him, and seeing his emotion gently touched his arm with her hand. This she did to reassure him, for she saw that he was ashamed of having to declare that he was a tradesman. As for herself, she had made up her mind to bear with this, if she found, as she felt sure she would find, that the trade was one which would not degrade either him or her. Hitherto, indeed,—in her early days,—she had looked down on trade; but of what benefit had her grand ideas been to her when she had returned to England? She had tried her hand at English genteel society, and no one had seemed to care for her. Therefore, she touched his arm lightly with her fingers that she might encourage him.

He paused for a moment, as I have said, and became red; and then feeling that he had shown some symptoms of shame—and feeling also, probably, that it was unmanly in him to do so, he shook himself slightly, raised his head up somewhat more proudly than was his wont, looked her full in the face with more strength of character than she had yet seen him assume; and then, declared his business.

'Madame,' he said, in a very audible, but not in a loud voice; 'madame—*je suis tailleur.*' And having so spoken, he turned slightly from her and looked down over the valley towards Le Puy.

*   *   *   *   *   *

There was nothing more said upon the subject as they drove down from the rock of Polignac back to the town. Immediately on receiving the announcement, Mrs. Thompson found that she had no answer to make. She withdrew her hand—and felt at once that she had received a blow. It was not that she was angry with M. Lacordaire for being a tailor; nor was she angry with him in that, being a tailor, he had so addressed her. But she was surprised, disappointed, and altogether put beyond her ease. She had, at any rate, not expected this. She had dreamed of his being a banker; thought that, perhaps, he might have been a wine merchant; but her idea had never gone below a jeweller or watchmaker. When those words broke upon her ear, 'Madame, *je suis tailleur,*' she had felt herself to be speechless.

But the words had not been a minute spoken when Lilian and Mimmy ran up to their mother. 'Oh, mamma,' said Lilian, 'we thought you were lost; we have searched for you all over the château.'

' We have been sitting very quietly here, my dear,
looking at the view,' said Mrs. Thompson.

' But, mamma, I do wish you'd see the mouth of the
oracle. It is so large, and so round, and so ugly. I
put my arm into it all the way,' said Mimmy.

But at the present moment her mamma felt no
interest in the mouth of the oracle; and so they all
walked down together to the carriage. And, though
the way was steep, Mrs. Thompson managed to pick
her steps without the assistance of an arm; nor did
M. Lacordaire presume to offer it.

The drive back to town was very silent. Mrs.
Thompson did make one or two attempts at conversation, but they were not effectual. M. Lacordaire
could not speak at his ease till this matter was settled,
and he already had begun to perceive that his business
was against him. Why is it that the trade of a tailor
should be less honourable than that of an haberdasher,
or even a grocer?

They sat next each other at dinner, as usual; and
here, as all eyes were upon them, they both made a
great struggle to behave in their accustomed way. But
even in this they failed. All the world of the Hôtel
des Ambassadeurs knew that M. Lacordaire had gone
forth to make an offer to Mrs. Thompson, and all that
world, therefore, was full of speculation. But all the
world could make nothing of it. M. Lacordaire did
look like a rejected man, but Mrs. Thompson did not
look like the woman who had rejected him. That the
offer had been made—in that everybody agreed, from

the senior habitué of the house who always sat at the head of the table, down to the junior assistant garçon. But as to reading the riddle, there was no accord among them.

When the dessert was done Mrs. Thompson, as usual, withdrew, and M. Lacordaire, as usual, bowed as he stood behind his own chair. He did not, however, attempt to follow her.

But when she reached the door, she called him. He was at her side in a moment, and then she whispered in his ear—

'And I, also—I will be of the same business.'

When M. Lacordaire regained the table the senior habitué, the junior garçon, and all the intermediate ranks of men at the Hôtel des Ambassadeurs knew that they might congratulate him.

Mrs. Thompson had made a great struggle; but, speaking for myself, I am inclined to think that she arrived at last at a wise decision.

THE END.

By the same author

The Clash of Tongues

(A Commentary on 1 Corinthians 14)

This work deals not only with the regulation of gifts of the Spirit and their relevance for today but also with some of the deeper principles underlying their use. It raises fundamental questions which are sometimes overlooked:

- How can an individual be edified through speaking something which he cannot understand?
- What is the point of speaking in this way when the hearers do not understand either?
- Is there a spiritual means of communication between the human spirit and God which by-passes the intellect and yields benefit?
- Why did Paul have to make regulations at all? If the gifts are Gifts of the Spirit, how can error creep into their use?
- Do the regulations not clash with the direct unctioning of the Spirit upon an individual?
- Tongues according to verse 2 of 1 Corinthians 14 are Godward. Why then is interpretation in modern times so often manward? Surely if God is addressed in one, He will be addressed in the other. Is there Scriptural justification for the present-day practice?
- Was there a difference between the tongues of Acts 2, which were understood by foreigners, and the 'tongues' of 1 Corinthians 14 which 'no man' understood?

These and other points are dealt with as they arise in the text, and it is hoped that both spiritual and intellectual benefit may be derived from the perusal of the solutions offered.

Due for later publication this book, while of general interest, is expected to appeal particularly to serious students of the New Testament.

BOOK ORDERS

The books advertised on the previous pages are being made available to Christian booksellers throughout the country, but if you have any difficulty in obtaining your supply, you may order directly from New Dawn Books, c/o 27 Denholm Street, Greenock, Scotland PA16 8RH.

············· ORDER FORM ··············

Please send me the books indicated below:

Quantity	Title	Price
	Reflections on the Baptism in the Holy Spirit	£2.25
	Reflections on the Gifts of the Spirit	£2.75
	Reflections on a Song of Love (A commentary on 1 Cor 13)	£1.25
	A Trumpet Call to Women	£2.50
	Consider Him (Twelve Qualities of Christ)	★
	Battle for the Body	★
	The Clash of Tongues (A commentary on 1 Cor 14)	★
	There Shone A Great Light (The Christmas Story)	★

★ Prices to be announced

Signature ....

Address ....

....

....

When ordering please send purchase price plus 30p per book to help cover the cost of postage and packaging.